NOT IN THE FLESH

ruth
rendell

NOT IN THE
FLESH

HUTCHINSON

LONDON

Published by Hutchinson 2007

2 4 6 8 10 9 7 5 3 1

Copyright © Kingsmarkham Enterprises Ltd 2007

Ruth Rendell has asserted her right under the
Copyright, Designs and Patents Act 1988 to be
identified as the author of this work

First published in Great Britain in 2007 by
Hutchinson
Random House, 20 Vauxhall Bridge Road,
London SW1V 2SA

www.randomhouse.co.uk

Addresses for companies within The Random
House Group Limited can be found at:
www.randomhouse.co.uk/offices.htm

The Random House Group Limited Reg. No. 954009

A CIP catalogue record for this book
is available from the British Library

ISBN 9780091920593 (Hardback)
ISBN 9780091920609 (Trade paperback)

The Random House Group Limited makes every
effort to ensure that the papers used in its books are
made from trees that have been legally sourced from
well-managed and credibly certified forests. Our
paper procurement policy can be found at:
www.randomhouse.co.uk/paper.htm

Typeset by Palimpsest Book Production Ltd, Grangemouth, Stirlingshire
Printed and bound in Great Britain by Clays Ltd, St Ives plc

For Patricia Nassif Acton, with love

CHAPTER ONE

Tom Belbury died in May and now that summer was over his brother missed him more than ever. Neither of them had married so there was no widow and no children, only the dog Honey. Jim took Honey to live with him, he had always liked her and it was what Tom had wanted. When he knew he hadn't long to live he worried a lot about Honey, what would happen to her after he was gone, and though Jim assured him repeatedly that he would take her, Tom said it again and again.

'Haven't I promised over and over? You want me to put it in writing and get it witnessed? I will if that's what you want.'

'No, I trust you. She's a good dog.'

His trust hadn't been misplaced. Jim lived in the cottage that had been the brothers' parents' home and there Honey went to live with him. She was no beauty, owing her ancestry to an apparent mix of spaniel, basset hound and Jack Russell. Tom used to say she looked like a corgi and everyone knew corgis were the Queen's dogs, having so to speak the royal seal of approval, but Jim couldn't see it. Nevertheless, he had grown attached to Honey. Apart from fidelity and affection, she had one great virtue. She was a truffle dog.

Every September, at the beginning of the month, Tom and Honey used to go into one patch of woodland or another in the neighbourhood of Flagford and hunt for truffles. A lot of people scoffed. They said truffles couldn't be found in Britain, only in France and

Italy, but there was no doubt Honey found them, was rewarded with a lump of meat, and Tom sold the truffles to a famous London restaurant for £200 a pound.

Jim disliked the taste but he liked the idea of £200 and possibly more. He had never been truffle-hunting with Tom but he knew how it was done. This was why a mild and sunny morning in late September found him and Honey in what their neighbours called the posh part of Flagford where Flagford Hall faced Athelstan House across Pump Lane, each amid extensive grounds. They had no interest in these houses or their occupants. They were heading for Old Grimble's Field which filled the corner between the gardens of Athelstan House and two identical detached houses called Oak Lodge and Marshmead.

Like the Holy Roman Empire which Gibbon said was neither holy, Roman nor an empire, this open space wasn't a field, nor was Grimble particularly old or really called Grimble. It was an over-grown piece of land, about an acre of what estate agents describe asa corner plot. Due to years of inattention, saplings had grown into trees, shrubs into bushes, roses and privet and dogwood into hedges and trees had doubled in size. Somewhere in the middle of this burgeoning woodland stood a semi-derelict bungalow which had belonged to Grimble's father, its windows boarded up, its roof slowly shedding its tiles. Tom Belbury had been there truffle-hunting with Honey the year before and pronounced it rich in members of the genus *Tuber*.

Because Tom carried the rewards for Honey unwrapped in the breast pocket of his leather jacket, he usually smelt of meat that was slightly 'off'. Jim hadn't much liked it at the time but now he recalled it with affection. How pleased dear old Tom would be to see him and Honey heading for Old Grimble's Field in close companionship, following his old pursuit. Perhaps he could see, Jim thought sentimentally, and imagined him looking down from whatever truffle wood in the sky he found himself in.

Honey was the director of operations. Tom used to claim that she was drawn to a particular spot by the presence of truffle flies hovering around the base of a tree, and now she led Jim to a mature tree (a sycamore, he thought it was) where he could see the flies himself.

'Get digging, girl,' he said.

The irregular warty lump, about the size of a tennis ball, which Honey unearthed she willingly relinquished in exchange for the cube of sirloin steak Jim took out of a hygienic ziplock bag he had brought with him.

'This old fungus must weigh a good half-pound,' he said aloud. 'Keep on with the good work, Honey.'

Honey kept on. The truffle flies annoyed her and she snapped at the swarms, scattering them and snuffling towards where they had been densest. There she began digging again, fetched out of the rich leaf mould first a much smaller truffle, then one about the size of a large potato and was rewarded once more with pieces of sirloin.

'There's a lot more flies buzzing about over there,' Jim said, pointing to a biggish beech tree which looked a hundred years old. 'How about moving on?'

Honey had no intention of moving on. So might a diamond prospector refuse to abandon the lode where gems worth a fortune had already come to light, until he was sure the seam had been exhausted. Honey sniffed, dug, slapped at the flies with her paws, dug again. No more truffles were foraged and the object which she had unearthed was of no interest to her. It lay exposed on the chestnut-coloured soil, white, fanlike, unmistakeably what it was, a human hand.

Or, rather, the bones of a human hand, flesh, skin, veins, tendons all gone.

'Oh, my lord, girl,' said Jim Belbury, 'whatever have you gone and found?'

As if she understood, Honey stopped digging, sat down and put her head on one side. Jim patted her. He put the three truffles in the plastic bag he had brought with him for that purpose, placed the bag inside his backpack and removed from it his mobile phone. Jim might be an old countryman, once an agricultural labourer and living in a cottage with no bathroom and no main drainage, but still he would no more have gone out without his mobile than would his fifteen-year-old great-nephew. Unaware of the number of Kingsmarkham police station, he dialled 999.

CHAPTER TWO

The thing that had come out of the pit lay exposed for them to see, a bunch of bones that looked more than anything like broomsticks, a skull to which scraps of decomposed tissue still adhered, all wrapped in purple cotton. They had been digging for two hours, an operation watched by Jim Belbury and his dog.

'Man or woman?' Chief Inspector Wexford asked.

'Hard to say.' The pathologist was a young woman who looked like a fifteen-year-old model, thin, tall, pale and other-worldly. 'I'll tell you when I've taken a closer look.'

'How long has it been there?'

Carina Laxton eyed Wexford and his sergeant, DS Hannah Goldsmith who had asked the question. 'And how long have you two been in the Force? Isn't it about time you knew I can't give you an immediate answer when a cadaver's obviously been buried for years?'

'OK but is it months or decades?'

'Maybe one decade. What I can tell you is you're wasting your time taking all these measurements and photographs as if someone put it there last week.'

'Maybe Mr Belbury can help us there,' said Wexford. He had decided not to mention the fact that Jim Belbury was trespassing, had probably been trespassing for years. 'Did your dog ever dig here before?'

'Not on this spot, no,' said Jim. 'Over there where there's more bigger trees. Can I ask you if you reckon it's what you call foul play?'

Wexford was tempted to say, well, no, you can't, but he relented. 'Someone buried him or her, so you have to—' he began but Hannah interrupted him.

'Law-abiding people don't bury bodies they find lying about, you know,' she said sharply. 'Perhaps you should be on your way, Mr Belbury. Thank you, you've been very helpful.'

But Jim wasn't to be dismissed so easily. Finding Wexford sympathetic and everyone else – Hannah, the scene-of-crime officer, the photographers, the pathologist and various policemen – of no account, he began giving the chief inspector details of all the houses and their occupants in the vicinity. 'That's Mr Tredown's place next door and down there's the Hunters and the Pickfords. Over the other side that's Mr Borodin. I've lived in Flagford all my life. There's nothing I don't know.'

'Then you can tell me who owns this land.' Wexford extended his arm and waved his hand. 'Must be at least an acre.'

His politically correct sergeant murmured something about hectares being a more appropriate measurement 'in the present day' but no one took much notice of her.

'An acre and a half,' said Jim with a glare at Hannah. 'We don't have no hectares round here. Them belongs in the Common Market.' Like many people of his age, Jim still referred in this way to the European Union. 'Who owns it? Well, Mr Grimble, innit? This here is Old Grimble's Field.'

Though he might possibly be compounding a felony, seeing that the subterranean fungi in the bag properly belonged to this Grimble, Wexford thanked Jim and offered him a lift home in a police car.

'And my dog?' said Jim.

'And your dog.'

His offer gratefully accepted, he and Hannah moved away, heading for the road where police vehicles were parked along the pavement. It became, within a short distance, Flagford High Street, a somewhat too picturesque village centre where stood the thirteenth-century church, a post office and general store, a shop which sold mosaic tabletops, another purveying lime-flower honey and mulberry conserve, and a number of flint-walled cottages, one thatched and another with its own bell tower.

Wexford, in the car, said to Hannah that, for all the times he had been to Flagford, he couldn't remember noticing that piece of land before.

'I don't think I've ever been here before, guv,' said Hannah.

He had grown accustomed to her calling him that and supposed she had originally got it off the television. *The Bill,* probably. Not that he liked it, while admitting it was current usage, but the trouble was all his officers had learnt it from her and now no one kept to the old 'sir'. Burden would know who owned that land. He had a relative living in Flagford, his first wife's cousin, Wexford thought it was.

'There's not much to be done,' Hannah was saying, 'until we know how long that body's been there.'

'Let's hope Carina will know by later today.'

'Meanwhile I could find out more about this Grimble and if he owns the old house on it.'

'Right, but let me talk to Mr Burden first.'

Hannah directed one of her looks at him. She was a beautiful young woman, black-haired, white-skinned, with large brown eyes which softened into a quite disproportionate pitying sorrow combined with a desire to reproach him gently whenever he committed the solecism of using terms or styles she thought obsolete. '*Mister* Burden, oh, come,' her glance said while the perfect lips stayed closed. Their relative ranks made reproach impossible but glances were free. As Wexford himself might have said, a cat may look at a king.

It was a gentle sunny day, what weather forecasters were starting to call 'quiet' weather, the temperature high for September, all the leaves still on the trees and most of them still green. Summer flowers in pots and urns and window boxes still bloomed on and

7

on, more luxuriantly than in August. Frosts were due, frosts would normally have come by now but none had. If this was global warming, and Wexford thought it must be, it disguised its awful face under a mask of mild innocence. The sky had become the milky blue of midsummer covered with tiny white puffs of cloud.

He called Burden a moment after he got into the police station but the inspector's voicemail told him he was occupied in an interview room. That would be his interview with Darrel Fincher, the teenager found with a knife on him. You could predict, without hearing a word of their conversation, what the boy would say: that he carried the knife for protection, that going home from school or going out in the evening he wouldn't feel safe without a knife. It was 'all them Somalis', he would say. They were everywhere and they all had knives. That was what they called dark-skinned people these days, 'them Somalis' as they had once indiscriminately called Asians 'them Pakis'. Wexford turned his thoughts to the Flagford corpse. With luck, it wouldn't have been there for more than a year or two and would turn out to be that chap he could remember going missing a while back after a ram raid on a jeweller's or the old woman who lived alone in a Forby cottage. After failing to visit her for three months her daughter had remembered her existence but on going there had found her apparently long gone. One of them it would most likely be. Strange, he thought, that death and subsequent decay wipe away age and sex and every distinguishing feature so that nothing is left but bones and a rag or two. And a hand, unearthed by an enthusiastic mongrel. How comforting it must have been when men and women (or women and men, as Hannah would say) believed that the body is but a sheath for the spirit which, at the point of death, flies away to some afterlife or paradise. It would hardly matter to you then, if your faith were strong enough, that you met your death from the blade of a knife, a bludgeon or because your heart gave its final beat in the natural course of things.

He came down to earth from these post-mortem reflections when his office door opened and Burden walked in. 'That bit of land at Flagford where the dog-walker found a body? Of course I know who owns it. Everybody knows.'

'I don't,' said Wexford. 'And what d'you mean, everybody knows? It's not the Tower of London, it's not Harrods.'

'I mean this guy it belongs to tells everyone how hard done by he is by the planning people. His name's Grimble, John Grimble. He's even had a piece about himself in the *Courier*. He's obsessed. His father died – well, his stepfather it was – and left him the bungalow and the land it's on and ever since he's been trying to get planning permission to build houses on it. He thinks he's been badly treated – that's an understatement – because they'll let him build one but not more.'

'Where does he live?'

'The next street to me, worse luck. The dog-walker must have known.'

'He's not a dog-walker. He's a truffle-hunter.'

Burden's normally impassive face brightened. 'A *truffle*-hunter? How amazing. *Tuber aestivum, Tuber gibbosum, Tuber magnatum* or *Tuber melanosporum*?'

Wexford stared. 'What do you know about truffles, since I suppose that's what you're talking about?'

'I used to hunt for them with my dad and our dog when I was a boy. Found a good many too. My grandfather used a pig, a sow, of course. Truffles smell like the male swine sex attractant, you see, but the trouble is that pigs'll eat anything, so they tend to eat the truffles before you can stop them and that's a bit expensive when you consider—'

'Mike, sit down a minute.'

Burden, one of those restless people who perch rather than sit and fidget instead of relaxing, balanced himself on the edge of Wexford's desk. He had at last, regretfully, discarded his designer jeans and was wearing charcoal trousers with a knife-edge crease and a stone-coloured polo neck under a linen jacket. Wexford thought rather wistfully that when he tried to get himself up in casual gear he just looked like someone's dad going to a fancy dress party.

'Never mind truffles. How long has this obsessive owned the land?'

'Must be at least ten years. More like twelve. I don't suppose the people on either side like it much, having a sort of wilderness next door, I mean. Apparently, when old Grimble lived there he kept the place neat and tidy. His garden was quite famous locally. This one – John – Grimble has let the place turn into a wood. He doesn't even mow the grass. And he says things are going to stay as they are until he gets his planning permission. For two houses, that is. He'll never agree to pulling down that old ruin of a bungalow – it's called Sunnybank, by the way – and building one house. Or that's what he says.'

'What does he do for a living?'

'Something in the building trade. He's put up a few houses around the place and made a lot of money. If you see a jerry-built eyesore, it'll be Grimble's. He's retired now, though he's only in his fifties.'

'We'll go and see him.'

'Why not? If it turns out he's murdered one of the district planners our task is going to be easy.'

John and Kathleen Grimble belonged to that category of people who, after about forty, decide consciously or unconsciously to become old. While the cult of youth prevails in society, while to be young is to be beautiful, bright and lovable, they sink rapidly into middle age and even seem to cultivate the disabilities of the aged. Wexford's theory was that they do this out of laziness and because of the benefits incident to being elderly. The old are not expected to take exercise, lift heavy weights or do much for themselves. They are pitied but they are also ignored. No one asks them to *do* anything or, come to that, to stop doing anything they choose to do. Burden had told him John Grimble was just fifty years old, his wife two or three years younger. They looked, each of them, at least ten years older than that, anchored to orthopaedic armchairs, the kind that have back supports and adjustable footrests, placed in the best position for perpetual television-watching.

He nodded to Burden, his neighbour. In response to Wexford's 'Good afternoon, Mr Grimble,' he merely stared. His wife said she was pleased to meet them in the tones of an old woman waking from her after-lunch siesta. On the way there Burden had explained something of the obsession which contributed to Grimble's reputation, so Wexford wasn't surprised at his first words.

'I mean to say,' Grimble began, 'if I tell you something that may put you on the right road to catching a criminal, will you use your influence to get my permission?'

'Oh, John,' said Kathleen Grimble.

'Oh, John, oh, John, you're a parrot, you are. Now, Mr Burden – it is Mr Burden, isn't it? You hear what I say – will you?'

'What permission would that be?' Wexford asked.

'Didn't he tell you?' Grimble said in his surly grudging voice. He cocked a thumb in Burden's direction. 'It's not as if everybody don't know. It's common knowledge. All I want is to be told I can build houses on what's my own, my own land that my dear old dad left me in his last will and testament – well, my stepdad he was, but as good as a father to me. So what I'm saying is, if I scratch your back will you scratch mine?'

'We have no influence at all with the planning authority, Mr Grimble. None at all. But I must tell you that this is a murder case and you are obliged to tell us what you know. Withholding information is a criminal offence.'

A tall thin man, one of a race which is classified as white and would be horrified if otherwise designated, Grimble had skin discoloured to a dark brownish-grey, suffused about his nose and chin with crimson. A perpetual frown had creased up his forehead and dug deep furrows across his cheeks. He stuck out his lower lip like a mutinous child and said, 'It's a funny thing how everybody's against me getting permission to build *on my own land*. Everybody. All my old dad's neighbours. All of them objected. Never mind how I know, I do know, that's all. Now it's the police. You wouldn't think the police would care, would you? If they're for law and order, like they're supposed to be, they ought to want four nice houses put up on that land, four houses with nice gardens and people as can afford them living there. Not asylum seekers, mind, not the so-called homeless, not Somalis, but decent people with a bit of money.'

'Oh, John,' said Kathleen.

Wexford got to his feet. He said sternly, 'Mr Grimble, either tell us what you have to tell us *now* or I shall ask you to accompany us to the police station and tell us there. In an interview room. Do you understand me?'

No apology was forthcoming. Wexford thought Grimble could take a prize for surliness but it seemed the man hadn't even begun. His features gathered themselves into a bunch composed of the deepest frown a human being could contrive, a wrinkling of his potato-like nose and a baring of the teeth, the result of curling back his top lip. His wife shook her head.

'Your blood pressure will go sky-high, John. You know what the doctor said.'

Whatever the doctor had said, reminding Grimble of it caused a very slight reduction in frown and teeth-baring. He spoke suddenly and rapidly. 'Me and my pal, we reckoned we'd put in the main drainage. Get started on it. Get rid of the old septic tank. Link the new houses up to the main drain in the road. You get me? We got down to digging a trench—'

'Just a minute,' said Wexford, loth to remind him of his grievance but seeing no way to avoid it. 'What new houses? You hadn't got planning permission for any new houses.'

'D'you think I don't know that? I'm talking about eleven years ago. I didn't know then, did I? My pal knew a chap in the planning and he said I was bound to get permission, bound to. He said, you go ahead, do what you want. Your pal – meaning me – he may not get it for four houses but there's no way they'd say no to two, right?'

'Exactly when was this? You said eleven years ago. When did your stepfather die?'

Unexpectedly, Kathleen intervened. 'Now, John, you just let me tell them.' Sulkily, Grimble nodded, contemplated the television on which the sound had been turned down fully but the picture remained. 'John's dad – his name was Arthur – he died in the January. January '95, that is. He left this will, straightforward it was, no problems. I don't know the ins and outs of it but the upshot was that it was John's in the May.'

'That piece of land, Mrs Grimble, and the house on it?'

'That's right. He wanted to pull down the old place and get building but his pal Bill Runge – that's pal he's talking about – he said, you can't do that, John, you have to get permission, so John got me to write to the council and ask to put up four houses. You got all that?'

'Yes, I think so, thank you.' Wexford turned back to John Grimble who was leaning forward, his head on one side, in an attempt to hear the soundless television programme. 'So without getting the permission,' he said, 'you and Mr Runge started digging a trench for the main drainage? When would that have been? Mr Grimble, I'm speaking to you.'

'All right. I hear you. Them busybody neighbours, it was them as put a spoke in my wheel, that fellow Tredown and those Pickfords. Them McNeils what used to live at Flagford Hall. I know what I know. That's why I never pulled down my dad's old house. Leave it there, I thought to myself, leave it there to be an eyesore to that lot. They won't like that and they don't. Leave the weeds there and the bloody nettles. Let the damn trees take over.'

Wexford sighed silently. 'I'm right, aren't I, in thinking that you and your friend started digging a trench between where you expected the houses would be sited and the road itself?' A surly nod from Grimble. 'But your application for planning permission was refused. You could build one house but no more. So you filled in the trench. And all this was eleven years ago.'

'If you know,' said Grimble, 'I don't know why you bother to ask, wasting my time.'

'Oh, John, don't,' said Kathleen Grimble, slightly varying her admonition.

'We dug a trench like I said, and left it open for a day or two and then those bastards at the planning turned me down so we filled the bugger in.'

'I'd like you to think carefully, Mr Grimble.' Wexford doubted if this was possible but he tried. 'Between the time you dug the trench and the time you filled it in, was it' – he paused – 'in any way interfered with?'

'What d'you mean, interfered with?' Grimble asked.

'Had it been touched? Had anything been put in it? Had it been disturbed?'

'How should I know? Bill Runge filled it in. I paid him to do it and he done it. To be honest with you, I was too upset to go near the place. I mean I'd banked on getting that permission, I'd as near as dammit been *promised* I'd get it. Can you wonder I was fed up to my back teeth? I was ill as a matter of fact. You ask the wife. I was laid up in bed, had to have the doctor, and he said no wonder you're in a bad way, Mr Grimble, he said, your nerves are shot to pieces and all because of those planning people and I said—'

Wexford almost had to shout to get a word in. 'When was permission refused?'

Again it was Kathleen who answered him. 'I'll never forget the date, he was in such a state. He started the digging end of May and the second week of June they wrote to him and said he could build one house but not more.'

Out in the little hallway, shaking her head, casting up her eyes, and with a glance at the open door behind them, she whispered, 'He's still on the phone to his pal most days. After eleven years! That's all they talk about, those two, that blessed planning permission. It gets you down.'

Wexford smiled non-committally.

Rather shyly, she peered up into his face. She was a little woman with thinning reddish hair, round wire-rimmed glasses sliding down her nose. 'I don't know if I ought to ask but how did you know there was a dead body in there? It wasn't that truffle man, was it? I thought he'd died.'

Wexford only smiled.

'If John thought that he'd go mad. He hates that truffle man. He hates trespassers. But if he's dead that's all right.'

'I 've a feeling,' Wexford said when they were back at the police station, 'that we've got a mystery person – man or woman, we don't know yet – on our hands. Identification is going to be a problem. I shan't be surprised if we're still asking who this character is in three months' time. It's just a hunch but I do have these hunches and often they're right.'

Burden shrugged. 'And just as often they're wrong. His teeth, her teeth, will identify him or her. His or her dentition, I should say. It never, or rather, seldom, fails.'

'I'm not telling the media anything till Carina gets back to me. It's not a good idea, confronting them with a cadaver we can't even say was a man or a woman. We can't say how he or she died or whether foul play, as they always put it, is suspected or not.'

'What is it you always say?' said Burden. 'A body illicitly interred is a body unlawfully killed.'

'Pretty well true,' said Wexford, 'but not invariably.'

'By the way, the kid with the knife said his mother *gave* it to him. She's called Leeanne Fincher. She said it made her feel better when he was out of the house knowing he'd got a weapon. I think I'll go round and see her on my way home.'

Wexford too went home. He walked. Dr Akande had told him it was time he paid attention to that long neglected piece of machinery, that once-efficient pump, his heart. Not in the half-hearted (half-*hearted*!) way he had in the past, dieting in a feeble fashion, forgetting the diet in favour of indulgence in meat and cheese and whisky, exercising in ever-decreasing spurts, letting Donaldson drive him whenever it rained or the temperature fell below fifteen degrees, running out of statins and not renewing his prescription. Now it was a walk to work and a walk home every day, a double dose of the Lipitor, a single glass of red wine every evening and cultivating a liking for salads. Why did all women love salads and all men hate them? You could almost say that real men don't eat green stuff. He had refused adamantly and rudely to join a gym. Burden went to one, of course, bouncing up and down on cross-trainers and walkways – or was it crossways and walk-trainers? – and pumping metal bars that weighed more than he did.

The walk was downhill in the morning and uphill in the evening. He often wished the reverse was true. He had even tried to find a new way of doing the journey so that, if not downhill, it was flat all the way, surely a possibility if one's route went round the side of a hill. It might be a possibility but it wasn't discoverable in the terrain of Kingsmarkham. He turned the corner into his own street and approached the house where Mr and Mrs Dirir and their son lived. It was called Mogadishu which Wexford knew he should have found touching, exiles reminding themselves daily of their native land. Only he didn't. He found it irritating, not, he told himself, because it was such a very un-English name for a house, but because it had a name at all. Most, if not all, of the other houses in the street had numbers only. But he wasn't quite sure that this was the real reason. The real reason would be racist and this bothered him for he sincerely did his best, constantly examining his conscience and his motives, to avoid even a smidgen of race prejudice. If it underlay his feelings about the Dirirs, it could perhaps be attributed to the undoubted bias in the town and no less among the police, against immigrants from Somalia. There was a small colony of them in Kingsmarkham, mostly law-abiding, it seemed, though they seemed as a race to be secretive people, modest, quiet, religious – some Christian, most Moslem – industrious and reserved. The bias rested on the fact or the suspicion or the unfounded prejudice, that their sons went about armed with knives.

When the Dirirs and their son came round for a drink – in their case Dora's latest health fad, pomegranate juice or, as they preferred, fizzy lemonade – they all got on well, even if conversation was a little stilted. They spoke good English, were considerably better educated, he had thought ruefully, than he was, and all of them anxious for the betterment of their community's fortunes. Mrs Dirir constituted herself a kind of social worker among her fellow immigrants, keeping an eye on their health, their work opportunities, their financial state and the welfare of their children. Her husband was a civil servant in the local benefit office, her son a student at the University of the South in Myringham.

Wexford had noticed that while he and Dora called everyone else they knew in the neighbourhood by their given names, the Somali couple were Mr and Mrs Dirir just as they were Mr and Mrs Wexford. If Hannah Goldsmith had been aware of this she would have called it racism of the worst kind, the sort that decrees meting out an extravagant respect to people of a different colour from oneself; a respect, she would say, that in the half-baked liberal masks contempt. Wexford was pretty sure he didn't feel contempt for the Dirirs, rather a puzzlement and a failure to find any common ground between them. He thought he might try calling Mr Dirir Omar next time he met him, and Mrs Dirir Iman, and as he was wondering how he might achieve this, Mrs Dirir emerged from her front door for no reason that he could discern but to say, 'Good evening, Mr Wexford.'

There was no time like the present. It still took a bit of nerve to say as he did, 'Good evening, Iman. How are you?'

She seemed somewhat taken aback, said in a preoccupied way, 'Fine. I am fine, thank you,' and retreated into the house. He worried all the rest of the way home that he had been too precipitate and offended her.

Next day Carina Laxton told him the body found on Grimble's land had once, between ten and twelve years before when it was still alive, been a man. Whoever had killed him had wrapped his body in some kind of purple cloth before burying him. What he had died of she couldn't tell and warned him with a frown that it was possible she might never be able to tell. It was policy now to have two pathologists conduct the autopsy and Dr Mavrikian had also been present. Scanning the report, Wexford saw that he also had little faith in ever finding the cause of death. The only clue to that cause was a crack in one of the dead man's ribs.

CHAPTER THREE

He had gathered his team together to give them a rundown on the thin facts as he knew them, but he left the demonstration on the much-magnified computer screen to DS Hannah Goldsmith. He was no good with computers and now never would be. The picture which had come up was a plan of the area, comprising Old Grimble's Field, the land and house on the western side of it, the house facing and the two houses on its southern side. Hannah made the arrow move on to the spot where the body had been found and then, with mysterious skill in Wexford's eyes, to each dwelling in the vicinity and the two cottages on the Kingsmarkham Road.

'The people who live at Oak Lodge are a married couple called Hunter and next door to them at Marshmead, James Pickford and his wife Brenda on the ground floor and in the upper flat, their son Jonathan and his girlfriend Louise Axall. The older couple, Oliver and Audrey Hunter, have been there since the house was built about forty years ago. They are very old, keep themselves to themselves and have a resident carer. As you may know, Flagford is locally known as "the geriatric ward". The place opposite, Flagford Hall, belongs to a man called Borodin, like the composer.'

Blank looks and silence met this disclosure, most of them being aficionados of Coldplay or Mariah Carey. Only DS Vine, the Bellini and Donizetti fan, nodded knowingly. Hannah shifted the cursor to a point across the Kingsmarkham Road, the diamond on her hand no one had seen before blazing as it caught the light. 'He's a weekender, lives in London, and in any case, hasn't owned Flagford Hall for more than eight years.' The arrow moved again, flitting from plot to plot. 'Two of the cottages are also occupied only at weekends, the other one by an old lady of ninety. With the exception of the house next door to Grimble's.'

As the arrow moved to the large Victorian villa and the diamond flashed once more, the voice of DC Coleman, deep and resonant, sounded, 'You know who lives there, guv? That author – what's he called?'

'Thank you, Damon,' Wexford said in a tone that implied anything but gratitude. 'Oddly enough, I do know. I've read his books – or one of them. Owen Tredown is what he's called. The other members of the household are his wife Maeve and a woman called Claudia Ricardo. Tredown's lived there for twenty years at least. Those are the neighbours and all of them need to be visited today. You, Damon, can concentrate your efforts on our records of missing persons.'

'They only go back eight years,' Burden said.

Wexford had forgotten. Vaguely he remembered that before they became fully computerised – went on broadband, was that the expression? – they hadn't the space for storing the reams of paper records. It was different now.

'Well, check eight years back,' he said, his voice sounding lame.

There was nothing, in fact, to be ashamed of in keeping a list of local disappearances for so short a period. It was standard practice before the National Missing Persons Bureau was established. Though it covered a relatively short space of time, it would be a long list, Wexford knew. People went missing at an alarming rate, nationwide something like 500 every day, locally one a day – or was it one every hour? And not all of them by any means were sought by the police. Alarm bells rang when the missing person was a child or a young girl. Every available officer was needed to hunt for lost children. Women in general, when they vanished, aroused concern and attention. Young men, indeed able-bodied men of any age but for the very old, were a different matter. This man, Carina Laxton had told him earlier, was probably in his forties. When he disappeared his nearest and dearest must have missed him, if he had nearest and dearest, and perhaps searched for him, but even if his disappearance had been reported, the police would not have done so. It was generally assumed that when a man left home, even left home without saying goodbye or leaving a note, he had gone off to make himself a new life or join another woman.

The post-mortem had uncovered no clue as to how the man, now inevitably labelled X, had met his death. One of his ribs was cracked but apart from that, no marks had showed on his bones. He had been five feet eight inches tall. This measurement, Carina told him scathingly, was for Wexford's ears only. In her report she would give his height in centimetres. The skull was intact. Fortunately, enough 'matter' remained, including marrow in the long bones, to extract DNA for help in identification. The wisdom teeth were missing but apart from that he had a full set, though with many fillings.

Why did he assume identifying X would be such a difficult task? Some kind of intuition, perhaps, which people said he had but which he couldn't accept himself. Surely, one should always rely on the facts and the facts alone. It was far too early to have any idea of who those bones might once have been, still less who dug the grave and put them there. Some of this he said to Hannah Goldsmith before she left to question the occupants of the cottages.

He liked Hannah who was a good officer and, being interested in her welfare, he took her left hand in his and asked her if congratulations were in order.

She didn't blush. Hannah had too much poise and what she would have called 'cool' for that. But she nodded and smiled a rare and radiant smile. 'Bal and I got engaged last night,' she said.

After he had said, in accordance with a long-forgotten traditional etiquette, that he hoped she would be very happy, he thought how absurd it was (by those ancient standards) that two people who had been living together for the past year should betroth themselves to each other. But engagement, as someone had said, was

21

the new marriage and for all he knew, she and Bal Bhattacharya might never marry but remain engaged as some people did through years together and the births of children till death or the intervention of someone else parted them.

'How's Bal?'

'He's fine. Said to say hallo.'

Wexford was sorry to have lost this fiancé of hers who had left to join the Met, the two of them occupying a flat near the Southern line, halfway between here and Croydon. Bal had been valuable, in spite of lapses into puritanical behaviour and wild heroism.

Bill Runge was as jovial and extrovert a man as Grimble had been recalcitrant. Sturdily plump and looking younger by a dozen years than his friend, he worked at Forby garden centre, where Wexford and Burden found him inside the main gate, arranging bags of daffodil and narcissus bulbs.

'Poor devil,' he said. 'I don't mind telling you, there's times when I feel like telling him to give it a rest. I did try, I did tell him once. Give over, John, I said, it's not worth it. Life's too short. Sell the place like it is. Take the money and run, I said, but he was so upset. In the end I had to apologise.'

'Tell us about the trench you dug, Mr Runge.'

Bill Runge attached a price ticket to a packet of anemone corms, wiped his hands on the plastic apron he wore and turned to them. 'Yes, well, we'd dug this trench for the main drainage. Mind you, I said to him, John, I said, leave it. Don't do it now. Leave it a couple of weeks. Be on the safe side. But he was so sure, poor devil. Then came the bombshell. No permission for four houses. Just the one he could build, on the site where his old dad's was. I thought he was going to have a nervous breakdown and maybe he did. Maybe that's what it was.'

'You filled it in for him, I believe.'

'I didn't want to. I could have done without that, I'm telling you, but he got in such a state. It'd break his heart to go near the place, he said. He said he'd pay me for doing it and – well, things weren't easy. My daughter was only twelve then. She wanted to go on a school trip to Spain and the education people don't pay for that. So I said yes to John and got started. It took me a couple of days. I could only do it in the evenings.'

'Let me get this clear, you hadn't put the pipes in the trench?'

'Oh, no, nothing like that. He'd got them on order but they hadn't come, thank God. Well, I filled in the trench, end of story.'

'Not exactly, Mr Runge. Tell me something. Think carefully. Did you shovel the earth back by putting in a layer the length of the trench and then going back to the beginning and putting in another layer and so on until it was filled up? Or did you fill the trench completely as you went along?'

'Come again?'

Wexford did his best to put his questions more clearly but, by the look on Runge's face, failed again. Burden came to his rescue by producing from his pocket a ballpoint and his notebook. 'Let me draw it,' he said.

A neat sketch was quickly achieved, three separate cross-sections of the trench depicting how it would have appeared a quarter filled, half-filled and completely full. Nodding, comprehending at last, Runge settled for the middle version. He had half-filled the trench, gone home when it got dark, returned to finish the job next day.

'You say you worked in the evenings,' said Wexford. 'It was June and the evenings would have been light till late.'

'June, it was. Didn't get dark till half-nine.'

'Can you pinpoint the date, Mr Runge?'

'It was 16 June. I know that for sure. It was my boy's birthday, he was seven, and he was mad at me for staying out working late. I made it up to him, though.'

It always brought Wexford pleasure to come upon a good parent, something which happened all too seldom. He smiled. 'Did you see anyone while you were working? I mean, did anyone come into the field? Did anyone talk to you?'

'Not that I recall.'

'People do cross that field, walking their dogs.'

'Maybe, but don't let poor old John know it.' Runge put up one finger, as if admonishing himself. 'I tell a lie,' he said. 'There was one person who came to talk to me. Mrs Tredown. Like one of the Mrs Tredowns, the young one, not that she's very young. Came across the field from her place. I said good evening to her. Very polite I was which is more than she was to me. I don't remember her exact words, I mean it was eleven years ago. "So he can't build his houses," she said, something like that. "I'm glad," she said, "I'm overjoyed. I'd like to dance on his effing trench," she said, only she didn't say effing. I reckon that's why I've remembered, her language and her supposed to be a lady. "We won," she said, "God is not mocked." I reckon she isn't all there, two sandwiches short of a picnic, like they say.'

'By "we won" she meant the neighbours' opposition to Mr Grimble's plan had succeeded?'

'That's about it.'

Burden said, 'I think you'd have told us if anything had been put into the trench overnight? Or if you'd seen anything untoward about the trench?'

'I would have, yes. I know what you're getting at. I saw about it on telly. I mean, a skeleton wrapped in purple rags, that's not the kind of thing you wouldn't notice, is it?'

Returning to the car, Wexford said to Burden, 'What did he mean by "one of the Mrs Tredowns", do you know?'

'Search me.'

Wexford asked his question again when they were back at the station. The fifth person he asked knew the answer. Barry Vine laughed, then said, 'He lives with his two wives. It's not like bigamy, him and the first one got divorced all right and I don't suppose there's any how's your father, if you get my meaning. Not with the first one anyway. And Tredown's not a well man.'

'You mean his ex-wife came back to live with him and his second wife?'

'Something like that, guv. I don't know the ins and outs of it.

24

They're a weird lot but I think they all get on. Tredown's ill now. Heart, I think, or it may be cancer. We'll have to talk to them, won't we?'

The Olive and Dove, not many years ago a quiet and conservative country inn with one bathroom to five bedrooms, a public bar as well as a saloon, prawn cocktail, roast lamb and apple pie served for lunch and music unheard within its precincts, had gradually become a smart and fashionable hotel, awarded four stars in the *Good Hotel Guide*. Once it had stood at the entrance to Kingsmarkham, overlooking the bridge that crossed the Kingsbrook (a sizeable river notwithstanding its name) and it was still where it had always been, though the bridge had been widened and the shopping area extended to where once there had only been great beech trees, water meadows, and a cottage or two. The beech trees were still there, though now they grew out of the pavement, and the water meadows had retreated a quarter of a mile or so. As for the cottages, they were now weekenders' residences, newly thatched and double-glazed.

Among its new bathrooms, its sauna, spa, Crystal Bar and Moonraker's Bar, its work-out room, its IT room called, for some unknown reason to non-francophones, Chez L'Ordinateur, its winter garden and its 'quiet room,' the old snug remained. Rumour was that the Olive had retained it solely – or at any rate, partly – at the request of Chief Inspector Wexford, backed up by its best barman who said if it went it would be over his dead body. 'We don't want any more dead bodies round here,' was Wexford's rejoinder but now they had one and it was eleven years dead.

'So we can pinpoint death to eleven years ago last June,' Burden was saying as he carried to their table Wexford's requisite red wine and his own lager. 'What do we think happened? Sometime at the end of May Grimble and Bill Runge started to dig the trench but on the 12th Grimble's application was refused. I checked with the planners. Four days later, on the 16th, Runge filled in half the trench. After dark, X's killer or an accomplice lifted out some of the earth, laid the body, wrapped in a purple sheet, inside and replaced the earth. There'd be nothing to show the trench had been tampered with. Next day Runge finished filling it in.'

'Something like that. Was it a sheet?'

'That's what the lab says. It's in rags but once it was a purple sheet.'

'Who has or had purple sheets, I wonder? The whole job would have been easy enough. The toughest part would have been carrying the body. He's not likely to have been killed out there.' Wexford took a small draught of his claret. 'It's funny, I know it can't be like that, but I fancy I can see this stuff flowing into my arteries and magically melting all that nasty gunge that clings to their walls. Of course it's not at all like that.'

'No, it's not,' said Burden. 'My brother-in-law had a thing called a colonoscopy and he watched what they were doing on a screen. He said his intestines looked like they were lined with pink satin.'

'Modern medicine is wonderful. I just wish we didn't have to hear about it day in and day out. In the Middle Ages they say people brought God into the conversation all the time and with the Victorians it was death. We talk about our insides. Ah, well. Now, we have a precise date for the burial, if not the death. Probably death occurred hours or, at most, days before. Whoever killed X must have known about the trench. It's not visible from Pump Lane or the Kingsmarkham Road.'

'It would be visible from windows.'

'Yes, we shall have to check that. I'd guess Athelstan House, Oak Lodge and Marshmead, wouldn't you? Possibly Flagford Hall too. Was he a local man, Mike? Or was he here on a visit? Eleven years is a long time. We're going to get pretty tired of that phrase before we're done. Most of them, young or old, walked across that land regularly. However much Grimble dislikes it, all the houses that abut on to the field have got gaps in their fences or even gateways that give them access.'

'Have we taken into account the predecessors of those residents who weren't there eleven years ago?'

26

'Barry's working on it,' said Wexford, 'with help from the Hunters. I'm hoping they're the sort of old people who know everything about who lived where since time immemorial. They haven't a clue about what happened yesterday or their own phone numbers but when it comes to years back, they're recording angels.'

'Who's seen the Tredowns?'

'I'm reserving them for myself. They're my tomorrow morning treat. Want to come? I want Hannah to have a look at our sparse missing persons list along with Lyn.'

E ight years before, although quite a large number of men remained missing in the greater mid-Sussex area, there were only two in Kingsmarkham and its environs, which included Flagford. Trevor Gaunt was listed as being sixty-five at the time which made him an unlikely candidate.

'Unless Carina Laxton is way out with her calculations,' said DC Lyn Fancourt. 'I never will understand how they can say someone's been eight or ten or, come to that, twenty years dead just by poking about with bones. Or how old they were.'

Hannah laughed. 'They can, though. You just have to accept it. She could be a year or two out on the age but not twenty years. This old boy isn't our man. He probably dropped dead somewhere,' she said with the callousness of youth, 'and they never found the body. Who's the other one?'

'A guy called Bertram Farrance. This list doesn't give much in the way of detail, does it? I mean, all it gives is his age, which was thirty-eight, his address and that he was reported missing by his wife.'

'What do you expect? You see the telly. You know what they all say. "He went out to buy the evening paper at five and when he hadn't come back by six I was devastated, I didn't know what to do. He'd never done that before," et cetera, et cetera.'

'It can't always be like that,' said Lyn, laughing.

'You could get over there – where is it? Station Road? – see if the woman's still there.'

It went against the grain with Hannah to refer to any woman, even though she might have been married for forty years, was called Mrs and had taken her husband's name, as a wife. She had an even stronger objection to 'lady', a word she had found out came from the Anglo-Saxon *lafdig*, meaning 'she who makes the bread'. Lyn Fancourt thought she was quite right and admired her for the stand she made but, just the same, wasn't it a bit silly?

'I love your ring,' she said.

'Between ourselves, I could have done without. I feel quite committed enough to Bal without wearing a shackle on my finger. But he wanted it, so what can you do? There's no need to get married, just because you wear a ring.'

Lyn walked down to Station Road. It wasn't far and walking was good for her. When she had weighed herself that morning she found she had gained sixty-two grams. It wasn't that much but it troubled her and she tried to think what extra calories she had consumed in the past few days. Literally the past few days because she had weighed herself on Sunday and only by a tremendous effort of will restrained herself from stepping on to the scales on Monday and Tuesday as well. Karen Malahyde would tell her she was getting obsessed but it was all right for Karen and for Hannah too. They were naturally thin. Such strength of character was needed to stop counting calories, keep off the scales and, more that that, stop thinking about it all the time! Stop thinking about it, she said to herself and she went up to the green door which opened directly on to the pavement and rang the bell.

Nothing could have been easier, except that the result got them no further. The woman who answered the door answered her question without inviting her in. 'He's not missing. He's upstairs. You want to see for yourself?'

'Well, yes.'

A shriek from the woman, shrill enough to shatter glass, summoned him. 'Bertie! Come down here, Bertie.'

'What happened?' Lyn asked. 'Did he just come back?'

'After about a year he did. Said he'd lost his memory. I don't let him out alone now. He wants to go out, I say, OK Bertie, but I'm coming with you. And that's what I do. He's not been out alone once since he came back.'

The man who came downstairs looked as if he was of African or Afro-Caribbean origin. He was short and rather fat, wearing camouflage pants and a loose black t-shirt. He didn't speak but confirmed his identity when she asked him. She asked for photographic ID and, rather to Lyn's surprise, Mrs Farrance, if that was who she was, produced a passport. The man was unmistakeably Bertram Farrance. Lyn handed the passport back.

'OK, is it?' said Mrs Farrance, amiably enough. Her voice rising several decibels, she shouted at her husband, 'OK, back upstairs, Bertie. Off you go.'

Telling the story to Hannah, Lyn hoped to make her laugh but the sergeant seemed admiring of Mrs Farrance rather than amused. 'Of course I'd prefer to see a couple equal partners,' she said, 'but if there had to be inequality – in the case of a very feckless or weak man, for instance – I'd rather see the set-up these Farrances have. That way things get done. I expect this woman is very efficient and managing.'

It was DS Barry Vine who had talked to Jonathan Pickford's mother and was told her son and his girlfriend both worked in banking and commuted by train to London each day. He was twenty-nine and she was thirty. Both of them had been at university eleven years before and had only lived in this house since Brenda and her husband had converted it into two flats four years ago.

'But you and your husband were here eleven years ago?'

'We've been here since we were married.' She took him into the living room of their ground-floor flat and showed him from a window Grimble's Field next door and the boarded-up derelict bungalow. This morning, because it had rained most of the night, the land looked particularly green and lush, the bungalow half-hidden among the trees, the only incongruous note the crime tape, enclosing the area where the body had been found. 'When old Mr Grimble was alive,' she said, 'he had such a lovely garden. And he went on working in it, keeping it immaculate until a week before he died. His lawn hadn't got a weed in it. Over by our fence he grew his vegetables and had his kitchen garden and on the other side, near the Tredowns, he had his fruit trees. I remember how he used to give us Cox's apples and Bramleys. For cooking, you know.' She peered into Barry's face, in case perhaps he had never heard of an apple pie. 'The trees are still there, of course, but John Grimble's never pruned them, never done a thing, so of course they don't bear. Isn't it a shame?'

'If you can cast your mind back eleven years, Mrs Pickford, precisely eleven years to June, can you remember anything unusual happening on that land? Anything at all, it doesn't matter how small.'

She seemed rather a timid woman. Suspicious too. It was as if she feared he was trying to catch her out in some misdemeanour. 'Ought I to remember? What kind of thing do you mean?'

That, obviously, he couldn't tell her. She was a woman who might easily have ideas put into her head. He looked patiently into the broad pale face, powdered and clumsily blotched with pink. She wasn't carrying excessive weight but seemed tightly corseted and was rather breathless. She laid one heavily ringed hand against her upper chest as if to quieten a threatened gasping. 'There were the farm workers. My husband called them *itinerant* workers. They come at fruit-picking time in caravans, you know, and one year they camped on Mr Grimble's field and made an awful mess. Is that the kind of thing you mean?'

'It might be,' he said cautiously. 'Do you remember which year that was?'

'Maybe ten years. Could have been eleven.'

That was better. 'What time of the year would it have been?'

She looked at him helplessly. 'Well, it was always June or September they came. June for the strawberries and autumn for the apples and pears.'

Barry persisted. 'Which was it that year? Can you remember?'

And she did, her already pink face flushing with the effort. 'Old Mr Grimble, Mr *Arthur* Grimble, he was dead by then. He'd died in the winter. His son never did a thing to that garden but all the roses were in bloom just the same. And when the fruit-pickers camped there in their caravans – they used to hang their washing on the trees, that wasn't very nice – where was I? Oh, yes, when they camped there Mr Grimble, young Mr Grimble that is, he came and drove them off with sticks. Well, they looked like guns to me but my husband said they were sticks.'

'That was before the trench was dug, was it?'

'Yes, it must have been. That's why Mr Grimble and his friend came over, that's how they knew the caravans were there. Mr Grimble told my husband they meant to survey the land for where the main drains should go and what did they find but all those people camping. I don't mind telling you I never cared much for Mr Grimble but when it came to trespassing I was completely on his side.'

'All that is very helpful, Mrs Pickford. Perhaps you could tell me if you remember anyone – a man – disappearing round here around that time.' The word alarmed her, he could see, and he modified it. 'Well, going away. Someone you know who went away and you didn't see them again.'

'Oh, no. I'd have said. When you asked me if I remembered anything unusual happening I'd have said. That would be very unusual, wouldn't it?'

The Hunters next door looked old enough to be Brenda Pickford's parents and she, as Barry said to himself, was no spring chicken. The front door was opened to him by a carer. He found the ancient pair sitting opposite each other before a fireplace, in which there was a vase of dried flowers instead of a fire. Barry thought there was something pathetic about their placing themselves in that particular spot, out of habit presumably, because all their lives until recently it had been normal practice to sit in front of an open fire. Pathetic perhaps but not tragic, for the room was insufferably hot

31

by his standards, yet both of them, shrunken and wasted, were wrapped in layers of cardigans, scarves and shawls, the old man as much as his wife. Audrey Hunter's eyes were shut and Barry would have thought her asleep but for the hand in her lap which moved and trembled, describing figures of eight on the blanket which covered her knees. Her husband's eyes were a watery sky blue, artless, innocent and uncomprehending.

'He's ninety-six and she's ninety-three,' said the woman. 'You needn't look like that. They're deaf, they can't hear you.' She bellowed into Mr Hunter's ear, 'Here's a policeman come to ask you about Old Grimble's Field.'

'What's that?' the old man muttered as Barry had known he would. Eventually, the question having been shouted twice more, he said, 'Eleven years? I was only eighty-five then. I could get about then.'

His wife continued doodling invisible shapes on her lap. She opened her eyes, put her free hand out to the carer and whispered, 'What's happening?'

'Nothing, sweetheart,' said the carer. 'Nothing for you to worry about.' To Barry she said in a more peremptory tone, 'You won't get anything out of them, you know.'

He persisted for a little longer but in vain.

'What did I tell you?' The woman was triumphant as she showed him to the front door.

He got into his car. The interview had rather shaken him. Wexford had been over-optimistic about the Hunters. Inevitably, Barry thought of modern medicine and healthier lifestyles keeping everyone alive much longer so that by the time he reached retirement age there wouldn't be thousands but tens, hundreds, of thousands of people like the Hunters. Alive but not living, ancient and disabled by time, deprived by the years of memory, hearing, sight and most movement but still alive. He, too, maybe one day. The carer, when she told him he needn't look like that, must have referred to his expression of pity mixed with horror.

*   *   *

32

H annah and Lyn went to the canteen for lunch, Lyn forcing herself to choose the spring salad and trying to keep her eyes from Hannah's ham and cheese pancakes with sauté potatoes. On the other side of the room, alone at a table, Hannah had spotted PS Peach of the uniformed branch. Peach had taken what he called 'a shine to' Hannah. He meant he had fallen in love with her, as he truly had, but to say so aloud would sound too serious and emotional for him even to dream of. Once, a few months back, he had declared himself in a way few men do these days, by telling her he liked her and wanted to take her out with him with engagement in view. Hannah thought he must be the only officer in Kingsmarkham police station who didn't know about her and Bal Bhattacharya. She told him and he was visibly upset. Since then, if he hadn't avoided her, he had kept his distance. Just the same, 'I don't want to catch his eye,' Hannah to Lyn.

So it was much to the surprise of both girls when they saw him on his feet and heading their way, plate in one hand and glass of Coke in the other. A blush suffused his face as he approached but he asked coolly enough if he might join them. Only the very rude and brutish ever say no to this request. Hannah said, 'Of course,' and Lyn said, 'You're welcome, Peachy. Sit down.'

Peach must have had at least one given name but no one knew what it was. He was always called Peachy, even by Wexford, and the name wasn't inappropriate, bestowed as it was on a man with plump pink cheeks and fair hair.

'I don't want to intrude,' he said, pausing to allow both women to demur, 'but I've not come over just because I was – well, wanting company or anything like that.' He looked at Hannah and quickly looked away. 'I've got something to tell you about this case. I mean, the body in Grimble's Field. Well, not tell you about it, tell you what I've done.'

'What you've done, Peachy?' said Hannah.

'What I've made, rather. It's this missing persons thing. We've only got records going back eight years, right?'

'Right.'

'Well, I've got them going back thirteen.'

'*You* have?' Lyn was afraid she had sounded rude and she quickly said, 'What d'you mean? You've found an earlier record?'

'No, I've made one. It was like this. I'll explain.' Peach had abandoned his spaghetti bolognese and pushed away the plate. 'That was when I first came here. 1993. We'd just got computerised. I mean the station had and – well, I was – I am – pretty good on computers, though I say it myself. Nothing out of the way, I'd done a course. I didn't have much use for it in here, not on the beat like I was, but I had access to a computer, of course I did, and I noticed we only kept records of missing persons going back eight years – it was like that then too – only going back to 1985.' He paused and looked into Lyn's face to avoid having to look into Hannah's. 'So I thought, I know what I'll do, I'll keep records myself. I'll do it here and transfer it to my own laptop at home just to be on the safe side.'

'And you did?'

'Well, yes I did.'

'From '93 till now?'

'That's right. It's quite a list. More women than men, though.'

Hannah said, 'You're a marvel. Peachy. The guv will be over the moon.'

'Will you tell him?' At praise from Hannah, Peach had blushed to the colour of a Mediterranean example of the fruit from which his name came, a rich rose shading to crimson.

'Certainly not. You must do that. Don't you want the credit?'

CHAPTER FOUR

E ighty names were on Peach's list, fifty-seven of them women
and girls. To Wexford's pleasure – he had warmly congratu-
lated Peach on his achievement – he had not only included
dates, ages and addresses but descriptions and, to a certain extent,
idiosyncrasies.

'It reminds me of the days when you used to have to put "distinguishing marks" in your passport,' Wexford said, a printout in his
hand. 'There's a chap disappeared he says has a wart on the lobe of
his left ear and another one got six toes on one foot.'

'Sounds nauseating.' Burden was in a gloomy mood this morning.
'I suppose Peach did all this in what one might call the firm's
time.'

'Oh, come on, Mike. It was the firm's business.'

'Maybe, but no one instructed him to do it. For all we know it
may not be accurate. And we haven't finished local enquiries yet.
Peach's stuff may not be needed.'

Wexford made no reply. They were on their way to Flagford, their
destination Athelstan House, home of the Tredowns.

O n the previous evening Wexford had reached home to find his
wife reading a novel called *The Son of Nun*.

'Is that one of Tredown's?'

Dora looked up. 'It's an early one, published twenty years ago.

You said you were going to see him tomorrow, so I got it out when I was in the library.'

'Sounds like unseemly goings-on in a convent. Who was the son of Nun, anyway?'

'Joshua, apparently, though I haven't got to him yet.'

'It's characters like that Joshua who turned me against religion when I was young,' said Wexford. 'All he did was fight battles in the name of the Lord and when the Lord told him to slaughter all the inhabitants of a city, he did slaughter them along with their children and babies and their oxen and their asses. If he was around today we'd call him a war criminal.'

'Things were different then,' said Dora vaguely. 'Does Tredown always write about biblical subjects?'

'Don't ask me. I only read one. That was about Esther and that despot she married. The only character I liked was his first wife he divorced because she defied him. Talking of wives and defiance, is there anything to eat?'

'When have you ever come home, Reg, and found nothing to eat?'

'I only asked,' said Wexford. 'D'you want a drink first? I must have my requisite red wine.'

Later on, after she had gone to bed, taking *The Son of Nun* with her, he looked through his bookcases and found the only book of Tredown's they possessed, *The Queen of Babylon*. He hoped this case wasn't going to take a turn which would necessitate his reading any more of them. Opposite the title page were listed Tredown's works. *The Son of Nun*, *The People of the Book*, *The Widow and her Daughter*, *The First Heaven*. This last, he remembered reading somewhere, was hailed as Tredown's masterpiece for which he had won something called the Fredrik Gartensen Fantasy Prize. Which biblical genocide or monstrous injustice did that chronicle, he wondered, as he shut up the book and went to bed.

Now he was on his way to see its author. There was very little traffic about. Donaldson had chosen to take the back lanes instead of the Kingsmarkham Road. They drove through lush green byways where the leaves were beginning to turn to pale gold and the fuzzy tangle of old man's beard covered the hedgerows. The cattle in the meadows browsed calmly in the mild sunshine but in a broad paddock a glossy bay horse and a grey raced each other round its perimeter, manes flying.

'It would be nice to walk across there with a dog,' said Wexford, 'down into the valley and up the other side on to the Downs.'

Burden looked at him. 'You don't like dogs.'

'Not much, but you have to have an excuse for that kind of thing.'

'He's seriously ill, you know.'

'Who is?'

'Tredown. Jenny told me. Liver cancer. I think it is.'

Wexford said nothing. He thought about cancer, the way so many people he knew and Dora knew who had it or had had it but got better. Yet all the other people who hadn't got it still went about talking of cancer as if it was a death sentence, the end of the world, a fate worse than death itself. One day they wouldn't any more, he supposed. He was aware that Donaldson was getting out of the car to open a pair of gates. They had arrived.

A driveway went up between trees with overhanging branches. Between their trunks, on the left-hand side, Grimble's Field could be seen, very green this morning and, as always, providing exercise for a man and a dog. The decaying bungalow lay among the encroaching trees as if it were dead itself, waiting only to be picked up and removed to a grave of its own.

The Athelstan House drive widened into a broad gravelled space. Seen close to, the house was unprepossessing, large, ill-proportioned, mainly of purplish red brick, roofed in bright blue-grey slates and with Gothic ogee-topped windows of buff-coloured stone. The front door might have been a church doorway, dark brown, black iron-studded and with a curved, purely ornamental handle. Wexford had the curious impression that it was a house of too many colours. And they were colours that clashed, all the ill-suited brown and purple and blue and cream jumbled and jangling together. Its being set

37

against a rich backcloth of dark greens and autumn golds didn't help matters. He thought how much he would have disliked living in it and then he rang the bell.

A phone call had warned Maeve Tredown of their coming. She still looked surprised as if she had expected very different-looking men, Sherlock Holmes and Watson perhaps, or two uniformed comedy cops.

'You'd better come in,' she said. 'Please wipe your feet.' She seemed to realise that outside it was a fine, warm and above all dry autumn day, and added, 'No, I see. It isn't raining, is it?'

The inside confirmed Wexford in his opinion that Victorian builders (architects?) had gone out of their way to make their interiors hideous. This must have been what Lewis Caroll had in mind when he used the word 'uglification'. The hallway was a passage, not particularly narrow but made to look narrower by the height of its ceiling and the vertical-striped green and yellow wallpaper. A kind of mosaic of black and ochre tiles covered the floor. As if an attempt was being made to conceal as much of the decor as possible, enough coats and capes and raincoats and mackintoshes and cagoules and anoraks and duffels and cardigans hung on ranges of hooks to protect twenty people from the weather, while appropriate footwear, boots and shoes and trainers and even something Wexford hadn't seen for years, galoshes, stood in pairs on the yellow and black tiles. What room remained against the walls was occupied by suitcases and shopping bags.

'In here,' said Maeve Tredown, opening a door.

It was a large room and, in spite of the warmth outside where the temperature was rising up into the twenties, very cold. Its window faced north and overlooked a lawn surrounded by trees, predominantly evergreens. The furniture was unnoticeable, nondescript chairs and sofas and tables. The carpet, patterned in reds and browns, reminded him of nothing so much as a dinner plate off which someone had just eaten a meal of fish and chips with tomato ketchup and a good sprinkling of vinegar. What dominated the place were books, hundreds of them, possibly thousands, in unglazed bookshelves which covered three walls from floor to ceiling. The fourth side of the room was mostly a window and one in dire need of cleaning. Looking out, her back to the room, stood a tall thin woman with long black hair.

'You'd better sit down.'

Maeve Tredown spoke as if she begrudged every word she uttered. She was small and round with a face like a pretty piglet's and dyed blonde hair, a surely harmless and inoffensive woman. Just the same, Wexford felt that if he had been shown a photograph of her and told she was the matron of a notoriously cruel old people's home or the director of a brutal boot camp, he wouldn't have been surprised. It was all to do with her economical and clipped speech, the iciness in her light blue eyes and the severe grey flannel suit she wore.

'I don't know what it is you want.' She glanced in the direction of the other woman, seemed to be considering whether there was any point in introducing her, and finally decided that there was no help for it. 'Claudia,' she said, 'I suppose these men are as likely to want to talk to you as to me.'

In turning round, the black-haired woman caused something of a shock. From the back she might have been twenty-five. When she faced them, even in the shadow which fell across her face, she at once became close on sixty. She was extravagantly thin, with the thinness which is natural and unaffected by dieting or overeating, and her face was deeply lined. She came up to them, held out a long-fingered, rope-veined hand, smiled and was immediately transformed into a ravaged beauty.

'How do you do? I'm Claudia Ricardo. Well, I was Tredown when I was married to Owen but I reverted when we were divorced. Ricardo was my maiden name, though I wasn't actually a maiden for very long.'

Burden was less able to deal with this sort of thing than Wexford. He resorted to ignoring it and speaking in the stolid gloomy tone of a copper on the beat. They had, he said, some questions they would like to ask. Wexford would probably have enjoyed himself at Mrs Tredown's expense and engaged in repartee with Claudia Ricardo, but Burden's technique may have been more effective. 'We'd like to speak to Mr Tredown as well.'

'No can do,' said Maeve in a phrase Wexford hadn't heard for years.

'Yes, I understand he's ill,' Wexford said. 'We'll disturb him as little as possible.'

'It's not that he's ill. He is but that's not the point. He's working.' Claudia Ricardo gave another of her smiles, a less charming one this time. 'My wife-in-law – that's what we call each other – likes to keep his nose to the grindstone. I mean, his books are our bread and butter. She cracks the whip, don't you, Em darling?'

It was Maeve Tredown who smiled this time. She appeared not to be the least offended but fixed Claudia with a conspiratorial smile, accompanied by a companionable wrinkling of the nose, a kind of what-a-one-you-are expression.

Wexford thought he preferred her when she was taciturn. 'Very well. It's not necessary to see him today,' he said. 'Perhaps you can answer a few questions. No doubt you know a body was discovered in Grimble's Field. We're having some difficulty of identification. Are you aware of anyone going missing in the area about eleven years ago?'

'How would we?' This was Maeve who had seated herself on a slippery black leather sofa with Claudia beside her. 'What has that dump to do with us?'

'Probably nothing but do you know of anyone being missing round here? It would be eleven years ago last May or June.'

Few people are able to utter an unadorned no but Maeve Tredown managed it. 'No.'

Claudia aimed at being more helpful. 'That would have been soon after I came to live here,' she said. 'I married again after the divorce but that didn't work out either. Maeve asked me if I'd like to come here and live with them. Nice of her, wasn't it? A bit odd, you might say – well, you would say, but very nice. We'd always got on, far better than I did with Owen, though that was a lot better when I wasn't married to him.'

Why tell them all this? Wexford had no idea. Because it amused her? Because she had decided they were both dense plodders? 'You must have seen Mr Grimble and his friend digging a trench across the field.'

'We saw *that*,' said Maeve, becoming more expansive. 'I was delighted when they refused him planning permission.'

'Me too.' Claudia bounced up and down on the leather seat, like a child offered an unexpected treat. 'I had a little holiday in my heart. Don't you think that's a nice expression? I almost had an orgasm when I heard.'

Maeve said suddenly, 'There was that cousin or brother-in-law or some relative of Grimble's who went missing around then. I've just remembered,' as if someone had asked. 'I can't tell you who it was but everybody knew. I expect that's who it is.'

'That's exactly right,' said Claudia with a merry laugh. 'Yes, I expect Grimble killed him and put him in the trench. I'm *so* sorry you can't see Owen now. Could you come back another time? Actually it's lovely to have some male company, isn't it, Em?'

'How did they know the body was in the trench?' said Burden on the way back.

'We told them.'

'Well, not exactly. You just said Grimble and his friend were digging a trench.'

'Oh, come on, Mike. Whatever you think of them, they're not stupid. Anyone would pick that up. Besides, it said a body was in a trench on the local TV news. I'm more interested in this missing relative Grimble didn't mention.'

'Maybe he's on Peach's list,' said Burden.

He was. He was one of the two men who had gone missing at the relevant time, Peter Darracott and Charlie Cummings. Hannah Goldsmith and Lyn Fancourt had spent the morning tracking down their families and discovered that Peter Darracott, who had disappeared from home in May 1995, was John Grimble's second cousin, his natural father's cousin's son.

His wife had gone away on holiday with her next-door neighbour to Tenerife, a ten-day package. If she wanted foreign holidays, Christine Darracott told Hannah, she'd always had to go with a friend. Her husband was afraid of flying.

'I used to tell people he got airsick,' she said and her face became vindictive. 'I used to, but if anyone asks me now I tell the truth. I'm done with shielding him from everything. He was scared shitless if you want the truth.'

'You came home and found him gone, Mrs Darracott?' Home was a terraced house in Pestle Lane, parallel to Kingsmarkham High Street. 'Hadn't he even left you a note?'

'Nothing. Not a sausage. Mind you, he left me the bed he hadn't made and his dirty dishes and full ashtrays everywhere. But that was normal.'

'He'd taken a lot of his clothes,' Hannah told Wexford, 'and things they owned in common, a radio, a little portable TV – oh, and a hairdryer. What does a man want with a hairdryer?'

'Much the same as what a woman does, I suppose. Maybe he'd got long hair. You mustn't be sexist, DS Goldsmith.'

Hannah had the grace to laugh. 'The truth is he took it out of spite. Why women get married I never will know.'

'Well, you're going to,' said Burden, 'unless that ring's purely for ornament.'

'We shall see,' said Hannah, unfazed. 'She told me Peter was Grimble's second cousin, whatever that means. Apparently, there's a huge family, spread out everywhere. She reported Peter as missing but she doesn't appear to have taken steps herself to find him. She more or less said it was good riddance. "One thing, he wouldn't have left the country," she said. "Too scared to get on a plane."'

'Did they know each other?' Wexford asked. 'I mean, Grimble and this Peter Darracott?' He turned to Burden. 'Do you know your second cousins? Do you, Lyn?'

'I wouldn't even know what makes someone your second cousin,' said Burden.

Lyn smiled. 'You'd know them if you were like me and hadn't got many relations. Apart from my mum and dad, my second cousin is the only one I've got.'

'According to Peach's list and comments,' said Wexford, 'Christine Darracott never heard from him again. It's always hard to imagine how this can happen, someone disappearing and being gone for good but it does, all the time. Of course it helps when their nearest and dearest would just as soon they never turned up. How about Charlie Cummings, Lyn?'

He had gone missing from the house in which he lived with his mother in December 1994. Both lived on the benefit, Charlie having some kind of disability, what would now be called, Lyn said, 'learning difficulties'. Apparently, both he and his mother were unable to read or write. The details Lyn had came from Mrs Cummings's neighbour, Mrs Cummings herself having died in 2000.

'Doris Lomax, that's the woman next door, said she died of a broken heart. There was quite a hunt for Cummings. I mean, you can see there would have been, with him not being normal and never going out much except to the village shop. That's where he went on that day in December. It was in the morning. He went to the shop to get a loaf and a packet of tea bags and he was – well, he was never seen again. Mrs Cummings went next door to Mrs Lomax and I gather Mrs Lomax sort of took charge. She phoned us and then practically the whole village turned out to hunt for him.'

'I remember this case,' Wexford said. 'I remember it well and you must do, Mike.'

'I got involved in the search. We turned the place over, looking for him. It was like a search for a child.'

'I suppose he *was* a child,' said Wexford sadly. I just hope, he didn't say aloud, that dreadful thing in Grimble's Field isn't him. I'd like to find he'd turned up, living in Brighton with a kindly woman as childlike as himself. 'And now, if you and Hannah and maybe Damon will start tracking down *previous* owners of houses in Pump Lane and the Kingsmarkham Road, you and I, Mike, will have another session with Grimble.'

A phone call to Theodore Borodin at his London home disclosed that Ronald and Irene McNeil had sold him Flagford Hall seven years before. It was a large house, almost a stately home, too much for the aging couple to cope with.

'They were getting on a bit,' Borodin said. 'The time was coming when they wouldn't be able to drive. They needed somewhere to live near the shops. The only one in Flagford's hopeless. Old McNeil was eighty and she wasn't much younger, and now I come to think of it, someone told me he'd died.'

'But they must have been there,' Damon Coleman said, 'when this murder and the subsequent burial took place.'

'Certainly they must have.' Borodin went on to describe in unnecessary detail what a state Flagford Hall had been in, what enormous sums of money he had been forced to spend on it, how costly was its upkeep, considering he only used it at the weekends, until Damon politely cut him short and thanked him for his help.

T he house, largish, detached, perhaps no more than eight years old, wasn't far from Wexford's own home. Damon passed it on his way there. The front door was opened by Irene McNeil herself, a heavy sluggish woman who looked every minute of her eighty-four years. Time had dragged down her features until chin blended in with neck and neck sagged over the collar of an unflattering grey blouse.

While Damon tried not to look at her log-like swollen legs, she stared searchingly at him and remarked in a throaty tone, 'I expected them to send someone more senior.'

Damon was certainly not paranoid, not even particularly sensitive, about being a black man in still predominantly white rural England. Still, interpreting as otherwise than racist Mrs McNeil's gaze, which travelled from his feet to the crown of his head and rested incredulously on the face which several woman had found exceptionally handsome, would have been impossible.

Having told him he had 'better come in', she led him through the ground floor, lumbering heavily. The interior was the reverse of what Damon expected, hi-tech and minimalist, built-in cupboards, ice-white walls, black tiles and pale wood floors. In the living room, Mrs McNeil's antiques and fifties armchairs sat uneasily against this stark background. Lowering herself on to a floral chintz sofa, she proceeded to list the reasons she and her husband had moved from Flagford Hall, a catalogue from which Borodin's explanation was absent. Her voice was the most plummy and upper class Damon had ever heard.

The neighbours were impossible, she said, particularly the Hunters and the Pickfords. She knew for a fact Mr Pickford senior had poisoned her cat and his saying (very rudely) that he hadn't laid a finger on it and even a twenty-year-old bird-slaughtering fiend belonging to her couldn't be expected to live for ever, was a tissue of lies. She had seen Mr Hunter watching her house through binoculars and taking photographs of herself and her late husband having tea in their garden. But the worst of all were those Tredowns. She was sure there must be a law against a man living with two wives, or if there wasn't there ought to be. It was the first Mrs Tredown coming back to live with him and the second Mrs Tredown that was the beginning of the end. That was when she and Mr McNeil started seriously thinking of moving, wrench though it was to leave a house they had occupied on their return from their honeymoon. She told, rather than asked, Damon to pass her the framed photograph from an occasional table with a piecrust edge.

'That was Ronald.'

'Your husband?'

'Yes, of course,' said Mrs McNeil. 'Who else would it be?'

Damon looked at the photograph of an elderly but still handsome man with a moustache, 'dressed up', as he put it to himself, in the requisite gear for going hunting, a kind of cap on his head and a red jacket he thought vaguely he ought to call pink.

'Very nice,' he said

It was evidently an inadequate response. Mrs McNeil snatched the photograph from him, said, 'Ronald was a wonderful man.'

Damon said he was sure of it, though there was something brutal in the pictured face and the hands clenched into fists. 'Did you know Mr Grimble?'

'The old one?' said Mrs McNeil. 'He wasn't the class of person one expected to be living in Pump Lane but, my goodness, he was an improvement on his son. Stepson, I should say. That one's real name, I mean his true father's name, was Darracott and we all know what the Darracotts are.' Damon, who didn't, listened patiently to the ensuing stream of invective on the subject of Mr John Grimble ('I call him Darracott') culminating in the monstrous behaviour of a son digging up his stepfather's garden when that parent was scarcely cold in his grave.

'Tell me about that,' said Damon.

'There's nothing to tell,' said Mrs McNeil, uttering the sentence most likely to cause exasperation if not despair in a policeman's heart. Fortunately, and Mrs McNeil was one of them, most people quickly find they have plenty to tell after all. 'He and this friend of his started digging a great – well, a sort of ditch or trench. It was high summer, you know, and they dug in an absolutely wanton fashion, right up through poor old Mr Grimble's garden, ruining a beautiful *Rosa hugonis* and a bed of calla lilies – I don't suppose you know what those are but no matter – and the friend finished the job, if he finished it. He only worked in the evenings, if you

46

can call it work. And then, of course, or so young Mr Pickford told my husband, he failed to get his planning permission and they had to fill it all in again.'

'I expect that pleased you.'

'It certainly did. The last thing I wanted was *four* houses built opposite me. All the same they would have been, all red brick with those picture windows, so-called. Of course that was before we knew we'd move on account of the disgusting behaviour going on at the Tredowns'.'

'You saw the trench they'd dug filled in again?'

'Oh, yes. I saw the man fill it in. He had his wireless on all the time, *full* on. I could hear it from Flagford Hall with all my windows shut. Those kind of people can't do anything without that pop music. Ronald used to say it makes them feel uneasy not having background noise.'

'Did you see anything odd at that time, Mrs McNeil? Anything, never mind how small, you thought at the time was – well, strange.'

'Not apart from that man's wireless set. But that's not odd these days, that's normal.' She hesitated. 'Well, there was one thing, though I don't really know that you could call it odd.'

'Try me,' said Damon.

'It was just the day after that man had finished filling in the trench. The first Mrs Tredown – she calls herself Claudia Ricardo but a person like that would call herself anything – she came across Grimble's Field with her dog. She had a little dog in those days, brought it with her. It's dead now and no one shed any tears about that. Well, she walked it across the field and when she came to where the trench was – there was a sort of line of bare earth if you see what I mean – she didn't walk over it, she walked round it, all the way down to the bungalow and up the other side as if she was avoiding that line of earth. I went over after she'd gone and I couldn't see any reason why a person would walk *round* it.'

'While you were living at Flagford Hall did you hear of anyone going missing? Disappearing?'

'Only that retarded man. What was he called? Cummings? He was simple, you know. Almost the village idiot.'

This phrase gave Damon a worse shock than would a stream of obscenities issuing from Mrs McNeil's mouth. He even made an involuntary sound, a kind of 'ouch' of protest. She spoke more gently than she had throughout the interview. 'Are you feeling unwell?'

'No, no, I'm fine.' He tried a smile. 'Thank you, Mrs McNeil, you've been very helpful.'

Walking him to the front door, her legs barely performing their prime function, she turned, peered at him and said, 'You speak very good English. What part of the world do you come from?'

This was a question Damon was quite used to being asked. It still happened all the time. 'Bermondsey,' he said.

Number 5, Oswald Road, home of the Grimbles, John and Kathleen, was one of those houses – or its living room was – which are furnished with most of the necessaries of life, things to sit on and sit at, things to look at and listen to, to supply warmth or keep out the cold, insulate the walls and cover the floors, but with nothing to refresh the spirit or gladden the heart, compel the eye or turn the soul's eye towards the light. The predominant colour was beige. There was a calendar (Industry in Twenty-first Century UK) but no pictures on the walls, no books, not even a magazine, a small pale blue cactus in a beige pot but no flowers or other plants, no cushions on the bleak wooden-armed chairs and settee, a beige carpet but no rugs. The only clock was the digital kind with large, very bright green, quivering figures.

John Grimble was sitting in front of the screen when Wexford and Hannah were brought in by his wife. The film which was showing had reached a torrid love scene, enacted in silence as the sound was off. Kathleen Grimble took her place in the other orthopaedic chair as if these positions and this contemplation of the picture had been ordained by some higher power. This time, though, she picked up the knitting which she had left lying on the seat of the chair, and, gazing in total impassivity at the writhing couple, began her mechanical and speedy work with needles and scarlet wool. Madame Defarge, Wexford thought. He could imagine her sitting on the steps of the guillotine, muttering 'Oh, John, don't' each time a head rolled.

'I'd appreciate your attention, Mr Grimble,' he said. 'We've something very serious to ask you.'

Grimble turned an irritable face to him. 'Give it five minutes, can't you, and I'll be with you.'

'Turn it off, please,' said Wexford, 'or I'll do it myself.'

But at that moment the actor on the screen picked up a knife from the bedside table and thrust it into the outstretched neck of his companion, causing Mrs Grimble to assert herself. 'Right, that's enough,' she said calmly. 'I'm not watching that sort of thing,' and grabbing the remote, she switched off, then turned off the set.

Grimble began a low muttered complaining which Hannah interrupted, 'Mr Grimble, you didn't tell us a relative of yours went missing in May 1995. A bit before the time you applied for planning permission to build on your field. I'm talking about Mr Peter Darracott of Pestle Lane, Kingsmarkham.'

'Is it all right for her to ask me questions?' Grimble said to Wexford. 'I mean, has she got the proper qualifications?'

Wexford saw the blood rush to Hannah's cheeks, sure sign of rage developing. He gave her a very small shake of the head. 'Very proper, Mr Grimble. Better than mine, in fact,' he said, thinking of Hannah's psychology degree.

'I suppose I have to take your word for it. What do you want to know for?' He was still addressing Wexford but it was Hannah who replied, the colour receding from her face.

'We already do know, Mr Grimble. When we last spoke to you, you didn't mention Mr Darracott.'

'Because I didn't know him, that's why.'

'But you knew he was your cousin.'

'My second cousin, if you don't mind. Oh, I can see what you're getting at. There was a body found in my field that's been dead eleven years. My second cousin went missing eleven years ago, so

49

they've got to be one and the same. Now I'll tell you something. Everybody knows Peter Darracott had been carrying on with the woman as worked in the chemist on the corner of Pestle Lane and that's who he went off with. And I for one don't blame him married to that Christine what had a tongue on her like a razor, nagged him from morn till night she did till he went spare.'

'Oh, John, don't,' said Kathleen.

'How well did you know him?' Wexford asked in a deceptively mild tone.

'About as well as most folks know their second cousins. Maybe we'd see each other at family funerals and that was about it. As matter of fact the last time I saw him was at my mum's funeral two years before he went missing.'

'It was good of him to come, John,' said Kathleen.

'Yes, well, my dad was his godfather and he thought he might be in the will, didn't he? He was unlucky there.'

'Some itinerant farm workers camped on that land eleven years ago. Was that with your permission?'

Grimble flared again. The very word 'permission' seemed enough to inflame him. 'Are you joking? They counted on me living over here what was five miles away. Some busybody must have told them. But I was too many for them. Me and Bill Runge come over to see where we'd dig that trench and there they was, their vans all over my field and their muck and litter. I got them off there pretty damn quick, I can tell you. Me and Bill went in there and got them off. If folks tell you we had guns it's a lie. Sticks we had and they put up no resistance. They was scared of us and no wonder.'

He must have got that bit about resistance off the TV, Wexford thought. 'Can you remember exactly when that was, Mr Grimble?'

'To the day, I can. It was May 31st and next day me and Bill started digging. Them bloody planners refused me permission 12 June and on 16 June Bill started filling up our trench. Nearly broke my heart it did. If you're thinking one of them might be them bones, you can think again. They was gone back to where they come from days before me and Bill ever stuck a spade in the sod.'

CHAPTER SIX

Sheila was just leaving when Wexford got home. He put his arms round her and kissed her, an embrace which also included the baby Anoushka in a sling on her mother's chest. 'Grandad kiss,' said Amy as Wexford picked her up.

'You don't have to go the moment I get in, do you?'

'I do. I've got a car picking me up here in two minutes. You're late, anyway, Pop.'

'I always am. Unpunctuality is the impoliteness of policemen. Not very good, I'm afraid, but I'm too weary for epigrams. When are you coming down again?'

'Next week. I've got a project on. Ma will tell you.'

The car came, sleek and black. The white-haired driver had the face of the old Italian actor, Rossano Brazzi. Wexford waved to the children and they waved at him out of a rear window and he went on watching until they were all out of sight. He turned away. His front garden was still a mass of flowers, awaiting the frost which never came. Fuchsias in tubs, the last of the dahlias and Michaelmas daisies in the borders. Nothing to do with him, he seldom if ever pulled out a weed or planted a seed, but all Dora's work. If he sometimes neglected his wife, and he feared he did, he appreciated her when her work came into flower. There was a graceful yellow thing in a tub called a *Thunbergia* that he'd forced himself to learn the name of, though he'd forget it again by the spring, and another yellow thing that was a shrub with flowers which smelt of oranges, but that was long over now.

Dora said, when she had received his wife-appreciating kiss, 'Did you see Sheila?'

'Just in time to watch them go. What's this project she was talking about?'

'Oh, that,' said Dora dismissively. 'Her *news* was that she's got the lead in this film that's based on your friend Tredown's great work.'

'Not my friend,' said Wexford, fetching himself a glass of red wine and her a glass of white. 'I haven't even set eyes on him yet. Do you mean *The First Heaven*?'

'I suppose so. It's a wonderful thing for her. She's to be the goddess of love and beauty. Oh, Reg, you should have heard her. You should have heard what she said. "And I was the check-in chick in that *Runway* serial for years and years," she said. "Haven't I come up in the world?"'

'I wish she stayed a bit longer. Shall we drink to her success?' They touched glasses and Wexford, seeing tears in her eyes, said quickly, 'So what *is* this project? I think of our other daughter having projects, not Sheila.'

'It's something to do with female circumcision, only she calls it female genital mutilation. It sounds awful. She says it's going on here.'

Wexford was silent for a moment. Then he said, 'It's against the law. There was a law passed a couple of years ago to stop people taking their daughters back to Africa to have it done. I hope there's none of it here. Did Sheila think there was?'

'She doesn't know. People are so secretive about it. There's quite a large Somali community in Kingsmarkham, as we know, and they practise it. You know how when everyone round here wants someone to blame for all the social ills, they always pick on the Somalis. I don't really know what female circumcision is. Do you?'

'Oh, yes,' said Wexford and, thinking he might need a second glass of wine, whatever Dr Akande said, he told her.

*   *   *

Of the names on Peach's list Charlie Cummings and Peter Darracott still remained unaccounted for and unless more bodies were discovered it seemed likely they would simply remain as missing persons and possible candidates for what had been found in Grimble's Field.

'We have to consider,' said Wexford, 'that he may not have lived here at all but have been here only on a visit, staying in the neighbourhood.'

He and Burden were having lunch in the new Indian restaurant. Its name was A Passage to India and they had chosen it mainly because it was next door but one to the police station where a handicrafts shop had once been. No one any longer wanted to work tapestries or buy embroidery frames and the shop, according to Barry Vine, had 'gone bust'. Burden looked up from the menu, an elaborate affair done in scarlet and gold on mock parchment.

'The first time the itinerant farm workers came to Flagford *was* eleven years ago in June, exactly as Grimble says. That was for the soft-fruit-picking and when he'd driven them off, Morella's fruit farm gave them a bit of land to camp on. That's where they were when they came back three years later in September. Whether it was the same lot I don't know. Probably some of the same lot and some new ones. Apparently the farmer – Morella's fruit farm, that is – was providing them with a proper campsite by that time. It's hard to keep tracks on these people. All we can say is that no missing person was reported to us.'

They gave their order to the waitress who smiled politely. She had difficulty with English but managed a 'Thank you very much.'

'We're checking on all the hotels,' Burden went on when she had gone. 'The difficulty there is that of course they don't keep records that far back. Still, why would anyone who came, say, on holiday, get himself murdered and buried in Flagford? I suppose whoever he was could have come here to blackmail someone who lived here.'

'Sounds like the Sherlock Holmes story Conan Doyle forgot to write. Let's say he was in possession of compromising photos of old Mrs McNeil and her lover old Mr Pickford and wanted £10,000 to keep them dark. So they asked him round, poisoned him in the Tio Pepe, and at the same time Grimble was very conveniently digging a trench for them to bury the body in. I don't think so.'

'It was only an example,' said Burden in a huffy tone, and then, very surprisingly, 'That girl who served us, she's called Matea, is probably the most beautiful woman I've ever seen.'

Wexford looked at him, his eyebrows raised. 'I don't believe my ears. You never say things like that.'

'I'm not being – well, salacious or whatever you call it. I don't fancy her, as you'd say in your crude way. I just think she's beautiful. I'd say it even if my own wife was having lunch here with me.'

'Really? Women don't generally like it much if you say that sort of thing about other women, however innocent and pure, as in your case, the motivation may be.'

Matea came out through the red and gold bead curtain at this point, bringing their lamb biryani and chicken korma. She was about eighteen, very tall, very slender and somehow her slenderness could be seen to be natural and not associated with starving herself. Her skin was the pastel gold of a tea rose, her features softly rounded and perfectly symmetrical, her hair waist-length, glossy and black and her eyes . . .

'I don't think I could describe them,' said Burden, contemplating a dish of yellow chutney.

'Oh, I could. How about ebony pools of fathomless depths or sloe-black windows of the soul? Come on, Mike, eat your lunch. What is she anyway? Middle Eastern? They don't make them like that in the outskirts of Stowerton.'

Burden didn't know or said he didn't. His wife's political correctness, though less intense than Hannah Goldsmith's, had affected him with an unease about ever categorising anyone according to their race.

*   *   *

T he shop on the corner of Pestle Lane and Queen Street still had the name Robinson's Chemists engraved on its window, reminder of ancient days, Burden said gloomily, before 'pharmacy' became the in word. Its proprietor was now a tall thin Asian man called Sharma and his shop a model emporium of cleanliness, order and efficiency. Gone were the tall stoppered vessels filled with dubious cobalt blue and malachite green liquids that used to stand in the window and gone too the trusses and mysteriously labelled 'rubber goods' which used to puzzle him as a child. As he remarked to DC Lyn Fancourt, he hadn't been inside the place for thirty-five years. A blonde girl assistant in a short pink overall over jeans was stacking shelves while another was in the dispensary at the back of the counter.

Palab Sharma had taken over the shop eleven years before and had taken over Nancy Jackson with it. 'She got married and left,' he said to Burden. 'It would have been two years after I came here.'

'Do you know who she married and where she is now?'

'My wife will know.'

Summoned by phone from the flat above, Parvati Sharma appeared, neither in a sari nor salwar kameez and veil but smartly dressed in a white shirt, short skirt and high heels. Though very pretty, she failed to match up to Burden's new standard of female beauty.

'I went to the wedding,' she said. 'I hadn't long been married myself. It was the first English wedding I ever went to and it was very nice.'

Burden asked her if the couple lived in Kingsmarkham.

'Sewingbury,' she said. 'I'm so sorry, I don't know where. She's Mrs Jackson now. I saw her in Marks & Spencer. She had her two little boys with her and I had mine. It was very nice. We said we'd have to meet and have a coffee or something but we never have – well, not yet.'

Burden thanked her and hustled Lyn away from where she was studying a display of slimming aids. 'Do you think those tablets really do suppress appetite, sir?'

'I doubt it,' said Burden and added, he who had seldom missed a meal in his entire life, 'You just have to eat less. Easy-peasy.'

Nancy Jackson, as Burden put it afterwards to Wexford, had done well for herself. If there was no comparison in his eyes with Matea, she was a good-looking young woman, blonde, sharp-featured, dressed in the young woman's uniform of skintight jeans and short tank top which left a three-inch gap of bare tanned flesh. If not quite the best part of Sewingbury, the home she shared with her husband and two small sons was in a quiet tree-lined road where every house had a double garage attached to it. She was welcoming, frank and cheerful. For a change, she was a woman who appeared to have nothing to hide and no chips on her shoulder.

She made Burden and Lyn a pot of tea and sat down with them at her teak kitchen table in her handsome kitchen, handing round a plate of carrot cake slices and chocolate chip cookies. Burden took a piece of cake, Lyn miserably succumbed to a cookie but refused milk in her tea.

'My twins are at school now,' she said. 'They're just five and I've got to go and fetch them at half-three but I can give you half an hour.'

'I believe you had a relationship with Peter Darracott, Mrs Jackson,' Burden said.

He must have spoken in a deliberately discreet way as if lowering his voice would ensure this statement wasn't heard by flies on walls. Nancy Jackson burst into laughter. 'You don't have to be careful what you say to me. Everyone knows I've been round the block a few times. Before I was married, I mean. Dave knows – that's my husband – and he says, "Well, I wasn't pure as the driven snow myself, darling," so you know what they say about the goose and the gander. But Pete Darracott. Of course he was married to that Christine and as a general rule I gave married men a wide berth but there was something about Pete. He was a postman, you know, hadn't got 2p to rub together.

'Me and my mum were living together but she turned a blind eye to my goings-on. Pete and I used to pop round to our place in the afternoons. He wanted me to go away with him, you know, but I was a bit wary. We could go up to his sister in Wales, he said, Cardiff it was. And do what? I said. And he said—'

'Mrs Jackson, when was this?'

'Oh, sure, it'd be a good idea to tell you that, wouldn't it? Have another biscuit,' she said to Lyn. 'Yes, well, it'll have been May '95, end of May. He said he'd stop with his sister and find a job and a place to live and write to me. The idea was that I'd join him. Well, he went. We had a last afternoon together first. Mum had a friend stopping at our place so we couldn't go there. So what d'you think we did? We went to old Grimble's place, that bungalow. Grimble was like Pete's cousin. I never saw him but he'd been round to Pete's house asking him to do him a favour, so we knew that bungalow was empty. It wasn't long after old Mr Grimble had passed on, so it wasn't bad. The bed was all made-up. It was OK for a quickie.' She broke off to giggle. 'He just went off after that, said he'd write and tell me when he'd got a place but he never did. I never heard a word, not a sausage, but to tell you the truth I didn't care that much. I'd met my Dave by then and I sort of knew he was the one for me. You know, don't you, when that happens?'

Burden thought how much less offensive this woman's sex talk was than Claudia Ricardo's. 'And you never saw him or heard from him again, Mrs Jackson?'

'Never. There's just one thing. Grimble asked Pete to help him dig a trench. I'll tell you about it. I've just got time before I pick up my twinnies.'

A man was kneeling on the floor at number 5, Oswald Road, examining the Grimbles' television set. Beside him on the floor, occupying the same sort of area as the armchair in which John Grimble habitually sat was a large cuboid cardboard box. As

Wexford and Hannah entered the room, led by Kathleen Grimble, the engineer, with the air of one breaking seriously bad news, remarked that he couldn't carry out repairs on the spot but would have to take the set away.

'You can't do that. What am I going to do without the telly?'

'Shouldn't be more than a day or two.'

'A day or two!' Grimble sat shaking his head in incredulity. 'You'll have to give me a lend of one.'

'I'll have to see,' said the man in a hopeless sort of voice. 'Give me a hand to get this into the box, will you? My back's not what it used to be.'

During the argument which ensued, Kathleen Grimble quietly offered her services and when she and the engineer had got the set into the box, she helped him drag it out to the front door. Grimble shouted after them, 'I want a loan of a set, mind, and I want it today. If it's not here by five I'm coming down the shop. And I want one of them as hangs up on the wall.'

Wexford had been enjoying all this too much to interrupt but now he did. 'You didn't tell us you asked your cousin Peter Darracott – I beg your pardon, your *second* cousin – to help you dig that trench across your late father's garden.'

'I didn't,' said Grimble, 'and why should I? He never done it. All he done was waste my time.'

'You'd know all about that. You've plenty of practice wasting ours. Tell us what happened. You went to Mr Darracott's house in May 1995 and then what?'

'Go on, John,' said Kathleen, 'do what the officer says. You've got nothing to hide, you know that.'

'That's why I don't want to do what he says,' said Grimble sullenly.

'If you won't, I will.'

Grimble seemed to be pondering his wife's words, perhaps thinking that if he left things to her, she might say more than was expedient.

'Come along, Mr Grimble,' said Wexford. 'If you don't want to go into it here we can always talk at the police station.'

This promise or threat had its usual effect. After staring in a kind of despair at the space which his television set had occupied, Grimble turned abruptly away and said in a rush, 'I went round to his and his wife was there, Christine, she's called, and I said to Pete, "D'you want to come over and give me a hand digging a trench on my property at Flagford what my dad left me?" And Pete said, "Digging it what for?" And I said, "For putting in the main drainage for the new properties I'm building." I never said I hadn't got no planning permission. It was no business of his.'

'Just take it a bit more slowly, would you, Mr Grimble?' said Hannah.

At fractionally less fast a pace, Grimble went on, 'She said, that Christine that is, "He'd want paying," and he told her to keep out of it and none too soon if you ask me. There wasn't no call for her to be there in the first place. Pete said, "I'd have to go over and see it. I'm not letting myself in for a job like that on spec," so I said, "OK," I said, "I'll run you over there tomorrow evening, right?"' **GALWAY COUNTY LIBRARIES**

As Wexford said later to Hannah, that was the only instance they had ever heard or were likely to hear of Grimble showing the faintest scrap of altruism and even then it was more for his own benefit than Peter Darracott's. 'And did you?'

'It was a bloody waste of time. He said he would but when the day come to start he never turned up, so I had to ask Bill Runge.'

Hannah asked him if he had ever seen Peter Darracott again. 'Not after he let me down, no I didn't.'

'Yes, you did, John,' said Kathleen Grimble. 'You saw him when he come over to Dad's place and said he'd changed his mind, he'd help out on account of he needed the money and you said, not on your nelly. It was when you'd finished the digging and the council said you couldn't build them houses. Must have been 16 or 17 June.'

Wexford said later to Burden, 'I got him to come down to the station and make a statement and we went through the whole thing again. Of course I suggested he might like a solicitor but he wouldn't.'

The problem is we don't even know if our corpse is Peter Darracott and we won't till we've got the DNA comparison done.'

'You mean Grimble actually gave a sample?'

'I didn't ask him. I know when I'm talking to a brick wall. Darracott's got a nephew, his sister's son, and he was happy to oblige. Some people get a thrill out of that sort of thing, you know. I wish we could come up with a motive, Mike. Why would Grimble kill Peter Darracott and bury him in his dad's garden? If Darracott had been the chief planning officer I could understand it.'

'I talked to Nancy Jackson today, she was called Nancy Saddler before she married—'

'Not more family connections,' said Wexford. 'Now those are what *I* call relationships.'

'All these people are sort of old Kingsmarkham, the Grimbles and the Darracotts and the Pages and the Pargeters – Christine Darracott was a Pargeter before she married. They've lived around here for generations, all farm labourers once. Well, the Grimbles were blacksmiths. My grandfather had a horse and I remember him taking it to a Grimble to be shod.'

'Was that the one with the truffle-digging pig? No, save it for later when we're having a nasty lunch in the canteen. Tell me what Nancy Jackson said. Imagine I can't read.'

They were having a cup of tea in Wexford's office, Burden perched, as was his wont, on a corner of the big rosewood desk. The morning had been warm and, when the sun came out, hot, but now a wind had got up, very blustery and chilling the air. The first raindrops of a shower dashed against the window. Burden finished his tea and put the cup back in its saucer.

'She says Darracott asked her to go away with him. This was in May '95. Apparently, he had an idea of going to Cardiff where he had family – his mother was Welsh – and getting a job on the buses there. Nancy wasn't at all keen on this idea. She's a bit of a snob, is Nancy. It was OK having a fling with Darracott but he wasn't husband material, she said. They used to go to her home where she lived with her mother—'

'Not more relatives, please, Mike.'

Wexford added water to the teapot and poured more for both of them. 'She sounds a tough cookie.'

'Hard as nails. Mr Jackson, by the way, owns a highly profitable garage and what he calls an on-the-spot repair shop in Sewingbury. Their house is worth a lot more than mine.'

'Good for Nancy. So what happened?'

'Rows, I gathered. Darracott trying to persuade Nancy and Nancy telling him to give up the idea, culminating in Darracott telling her he was going as soon as Christine had departed on this holiday to Tenerife.'

'Did she know anything about Grimble asking him to help with digging this trench?'

'Oh, yes. He couldn't make up his mind whether to do it or not and when he did it was too late. Planning permission was refused, something Nancy said cheered Darracott up no end. Everybody seems to have been happy about that except poor old Grimble. Now sometime at the end of May was the last time Nancy saw Darracott. They couldn't go to her place because her mother had an old pal staying. So where d'you think they went? Over to Flagford to the late Mr Grimble's bungalow. Sunnybank, it's called.'

'What, that derelict dump in Grimble's field? Not exactly a love nest, was it?'

'I suppose passion will always find a way. I don't know if it was locked up in those days, she didn't say – didn't know, I suppose. Remember Grimble meant to demolish it as soon as he got his permission. Anyway, they went there, she doesn't remember the date but it was before Grimble started digging, and Darracott told her he'd decided to go to Cardiff and stop with his other sister – sorry, Reg – until he'd got a job and somewhere to live. He'd write to her. He still hoped she'd join him. Nancy says he gave her his sister's address and phone number. She never heard a word.'

'The sister'd be another potential DNA donor, only we don't need her,' said Wexford. 'And that's it?'

61

'Well, no, not exactly. I'm not going to say this is just like a woman because you'd be down on me like a ton of bricks for being a sexist, but the fact is she didn't want the guy, she'd broken with him and as it happens she'd met Jackson by then. For all that, she didn't like it that Darracott hadn't written. She couldn't have meant much to him if he forgot her as soon as she was out of his sight. So she phoned the sister or tried to but the number was unobtainable. She wrote to him at that address and got no reply. And that was it.'

'Do we have the sister's name?'

'Dilys Hughes. Coleman's traced her to another address in Cardiff. The difficulty is she remembers very little about the summer of 1995. She was in hospital having a hysterectomy around that time. She does remember getting a letter from her brother some weeks earlier asking what were his chances of getting a job in Cardiff and accommodation. It was the first time she'd heard from him for years, she told Coleman. She answered his letter, putting him off, and she never heard from him again until some relative or other told her he'd gone missing.'

'So did Darracott ever go to Wales? Or did he go, find his sister was in hospital, and stay with someone else, stay in a B and B or something?'

'He may have been dead.'

'It's beginning to look like it,' Wexford said cautiously. 'We must hope this DNA test won't take too long. But what motive did Grimble have, Mike? Darracott was a postman. He hadn't any money or if he had it wasn't going to come Grimble's way. Don't tell me Grimble had his eye on Nancy Jackson because I won't believe it. One of the extraordinary things about Grimble is that he appears to be happily married to his Kathleen. Oh, he's a bad-tempered bugger. I suppose he could have struck Darracott in a rage over there in that field, bashed him over the head with a spade because he wouldn't help him and Runge fill the trench in.'

'We don't believe that, do we?' said Burden.

'I don't think we do. I'll tell you what, it might be wise to have a look inside that bungalow of Grimble's.'

'What for? He'll never let us, we'd have to get a warrant.'

'Then so be it,' said Wexford. 'We'll get one. I've just got a feeling not taking a look inside might be something we'd regret.'

CHAPTER SEVEN

W exford had picked up *The Son of Nun* and was leafing through it, reading bits of it and rereading them in consternation, when Sheila phoned.

'So you've got the lead in this Tredown epic?'

'Isn't it great? I'm to be Jossabi, the goddess of love and beauty. She was like a sort of Helen of Troy, you know. The wars in heaven all started because of her being stolen away. Of course you've read *The First Heaven*?'

'No, I haven't,' said Wexford. 'I've dipped into it but I don't like fantasy. If I read fiction I want to recognise the characters as real people, the kind of people I might know, not immortal gods and dinosaurs.'

'But, Pop, the point with *The First Heaven* is that the people all seem real. It's a marvellous book, you can't put it down.'

'I could. If it's anything like *The Son of Nun* I don't know why anyone wants to make a film of it. So what's all this about female genital mutilation?'

'You've such a big group of Somalis in Kingsmarkham I just thought I should target it in my campaign. Sylvia agrees. I've just been talking to her. The view our campaign takes is all the girls in this country between the ages of three months and twenty with origins in the Horn of Africa should be medically examined every year to check that they've not been mutilated. You could start that, get the GPs to agree to it and when they find a recent case you could get a prosecution going.'

'Get an accusation of institutional racism in the police going more like,' said Wexford. 'You can only do that sort of thing if you examine every girl, not just the African ones, and the NHS hasn't the resources. Oh, I hear what you say. I hate the practice as much as you do but I've got a more realistic attitude to what can and can't be done.'

'I'll tell you something,' said Sheila, huffy now. 'I bet you if these were little white girls there'd be a national outcry.'

He called Dora and left Sheila to her mother. By association, the role of a goddess of love and beauty reminded him of the girl in the restaurant called A Passage to India – Matea. Could she be Somali? And if she was . . . ? The idea of some old woman, using a sharpened stone and no anaesthetic, shearing away her delicate flesh, was so abhorrent that he made the effort to banish it from his mind and once more picked up *The Son of Nun*.

It was, he saw, a reissue. The novel had first been published in the mid-eighties and was one of a number Tredown had written on Old Testament themes. There were others based on the story of Samuel, the triumphs of David and the iniquities of Ahab and Jezebel. The sad story of Jephtha's daughter Tredown had retold under the title of *The First Living Thing He Saw* and he remembered how Jephtha had foolishly promised God that, in gratitude for victory in war, he would sacrifice the first creature he encountered when he returned and was in sight of home. The idiot might have calculated it would be his daughter, Wexford thought with contempt. Suggesting to Dora when she came off the phone that this hardly seemed to him likely to be a recipe for literary success, on the grounds that potential readers would assume they were being preached at, he added, 'But what do I know?'

'As much as any other reader, I suppose,' she said. 'They *weren't* very successful. That's why he – well, he changed tack and wrote *The First Heaven*. It's not like anything else he'd ever done. No Bible stories, more a sort of amalgam of Greek myths and Norse tales and prehistoric animals. That's what Sheila says. I haven't read it. It made him very popular.'

'And now,' said Wexford, unconvinced, 'it's going to bore thousands more for four hours on the screen. I can't bear to think of it.'

'You'll have to do more than think of it with your daughter in the lead. You'll have to see it – at least once.'

N ext day, among the documents which landed on his desk, one was that rarity, an old-fashioned handwritten letter sent through the post, the others the post-mortem report, compiled by Mavrikian and Laxton, and the report on a lab examination of the purple sheet which had wrapped the body of the man in Grimble's Field. Man begins to decay once life is gone but the man-*made* may endure for centuries. The eleven years this sheet had lasted – though now threadbare in parts – was like a minute gone in the life history of a sheet, Wexford said with some exaggeration. This one had come from Marks & Spencer. According to that company's records purple had been a fashionable shade and the colour of one of their ranges in the early seventies. It therefore seemed likely that it was more than twenty years old before it was used as a shroud. Possibly it had been used for this purpose because it had a hole or slit at one end about a foot from the hem. The slit was ragged round the edges and stained with a brownish substance which, on analysis, proved to be blood of the same group as that of the dead man.

The post-mortem report told him little he didn't know already. He was already aware that one of the ribs was cracked. Neither of the pathologists offered this as the cause of death, they couldn't tell the cause of death. What they had had in front of them was a skeleton with a simple break in a rib, but it afforded enough DNA to establish whether the corpse was that of Peter Darracott. He would have Christine Darracott in here to see if she could identify the sheet but that wouldn't be much help either. None of those neighbours seemed the sort of people who would use purple bedlinen. They were mostly elderly. They were middle class, the men professionals of some sort or another, the women stay-at-home housewives, the kind who would make up their beds in white linen, or daringly, in pale blue or pink. One of them was the writer of the letter he turned to next.

He saw at a glance that its purpose was to provide him with a possible identification. There had been many of these, but all the rest had come by email.

Long ago he had made-up his mind that in many respects the Internet was more trouble than it was worth. Half the country, it seemed, sat in front of screens all day, telling the other half their thoughts, hopes, aspirations, giving advice, requesting help, offering things for sale, inviting fraud by demanding and receiving credit card numbers, misleading the frightened and the lonely, and wasting the time of people like himself who had their jobs to do. Of course, it had its uses, like supplying information about every citizen and bringing up registers at the touch of a key. But the time-wasting factor really made itself felt in the screen-fillers which had come to him: those which told him of *female* relatives who had gone missing in 1981 or 2002, those telling him how interested they were in the investigation and had he a job for them, and others madly requesting meetings, including one from a woman who gave her vital statistics, hair and eye colour, age and education and job history, and suggested he and she have their first date next Tuesday.

The letter seemed to belong to a different era from the emails, was addressed 'Dear Sir' and signed 'Yours truly, Irene McNeil', a usage he had thought utterly gone. She told him she had 'remembered something since the visit of the coloured boy', was sure he should know about it and, having no idea how otherwise to communicate with him, was writing. She didn't trust the phone and never had done since childhood when her parents had 'the telephone installed' in 1933. The 'something' she recalled concerned 'old Mr Grimble's lodger'. This was the first Wexford had heard of Arthur Grimble having a lodger but whether this had any connection with the case seemed unlikely. He read on.

'I could see everything which went on from my front windows,' Mrs McNeil ended unashamedly.

Burden and Damon Coleman had a warrant to search Sunnybank. Grimble had been asked permission for them to enter and had refused, saying he hadn't been in the place himself for eleven years so he didn't see why the police should. This delayed things but not for long. Not usually given to flights of fancy, Burden said afterwards to Wexford that going in there made him think of explorers penetrating a jungle to discover some ancient tomb in the depths of a forest.

'I just hope the spirit of the place hasn't put a curse on you,' said Wexford.

Damon removed the screws which held in place the sheet of plywood over the front doorway. Underneath they expected to find the front door but there was only a cavity. Inside was semi-darkness and a strong smell of dry rot and wet rot, mildew, mould, lichen, putrefaction and general decay. Not all the windows were boarded up – there seemed no logic as to why some were and some were not – and in the first room they went into it was light enough to see that the place was still furnished but in the grimmest and most eerie way, the table and chairs coated with grey dust, cobwebs linking lampshade to mantelpiece to pictures, like some primitive electrical system of loosely strung cables. The windowpanes were cracked and the curtains which hung from a broken rail, ragged and stained. Damp had marked the ceiling with curious patterns, some shaped like parts of the human body, a leg here in a high-heeled shoe, a disembodied head, and others like maps of islands in an archipelago or close-ups of the surface of the moon.

On a dining table, the top of which was scarred with white rings made by hot cups and black channels made by cigarettes left to burn themselves out, stood a glass vase, its inside scummed with a brown deposit which supported the dried-up straw-like stems of flowers that fell into dust when Damon touched them. The smell

68

was stronger here, mostly coming, it seemed, from the mould on the walls where rising damp had erupted in crusts like brown scabs. It was a very strong smell and one almost impossible to ignore. Damon began sneezing.

'Bless you,' said Burden automatically.

'What are we looking for, anyway, sir?' Damon asked when the spasm had passed.

'Anything,' said Burden. 'I don't know. Signs of Arthur Grimble's lodger? He had a lodger, the lodger left or didn't leave. It's all a bit vague. When I asked Grimble if we could come in here he said nothing about this lodger. He just refused permission. I'm inclined to think he said it out of cussedness. He couldn't get his permission, so he wasn't going to give us any.'

The window in this room was intact but for a diagonal crack across one corner. Damon peered out of it into the greenish gloom and beyond at the grave and the police crime tape surrounding it. He tried a light switch but the power had long been cut off. It was only four in the afternoon but a kind of premature dusk had come and inside here they needed their torches. The light they gave showed the way to the kitchen. At the sight of it Burden made no attempt to suppress his shudder. It was more like a cavern than a place where food had once been prepared, dark, smelly, every surface beaded with condensation as if the furniture had sweated.

Damon's torch played on the single counter where lay, in a heap, blue jeans, an orange-coloured anorak, a well-worn t-shirt printed with some kind of animal or insect, wool socks and a pair of black and grey trainers.

'It looks as if our visit hasn't been in vain,' Burden said.

'Could this lot have belonged to X, sir?'

'Who knows? Not to either of the Grimbles, I'd have thought.'

Burden felt a tension that was almost a shiver run through him and he couldn't attribute it to the dampness or the smells. It was something else, something primitive, perhaps a discharge of adrenalin preparing him for fight or flight. He and Coleman went back into the passage and from there into the bedrooms, both of which were full of cheap, shabby, worn-out furniture, a single bed in one, a double bed in the other, old-fashioned washstands, one of bamboo, with basins and jugs from another distant age, parchment-shaded hanging lamps, the whole covered in grey shrouds of dust. On the double bed two pillows without pillowcases still lay, ochre-coloured and marked with the stains of saliva, sweat, and other human effluvia Burden didn't want to think about. A grey bedspread had been visited by moths and mice which had left behind them the usual evidence of their occupation.

'Darracott's love nest,' Burden muttered, though it wouldn't have been as bad as this eleven years ago when the missing man had brought Nancy Jackson here.

He opened a wardrobe door to release a new smell, mothballs and ancient dried sweat, the stench of the old man's clothes still left hanging there, two suits which might have been new in the forties, a sports jacket, coats and trousers. Burden closed the door again and they made their way into the bathroom, where the floor was deep in grey dust, the bath brown from iron stains and the lavatory pan stuffed with newspaper. A sliver of soap, rock-hard and split into blackened cracks lay above the basin and on a sagging wooden shelf was an old man's shaving brush, the bristles worn down to stumps.

Damon began sneezing again. 'Let's get out of here, sir.'

'Wait a minute. There's a cellar.'

A flight of steps led down into darkness. Burden went down first, switching on his torch. He let the beam play on what lay below. There was a small square of floor space and beyond that a doorway. All the others doors in the house were open but that door was shut. Burden said, with some kind of prevision, with fore-boding, 'Better not touch that doorknob.'

For 364 days a year he never carried a handkerchief. This was the 365th and for no known reason he had picked up a clean one when he went to put his shirt on. He wrapped it round his right hand, took hold of the door handle, tugged at it and finally wrenched it open. Inside was a small room perhaps measuring six feet by eight, where everything seemed coated in coal dust. A heap of coal lay in one corner, prompting Burden to ask himself when he had last seen coal – years and years ago. In front of it wood was stacked, pieces of timber and small logs, a pile of it, three feet high.

'Pull out one of those planks, Damon, could you? But go carefully.'

Damon went carefully, slowly tugging at the longest piece of timber until it came free, dislodging some of the logs and sending them tumbling. He pulled at another, smaller, board and heard the inspector's indrawn breath.

'There's something under there,' Burden said.

The torches set down on a shelf, their beams playing on the heap of timber, revealed what might have been a small piece of white rag. They carefully lifted logs one by one until hair came to light, black and coarse like the horsehair Burden had once seen stuffing an old sofa, then something which might have been a section of bone. What had been under the logs was half-exposed, Damon took a step backwards, grasped his torch and shone the beam directly downwards. By its light, he and Burden were looking down at the remains of a man, bones mostly, vestiges of grey flesh clinging to them, still dressed with horrid incongruity in whitish singlet and underpants. The black hair, the first thing Burden had seen, longish and shaggy, covered the back of the skull. Whoever he was appeared to have been dumped face downwards, the arms and legs spread in a starfish shape.

The smell in the house came from elsewhere. Here, only a kind of airlessness combined with a whiff of coal dust remained, for the body they were looking at had been there a long time.

'Is this the chap who didn't leave, sir?'

'Plainly, he didn't,' said Burden, 'but who he was, God knows. One thing's for sure. Just as you don't bury yourself, you don't hide yourself in a woodpile after you're dead.'

CHAPTER EIGHT

H is whole team were there, at the kind of meeting he usually held at nine in the morning. The time was seven in the evening and dark as midnight. They looked tired, even the very young ones. Burden was trim as ever in a stone linen jacket and jeans, his forehead pleated in a frown, his greying hair cut a fraction too short. Weariness makes some people look younger and Hannah was one of them, the colour gone from her cheeks, her eyes heavy, while Lyn's and Karen's faces, made-up as usual in the morning, were now shiny and pale as nature made them. Damon seemed the exception to the rule that black skins bleach to grey when exhaustion sets in and he still had that alert look, his eyes pitch-black and bright, the whites almost blue, which Wexford so liked about him.

He noticed that he alone among the men wore a tie. Barry's shirt under a thin zipper jacket was open almost to the waist, revealing a fleshy roll which, in women, he'd heard called a 'muffin top'. Like Hamlet he had been 'too much in the sun' and, from bridge to tip, his nose was burnt red from the long protracted summer, as was his tieless throat. Ties had almost disappeared, at least they had out here in the country, and Wexford wondered what inhibition or diffidence in himself made him need to go on wearing this weathered, worn and stain-spotted strip of synthetic fabric.

Wondered, but only for a moment, and then he began to address them. 'This afternoon,' he began, 'the body of a man was found in the derelict bungalow on Grimble's Field. Mike Burden and Damon Coleman went in there on a routine search and found the body in the cellar. We don't know who it is but Carina has seen it and says she'd guess it's been there a shorter time than the unidentified corpse in the trench. Nor can we say yet if there's any connection between these two bodies. We shall know more tomorrow when she's done the post-mortem.

'As for Peter Darracott, we are waiting for the result of the DNA test and we should get that tomorrow. Depending on that result, we may have to widen our search. If, for instance, the body in the trench isn't Peter Darracott. There appear to be no more missing or possibly missing males in the Kingsmarkham area who disappeared sometime in the spring of 1995. There is of course the possibility that the body in the cellar is Darracott's. I shall have John Grimble in here in the morning and question him about this second body found on his property. At the moment we have some reason to believe the death was the result of violence because the body was hidden in the cellar under a pile of logs. As yet we don't know what caused death or whether death occurred in the cellar. But the body had been hidden. Someone hid it and we know it's extremely rare to conceal a body that has met a natural death.

'The clothes he seems to have worn were in the kitchen. Two unusual features of this case are that the body was clothed only in a vest and underpants and that £1,000 in ten- and twenty-pound notes was in the pocket of a pair of jeans. The jeans were probably his but that still has to be established. Are there any questions?'

There always were. Hannah was the first to ask. 'Why did DI Burden and Damon go in there, guv?'

'A Mrs McNeil, the woman who used to live in Borodin's house, wrote to me with what looked like an absurd story about old Grimble – Grimble senior, that is – evicting his lodger but no one seeing him actually leave. Then John Grimble wouldn't let us go in there, which seemed a bit dodgy, so we got a warrant.'

She nodded, sighed, pushed back her long black hair behind

her ears. Barry Vine asked if the media had yet been told and Wexford said he'd tell them in the morning after his meeting with the chief constable. Then he'd hold a press conference when the post-mortem results – and with luck the DNA test result – came through.

Lyn had something to say but not a question. Theodore Borodin had come down for the weekend and she had been to call on him, an interview which yielded nothing of interest beyond his professing a total lack of curiosity about any of his neighbours, none of whom he seemed to know by name.

'When I was coming away and getting into my car one of Tredown's wives came out.' This gave rise to laughter, enough to make Lyn modify what she had said. 'I mean one of the Mrs Tredowns. She came up to me and said was it true they'd found a cadaver – that was her word, "cadaver" – in that house. She could see something had happened, what with all the crime tape round the place and police vehicles coming and going. I asked her what made her think it was a – well, a body, and she said something like, 'I knew it. They don't put that blue and white ribbon round a place because some lout's broken a window.' And she was very happy at the idea, I must say. "Man or woman?" she said. Of course I didn't tell her. I just said if there was anything any of the people living there needed to know we'd keep them informed and then I drove off.'

Wexford laughed. 'Well done,' he said. 'Right, that's that for now. We can't do any more tonight so I suggest you all go home and get a good night's rest. We'll start again in the morning.' But as Burden lingered when all the rest had gone, he said, 'Come and have a drink, Mike. The snug in the Olive, I think.'

Rain had fallen for most of the day but now the clouds had moved away eastwards and it was becoming a fine night, mild enough for lights to be on in the Olive's garden. A few drinkers, mostly young, sat at the tables under sunshades which would double as umbrellas if the rain began again.

'I don't like sitting outdoors,' said Wexford, squashing any al-fresco ideas Burden might have had. 'I never have. Nothing depresses me so much on a holiday as the prospect of a picnic. All those flies and wasps. I remember a picnic Dora and I had when the girls were little. The food was all laid out on a red checked tablecloth – funny how you remember these details – and this puppy, basset hound or beagle or something, came running up, grabbed a Swiss roll in its mouth and made off with it. The girls were entranced. Sheila thought we'd actually fixed it.' He laughed at the memory. 'She thought we'd arranged for the bloody thing to come and do that to *entertain* them. I almost wished we had.'

'That,' said Burden, ordering their drinks, 'is sort of like Christmas in reverse. I mean the way we *have* fixed Father Christmas, it's probably Dad dressed up, but kids think it really is some old guy from Lapland. Or they do for a while.'

Mike could still surprise him with his occasional insights. He smiled. 'That must have been quite a shock, finding those – er, remains in Grimble's cellar. I imagine your first thought was that here was the old man's lodger.'

'And my second and third thoughts.'

'It's a bit much, though, isn't it? This old man – how old was he, by the way? Eighty? – he murders his tenant and stuffs the corpse in the cellar. Or, because he's not strong enough to do that, lures him down into the cellar and there kills him. In six months' time the old man is dead and within weeks of his death the son is murdering another man and burying him in a trench some ten yards from where the other body is lying.'

'More than ten yards, Reg. More like twenty.'

'Ten or twenty, it doesn't make much difference. Does homicide run in the family? And if it does we have to suppose Grimble senior didn't wait until he was eighty and practically at death's door before he killed. So how many other unsolved killings are there along the way? And what are the motives in all this? *Cui bono?*'

'We don't know who benefits, do we?' said Burden. 'We don't yet know who either of these men are. We're not even near to finding out. The old man may have been dead before either of them died. We don't know what connection there was between them, if any.

'Isn't it rather odd that Mrs McNeil should have written to you about this lodger? She didn't mention him before when Damon first interviewed her. And when you come to think of it her story was pretty thin. I can understand she was bored and had nothing better to do than watch her neighbours' houses from morning till night but why seize on that? Why jump to the conclusion that a man's disappeared – a man she didn't know but thinks was called Chapman, no first name – just because she hasn't actually seen him depart?'

'You think she knows more than she's telling?'

'Well, don't you? Another funny thing is the £1,000. The clothes were shabby, those jeans were on their last legs.' Burden realised what he had said and laughed. 'Yet £1,000 was in the pocket?'

'And those notes had been in there for a decade.' Wexford shrugged. 'I can't say I look forward to a session with John Grimble in the morning and there'll be no wife there to "Oh, John" him.'

'Don't be too sure,' said Burden. 'What's the betting he brings her along? Do you want another couple of units of that red plonk?'

Wexford sat in his office at the rosewood desk (which was his own and not the property of the Mid-Sussex Police Force) contemplating the t-shirt which had been found in the kitchen of Grimble's bungalow. It had already been examined in the lab and put to rigorous testing.

On a white background was printed in black a scorpion, measuring twelve inches from head to curled-up forked tail. The lab gave its length in centimetres but Wexford refused to cope with that. Under the scorpion's tail was the name 'Sam' in block letters. The letters had been printed in red but had now faded to a dull pink. The only label inside the t-shirt was a tiny square of cotton bearing the letter 'M' for medium.

He left it lying there when Grimble was announced. Burden

would have won his bet if Wexford had done more than smile in response to the challenge, for Grimble had indeed brought his wife. She was without her knitting, and the devil finding no work for idle hands, hers wandered aimlessly about her lap, rubbed the surface of Wexford's desk and occasionally scratched portions of her anatomy.

Grimble listened with apparent surprise and growing distaste to the story of the discovery, related by Burden, in his late father's house. His wife's mouth fell open and one of those fidgety hands came up to cover it as if the solecism of relating such a story had been hers, not Wexford's.

'What's that thing?' He pointed an accusing finger at the t-shirt. 'What's that doing there?'

In a level voice, Wexford said, 'It was in your late father's house. In the kitchen. Is it yours?'

'Of course it isn't bloody mine.' Wexford had never seen Grimble so angry. 'Would I wear a thing like that?' He cocked his thumb in his wife's direction. 'And it isn't hers. I told you time and again I never set foot in that place after they never gave me my permission.'

'Now, John,' said his wife, 'you keep calm.'

Grimble took a deep breath, closed his eyes briefly and sighed. Unlikely as it seemed, it was apparent someone – probably Kathleen Grimble – had taught him a technique for dealing with rage. His face gradually lost the dark red colour which had suffused it. He began shaking his head slowly.

'I don't get it,' he said. 'What was that door doing shut?'

'Which door is that, Mr Grimble?'

'Door to the cellar. *He* said he found it shut. That door was never shut. My old dad kept that open all the years he lived there. I was a boy there, I grew up there, didn't I, Kath, and I never saw that door shut, didn't know it *could* shut.'

Perhaps believing some response was required, Kathleen Grimble said, 'There wasn't no need to shut that door.'

Grimble nodded. 'I reckon whoever it was went down there

snooping about' – his eyes wandered malevolently to Burden – 'they got it wrong. That door was never shut.'

Unwilling to enter into an undignified argument, Burden nevertheless saw himself heading that way. 'The door was shut,' he said as shortly and crisply as he could. 'That you have to accept. I found it shut and opened it myself. I had some trouble in getting it to open.'

'It never was shut before, that's all I can say.' As with many people who make this remark, it was far from all he could say but as he launched into a week-by-week, month-by-month account of the number of times he had been down the cellar steps and found the door open, Wexford briskly cut him short.

'All right. Thank you. Tell me about your father's tenant – a Mr Chapman, was it?'

Grimble's face distorted into a moue of disgust that anyone could mistake this man's real name for Chapman. 'Chadwick, Chadwick. Who told you he was called Chapman? They want their head tested. Chadwick, he was called.'

'Of course he was.' Kathleen was rubbing her fingertips together like someone crumbling bread. 'Never Chapman. Where did you get that from?'

Instead of answering her, Wexford said, 'Was his first name Sam?'

Uttering this innocuous three-letter word caused a similar explosion to that brought about by their mistake in Chadwick's surname. '*Sam?* You lot haven't done your homework, have you? Douglas was his name. My poor old dad called him Doug.'

'That's right,' said Kathleen with an approving smile for her husband. 'He did. Friendly to everyone, John's dad was. Kindness itself.'

'But he evicted this Chadwick?'

'No, he never. He wanted his rent. Kept him waiting weeks for it, Chadwick did.'

'Don't forget the piano, John.'

'I won't. You can be sure of that. Chadwick played that piano at all hours. Midnight, six in the morning, it was all one to him.

And that was only half of it. He left wet towels on the bathroom floor like he had a servant to pick them up for him. It was hard on my poor old dad, he was a sick man then, got the Big C, though he didn't know it, poor old devil. He wasn't going to evict him, was he? Not with all that rent owing. Chadwick did a moonlight flit, left his stuff behind. Dad was an honest man, he wasn't keeping nothing what wasn't his due, so he put all that junk outside the house and held on to the piano. It was his right, wasn't it? Chadwick's pal came back with a van and knocked at the door and asked for the piano and Dad said—'

Damon Coleman had come into the room and, speaking softly to Wexford, said, 'Miss Laxton's sent a note over to you, sir. I've got it here. I think it's the DNA test result.'

'OK. Thanks, Damon.' Wexford unfolded the sheet of paper and read the result. He looked up, said to Grimble, 'No doubt, you'll be glad to hear the body in your trench isn't that of your second cousin Peter Darracott.'

Grimble said in a contemptuous tone that he had never thought it was. 'That his DNA you've got there?'

'It's the result of comparing the body in your trench with Mark Page's DNA, yes.'

An electrifying change came over Grimble. It was as if he had literally seen the light and it had brought him not only revelation but huge pleasure and a kind of triumph. 'You took a whatsit – a sample or whatever – from that little bugger Mark Page?' When neither Wexford nor Burden said a word, he went on, 'My cousin Maureen Page's boy?'

'Yes, Mr Grimble. What is all this?'

'I'll tell you what all this is. Mark Page is adopted, that's what.'

They looked at him almost as bleakly as he had at them when he heard of the body in his father's house.

'Maureen couldn't have kids of her own. Her and her husband George Page, they adopted a girl first and then this kid Mark.'

'Mr Page said nothing about this,' said Burden.

'No, he wouldn't.' Kathleen Grimble had begun to giggle. 'He knows, of course he does. Known since he was four, he has. But he don't like it, he's like ashamed. He wouldn't tell you. Even if you asked he wouldn't.'

After that, the interview came to an abrupt end. Wexford asked only one more question and that was concerning the possible whereabouts of Douglas Chadwick. Surprisingly, Kathleen Grimble had an address for him. It appeared that whatever secretarial work had been required by Grimble senior (or, come to that, by Grimble junior) had been performed by Kathleen, the established ways of things in a world where women carried out the despised functions of housework, child-rearing and the exercise of the mind. She had written to him when he answered Grimble senior's original advertisement, which she also had drafted. That letter had been sent thirteen years before, so there wasn't much chance that whoever lived at the address now would have much idea of Chadwick's present whereabouts.

'If he has any whereabouts,' said Wexford.

'I could wring that Mark Page's neck.' Burden was still wrathful. 'Why didn't he say? Didn't he realise?'

'Speaking of necks, he's thick from his upwards. We'll ask Maureen Page herself or the sister Peter Darracott didn't go to when he said he had. And when dealing with this family, make sure she really is his sister and not someone his dead brother married or lived with or happened to be brought up by his parents. Remember old Grimble was young Grimble's stepfather, not his own father. And let's hope she's not a Seventh Day Adventist or a Jehovah's Witness who objects to giving us a spot of saliva.'

I t would have been hard for Wexford to get to Forby village hall by seven-thirty, or indeed any time before nine, but his attempts to cancel aroused wails of disappointment from his younger daughter.

Her 'Oh, Pop, you promised!' sounded very much the sort of thing she used to say when she was five. It still went straight to his heart. Her follow-up remark was a little more mature. 'Having a detective chief inspector there would mean so much to them.'

He tried a ridiculous reproof in Hannah's style, political correctness gone mad, and said, 'I question whether you ought to refer to an ethnic minority as "them", Sheila.'

Her indignant reaction made him laugh. 'You know I didn't mean—'

'I'll do my best to be there.'

Barry Vine had gone to Cardiff, Lyn Fancourt driving him, to secure the DNA sample promised by Dilys Hughes, née Darracott. Wexford's own attention had been turned to Douglas Chadwick, his forays into the Internet assisted by Hannah. He couldn't have done it without her. The address Kathleen Grimble had given him was in Nottingham, a street which sounded as if in a poor neighbourhood. Hannah frowned when he used those words, fearing worse to come.

'OK, did you ever hear of a Violet Grove in an upmarket residential area?'

'Well if you put it like that . . .'

'Number 15 Violet Grove. The family name is or was Dixon.'

'"Was" is right, guv. There's a Marilyn P. Williams and a Robert A. Greville there now.'

Wexford sighed. 'I suppose we'll have to go up there or get the Nottingham police in on this. Someone in the street may remember him. Do we know what he was doing in Flagford?'

Hannah had pursued the questioning of Kathleen Grimble with some difficulty. 'He was a student at Myringham University, guv. I've been on to them and they said he'd attended the university from 1993 to 1996.'

Wexford thought of the piano-playing. 'A music student?'

'Mechanical engineering. The degree is a BSc MEng.'

'He'd have been a mature student, over 40. Is there some record somewhere, I mean some register, of people with degrees in that?'

'I can find out, guv.'

While her fingers trawled through the Internet, he thought about the clothes that had been found in the house, the underclothes on the body, the scorpion t-shirt, orange anorak, jeans and socks, the trainers, which had been piled up on the kitchen counter. Why had this man, whoever he was, Chadwick or Darracott or Charlie Cummings, taken off his clothes and his shoes in the kitchen and gone barefoot down to the cellar in his underwear? Because he was looking for something? In that case, why not go down there fully clothed?

Hannah said, 'The Engineering Council are responsible for regulating the engineering profession.' She was reading from the screen. 'They run the National Register of Chartered Engineers. But wait a minute – once you've got your degree you have to go into something called the Monitored Professional Development Scheme and that's another four years. I'd no idea getting to be an engineer took so long, had you, guv?'

'I can't say I've ever thought about it.'

'These MPDS people have got a membership web page. Bear with me and I'm sure I'll find something.'

'And meanwhile,' said Wexford, 'I've got a meeting with Carina Laxton.'

She looked like a child with a prematurely lined face. Her pale hair was worn in two sparse plaits, her face free of make-up, her round glasses the kind that a myopic eight-year-old might wear. The white coat she wore had greenish stains down the front which were somehow more repellent than blood would have been. Not usually particularly sensitive to the squeamishness of policemen, she had for once covered up the remains on the table.

'What did he die of?' Wexford asked.

Carina raised her almost invisible eyebrows. 'How d'you know it was a man?'

'The size, the clothes in the kitchen. The body was wearing men's underwear.'

'OK. Jumping to conclusions a bit, weren't you? Still, it was a man. I don't know what he died of. It's difficult when someone's been dead so long. Quite possibly a natural death. Might have been his heart or a stroke. I can't tell because there's no heart and not much soft tissue in the skull. One thing I can tell you. He was a tall man, exceptionally tall, you're so out of date I know you don't care for the metric system. Say between six feet three and six feet five.'

'How old was he?'

'Mid-forties. Maybe forty-five. No more than fifty. As for when he died, it was between seven and ten years ago.'

'Not so long as the other one, then?'

'You said it, not me,' said Carina. 'Ask me again when I've done a more thorough job on him. I'll know more, I hope.'

He faced the media, told them most of what he knew about the two bodies without mentioning the error they had made in taking a DNA sample from someone who could not in fact be related to the dead man. He told them about the clothes without producing them. A description, he felt, was enough: a white t-shirt with a black scorpion printed on it, blue jeans, black trainers diagonally banded in grey, grey socks. He also said the purple sheet needed identifying, the one which had wrapped the body in the trench.

Hannah caught up with him as he was leaving the building at five past seven. He had just reached the automatic doors which had tentatively begun to open and closed again as he turned back.

'Chadwick's not registered as a chartered engineer, guv, and he's not on the MPDS register. But then I realised. We assumed it was a three year degree course but it's not, it's four years. He was only at the university till 1996, so it looks as if he dropped out.'

'Or was killed,' said Wexford.

'Or was killed, guv. It makes it more likely it's him, doesn't it?'

It took him a quarter of an hour to drive to Forby. He took the last remaining space in the village hall car park and walked up the steps to the front doors where a notice told him this would be the inaugural meeting of the Kingsmarkham African Women's Health Action Group. He had hoped to slip in unobtrusively and listen to the proceedings from a seat at the back, but he was no sooner inside than he was caught by his daughter Sylvia who seized him by the arm and hustled him up on to the stage.

A modicum of presence of mind enabled him to say how seriously the police took the problem of female genital mutilation and how much they would rely on the Somali community helping them in their task of prevention rather than prosecution. As he repeated the platitudes, meaningless promises that he had said and heard said a dozen times, he realised how little he really knew about this kind of circumcision. The applause from the audience rang hollowly in his ears as he stepped down from the platform and took the empty seat next to his wife. He had described it to her because she asked him, seen her face grow pale and heard her say, 'But, Reg, it can't be! Not millions of women,' and he had to say it was so without knowing more than the bare physiological facts.

Sheila was on the platform now, speaking about the early migrations of young women from the Horn of Africa. When British doctors and midwives had to carry out antenatal examinations, they at first believed that what they saw was congenital malformation and so routinely performed Caesarean sections. She then outlined, to an audience who mostly knew what she was talking about at first hand, how little girls, sometimes babies, had their labia and clitoris cut away with razors or sharp stones and the skin stitched up over the wound. Wexford had begun to feel slightly sick and looking round the room, wondered how many of these women had suffered in infancy or girlhood what had just been described.

Five or six seats away from him and a row behind sat the young waitress Matea whom Burden had so admired. It made him shudder to think that she might, in all probability, have suffered this. He knew that he shouldn't consider it a worse affront to a beautiful girl than to a plain one and he castigated himself. It was outrageous whoever might be the victim. There were more speakers, one talking about a conference on this subject she had attended in Kenya, another setting out what could be done to stop the practice here. Then the speeches ended and the audience was invited to ask questions. An elderly woman at the back put up her hand. Plainly she was more likely to have been from Sewingbury than Somalia, her hair was whitish blonde and her skin self-tanned. She asked if it wasn't wrong to interfere with a community's ancient traditions and Wexford was pleased with Sheila's answer.

'Would you have said that about foot-binding in China? Interference with ancient traditions put an end to that. One day perhaps interference will stop the artificial lengthening of women's necks in northern Burma.'

One of the few men in the audience asked what was men's attitude to the practice and was given what sounded to Wexford like anecdotal evidence. After that the question of a title for the new association was considered and the name Kingsmarkham Association Against Mutilation or KAAM, pronounced 'calm', was decided on. It was time for refreshments, glasses of red and white wine (ignored by the Somalis who were mostly Moslems), orange juice and fizzy water. For some reason, he had supposed, if he thought about it at all, that all these women would speak English reasonably well, so he was surprised when his neighbour Iman Dirir introduced him to a woman she called 'the interpreter'.

'We have no terms in Somali or English for these parts of the body,' she told him with a sad smile. 'The people need someone to explain the British laws to them. Most people who come here from Africa don't know there is such a law. They don't know circumcision is forbidden.'

She was tall and statuesque, far from young, but still beautiful in that goddess-like way more usually associated with Native Americans, the aquiline nose, the prominent cheekbones, the long neck and long hands. But as he again looked round him and surveyed all the women present, he saw that without exception all were either good-looking or extremely beautiful, their looks matched by their grace of movement and in the older ones, by their dignity. He sighed to himself because it sometimes seemed to him that man had only to see beauty in order to wish to ruin it.

He gave Mrs Dirir a lift home. She wore a long gown and the scarf but no all-enveloping jilbab as some of the women had. Alone with him, she was shy but when he mentioned his daughters she began to talk freely about how much she admired Sheila whom she had seen in a television serial rerun. They were nearly at her house when she said, in a breathless way as if she had been working up to this for some minutes, 'I have two daughters. They are grown-up now. I want you to know that we came here, my husband and I, when they were little to save them from mutilation. I was afraid because I thought we would be sent back but my husband is a scientist from Cairo University, so we were allowed to stay.'

'I'm glad,' he said. 'I'm very glad.'

A European woman in a long dress would have gathered up her skirts but Iman Dirir let her gown hang untouched, held her head high, and glided up the path. When she reached the door, she turned once, raised her hand in a gesture which was more graceful than a wave, and let herself into the house.

*　　*　　*

86

D ental records are useful only if you have some idea as to whose body you are looking at. These were Carina Laxton's words to Wexford. She told him that she could come a little closer to the death date of the body in the cellar. Between eight and ten years, she now thought. In the case of the body in the trench, she was prepared to fix on eleven years. Wexford was far from taking Burden's and Hannah's view that this was the remains of Douglas Chadwick on the grounds of who else could it be. For one thing, there was no evidence that he had met a violent death at someone else's hands and, for another, no apparent motive for Grimble father or son to have murdered him. The clothes, he thought, were the only clue as to who this was but so far, three days after a photograph of the t-shirt and the trainers had appeared in national newspapers and the *Kingsmarkham Courier*, no one had come forward to acknowledge recognition.

Dilys Hughes had provided a DNA sample to be compared to that of the body in the trench and this time the comparison would be sound. There was no doubt she and Peter Darracott were sister and brother, without the complications of stepfatherhood or adoption. As to dental records, the difficulty was that, according to Christine Darracott, her husband hadn't been to a dentist since he was at school and, as far as she knew, had had two fillings and one extraction when he was in his teens. The body in the trench had three fillings, and several extractions, but at different points in the dentition from where Christine said Peter's were.

Emails from well-meaning citizens flooded Wexford's computer. Hannah read them all carefully but had stopped printing them out. It wasn't until now that he had quite realised how many people simply vanished. Of course he was aware of the figures; statistics only begin to have much meaning when they apply to individuals, when the people who have been just numbers acquire names and ages and descriptions. The senders of the emails seemed to ignore the cut-off point of spring 1995 and wrote of a relative disappearing twenty years before or five years before. Many contributed stories of missing wives or girlfriends. The hundred and more Hannah read in one day all listed missing people, and then came one from a woman in Maidstone claiming to recognise the scorpion t-shirt. Hannah phoned her, then went to Maidstone to see her.

Janet Mabledon was in her fifties, a bright well-dressed woman who worked as secretary and receptionist at a medical centre. She had taken Wexford's email address from a television appeal for witnesses. A phone number had been given as well but she had decided, she told Hannah, that Kingsmarkham police would be overwhelmed with phone calls while they might seldom receive electronic messages. Hannah smiled but said nothing. She showed her the photograph of the t-shirt, the same picture as had appeared on several television news programmes.

'My elder son's name is Samuel,' Janet Mabledon said. 'Of course he's always called Sam. I had that t-shirt printed for him. There used to be a shop in Maidstone that printed t-shirts for you, any picture you wanted with a name, and they claimed the ones they did would be unique. Both my sons were very keen on – well, reptiles, I suppose you'd call them, when they were young, snakes and scorpions and alligators, all that sort of thing. Boys are. Sam and Ben were fifteen and thirteen at the time I had the t-shirts done.'

'Ben is your second son, Mrs Mabledon?'

'That's right. He's a research chemist now,' she said with pride, 'and Sam teaches at a university in the United States. It was twelve years ago I had the t-shirts done. Sam's had that scorpion with "Sam" printed underneath and Ben's had a crocodile with "Ben" under it. Ben loved his. I suppose I should have known Sam was too old for that sort of thing. He absolutely refused to wear it, never even tried it on.'

Hannah smiled. 'What happened to it?'

'Nothing for a while. Then I had a clear-out. Actually I was amazed to find it, it had never been worn. Ben had a girlfriend with a brother called Sam – it had got to be a very popular name – and we gave it to her for her brother. She lived at Myringham. That's near Kingsmarkham, isn't it?'

'When would that have been, Mrs Mabledon?'

'Oh, a long time ago. Ten years? I don't know where that ex-girlfriend is now but I can tell you her name. Her brother was at Myringham University when Ben knew her.'

'Where Douglas Chadwick was doing his engineering course,' Wexford said to Burden that evening. They were back in the snug at the Olive and Dove and their wives were with them. Some of their most valuable deductions were made over a drink in this quiet little room but the *Kingsmarkham Courier* saw these meetings in a different light. The newspaper took every chance to run a spiteful story about police negligence and laziness. Now that it was possible for one of its reporters to blunder into the snug 'by mistake' and take a photograph on his mobile, nowhere was private. But they had found, rather strangely, that if Dora and Jenny came with them, the press seemed to regard their visit as normal time-off social-ising and took no action. Hannah, of course, believed some monstrous chauvinism was involved here but found it difficult to say quite how.

Burden was drinking his usual lager, Wexford claret. He was uncomfortably aware of his wife's eyes on him as he fetched a second glass. She had already told him that whereas one glass of red wine was good for his heart, four or five were not and when he said, 'Can one have too much of a good thing?' scolded that his health was not, as far as she was concerned, a suitable subject for jokes. She herself was drinking what looked like red wine but was in fact cranberry juice. She and Jenny had pushed their chairs back from the table and were talking about KAAM, the newly-formed group.

Wexford had been interrupted and now he repeated what he had said about Myringham University and Douglas Chadwick. 'Her name's Sarah Finlay and she's a lecturer there. But in psychology, not mechanical engineering. I don't know whether it's a coinci-dence, Mike. There are an enormous lot of students at Myringham and she says she didn't know him. I talked to her on the phone.'

'What became of the t-shirt?'

'She gave it to her brother who didn't want it either. She broke up with Ben Mabledon soon after and she took it to the Oxfam shop.'

'Which Oxfam shop?'

'The one in Myringham. This was in '98. It's a long time ago and naturally there are different people in the Oxfam shop and no one would remember that far back, anyway. It's not as if they'd keep meticulous records of the old clothes they sold.'

'You don't think it's Douglas Chadwick, do you?'

'No, I don't,' said Wexford. 'Why would old Grimble have killed his tenant? Come to that, why would young Grimble have killed him? The old man wanted to be rid of him and he wanted his money, which is exactly what he couldn't accomplish by killing him. As for the money, he had the piano to sell. Presumably that was the arrangement. I'll go, the lodger would have said, you keep as much of my stuff as you want to cover the debt, put the rest out in the front and my pal will come and pick it up in his van. And that's exactly what old Grimble did. I don't think Chadwick comes into it. I think Chadwick's out there somewhere, in Wales or the north of Scotland or the Scilly Isles, playing the piano in a hotel lounge or working in a garage or taking another MEng course in a university in Northern Ireland.'

'Did you say Douglas Chadwick?'

Wexford turned slowly to smile at Jenny Burden. 'I did,' he said. 'Do say you know him, Jenny. Give us some much-needed revelation.'

'Well, if it's the same one, I used to know a Douglas Chadwick whose sister was a teacher in the first school I ever taught at. He was a jazz pianist – amateur, I mean – in a club.'

'It sounds like the same one. When was this?'

'Let's see. My first job was at a school in Lewes. That was before I came to Kingsmarkham, so it'll be fifteen years ago. Helen Chadwick and I used to go to this club and hear Douglas play and we all had a meal together once and I think we met in a pub. And then I got my job at Kingsmarkham Comprehensive.'

'Where is he now?' her husband asked.

'Don't know. I know where she is. And so do you. She got married like me and she's Helen Carver now.'

'You mean that woman who came on a visit and called to see us and brought those appalling kids who chopped the heads off all my dahlias?'

'That's who I mean, yes.'

Wexford laughed. 'I'm a feminist,' he said. 'I don't hold with women changing their names when they marry. It causes needless confusion. What happened to the brother, Jenny?'

'She didn't mention him that time her kids decapitated Mike's dahlias. I could ask her. I could phone her – well, now.'

'Don't issue any invitations,' said Burden.

It was eight-thirty in the evening. Jenny took her mobile out of her handbag and went out into the damp darkness of the Olive's garden. In the snug Wexford, Burden and Dora began speculating as to the present whereabouts of Douglas Chadwick and Wexford, because one of his problems would be solved, half-hoped Helen Carver would say she hadn't seen her brother since April 1996. He had disappeared from the face of the earth.

Jenny came back, looking very different from the smiling, rather excited woman who had gone optimistically off into the garden. 'I spoke to her. I said I'd heard Douglas was playing at some fringe theatre at a festival next month and I thought we might go. God, I wish I hadn't. She was nearly in tears. She said he'd died in a road accident two years ago.'

CHAPTER TEN

I f Helen Carver had wept for the loss of her brother, Dilys
Hughes seemed indifferent to the negative result of the DNA
comparison. She had been reading the *Sunday Times* when
Barry Vine arrived and from the way it lay open on the seat of an
armchair, had cast it aside reluctantly when he rang her doorbell.
'I've not seen him for fifteen years,' she said, 'and when I've heard
from him it's always been him wanting something.' She didn't ask
Barry to sit down. 'To be honest with you, it wouldn't have broken
my heart if it had been him in that ditch.'

'You've no idea where he might be now?'

'I told you. Last time I heard was when he wanted to come here
and that was eleven years ago. He thought he could bring some
woman with him, the cheek of him. He might as well be dead as
far as I'm concerned.'

Barry rather regretted coming to Cardiff, especially on a Sunday.
A phone call would have done just as well but he had thought the
woman would need the sensitive approach. Wexford was very keen
on understanding and empathy, though Barry suspected this was
a directive from above rather than his own opinion. But now there
seemed nothing more to be said. Peter Darracott's present whereabouts were of no importance if he wasn't the mystery man who
had been buried eleven years before.

'Ah, well, that's all then, Mrs Hughes,' he said. It had taken all
of three minutes after a two-and-a-half-hour journey

She had picked up the *Sunday Times* and had just enough courtesy to remain standing while she read it. 'Bye-bye. Take care.'

Of all meaningless tags that was the most banal, Barry thought as he let himself out. Were you more likely to look to right and left before you crossed a street or drive your car within the speed limit, because someone told you to take care? There was a shopping centre on the way to the station. He went in, found a music store with, as usual, a pitifully small classical section. Bellini was his favourite composer, though he sometimes made incursions into Donizetti. The kind of people who confused the two he despised. By a piece of luck the shop happened to have *La sonnambula* in stock. He knew it well but was quite happy to have it to listen to on the long journey back to Paddington, interrupted though it would be by other passengers rustling crisp bags while their mobiles played pop music. Outside a newsagent's he saw the *Sunday Times*. On its front page it advertised, in the News Review section, the story Dilys Hughes had been so absorbed in: *Gone Without Trace: The Lost Father* by Selina Hexham. Barry felt tempted to see it for himself and he bought a copy of the paper, realising as soon as he did so how heavy it was, all those sections, and he would have to carry them home.

Once in the train he riffled through the main section, just to keep himself up to date with the news, discarded all the rest but the News Review, which he kept, folded small in the pocket of the raincoat he had brought with him. He'd read it at home in the evening. The rest of the journey he spent in blissful enjoyment of Bellini.

'We now know that the remains in Grimble's bungalow aren't Douglas Chadwick,' said Wexford, 'but whoever he was the scorpion t-shirt was his. It certainly did belong to the man in the cellar. His hairs were on it, traces of his DNA were on it. It was his all right. The same goes for the anorak, the jeans and the trainers. Did he buy it from the Myringham Oxfam shop or did

93

someone buy it for him? And why has no one else come forward to say they've recognised that t-shirt at a later date? Did he take his clothes off before going into the cellar or did someone else take them off after he was dead? And why take them off?'

'Maybe he was going to have a bath,' said Burden but whether he was serious or being facetious wasn't clear.

'Then you'd have found him in the bathroom, not the cellar. Grimble said that cellar door was never shut. He'd never seen it shut. Why would he lie about that?'

'He might if he killed the chap in the cellar.'

'I don't see that,' said Wexford. 'If he'd killed the chap in the cellar, why mention it at all?'

The phone ringing put an end to this exchange of views. It was a Mrs Tredown to see him, said the desk sergeant's voice, adding rather awkwardly that what he actually meant was that it was two Mrs Tredowns.

'Have someone bring them up here, will you?' said Wexford and to Burden, 'You stay, Mike.'

Lyn Fancourt brought them in. Claudia Ricardo wore a long coat of asymmetrical patches in red, yellow, green and black over a badly creased white linen dress which also came to her ankles. On her feet were sandals with high wedge heels and laces cross-gartered. Her hair in a wild dense bush was in marked contrast to Maeve Tredown's smooth blonde 'set', lacquered into helmet shape and glossy as new paintwork. Maeve was in a calf-length check skirt and grey jacket, both rather shabby with a charity-shop look about them. But what struck Wexford about them when they began to speak was not the difference between them but the similarity of their speech and intonation. If you closed your eyes you couldn't have said whose voice it was, Claudia's or Maeve's. Only the content of what they said identified them. Although very unlike to look at, in certain ways they seemed to belong to the same type. Was that why Tredown had married first one and then the other? Or having lost or rid himself of Claudia, he had looked for her counterpart in Maeve?

94

They had come to tell him something Maeve said they had 'neglected' to mention before. 'When I spoke to that girl who came to see to Mr Borodin. The one that brought us up here just now.'

'You mean when you asked if it was true we'd found a body in the cellar of Mr Grimble's house? I believe you asked if it was a man or a woman.'

'Did you really, Cee? You are so awful.' Maeve's tone was that of a teenager.

'We can't always account for what we say,' Claudia said with a giggle. 'Naturally, I wanted to know. Who wouldn't? All those bodies next door. I wondered if they might have partaken in some sexy ritual.'

Burden said in the repressive tone Wexford knew signified his extreme displeasure, 'What did you come here to tell us?'

Maeve looked at him as if she had just realised a second man was in the room. 'Oh, yes, I remember you now. You came to the house with him, didn't you? Is it all right for you to ask me questions?' She pointed one sharp finger at Wexford. 'He's the head one, isn't he?'

These enquiries – they resulted in Claudia dissolving into giggles – neither Wexford nor Burden replied to. 'If you have something to tell us, please do so. Our time is limited.'

'Oh, is it?' Claudia put on an expression of disbelief. 'Well, if you say so. What was it you asked? Oh, yes, what did we come to tell you. Two things really. One is that Mr Chadwick – I don't know his first name – he was very friendly with Louise Axall, always round at her flat he was when her – well, he's not her husband, is he? – her paramour was away.'

'Let me stop you there, Miss Ricardo.' said Wexford. 'Miss Axall has only lived in the district for four years and Douglas Chadwick is no longer a subject of our investigations. He died two years ago.'

Maeve Tredown assumed the look of someone granted a revelation of the magnitude sustained on the road to Damascus. 'Douglas! That was his name. I'd entirely forgotten.'

'The second piece of information, Miss Ricardo?

'Yes, now where was I? Where was I, Em?'

'You were going to tell them about seeing that old bat Irene McNeil going into the house after old Grimble died.'

'That's it. She and that retarded boy and Grimble's pals, they were always in and out. Irene must be the nosiest old woman in the United Kingdom. As soon as they'd had the funeral she was in there. She lived across the road then, of course. We used to see her go in there time after time, didn't we, Em?'

'Absolutely, Cee, and bring stuff out with her. Her husband too. That man decimated the wildlife round here. If it moved he shot it. Shame, really.'

In absolute calm, Wexford said, 'Thank you very much, Mrs Tredown, Miss Ricardo.' He picked up the phone, said into it, 'Have DC Fancourt come up, will you?'

The two 'wives-in-law' began chatting to each other in low voices, punctuated by the occasional burst of laughter and little high-pitched screams. From what Wexford could hear of their conversation, he gathered Claudia was telling Maeve a joke involving fellatio and a banana. He sighed, said, 'We should like to talk to Mr Tredown. Will tomorrow morning be convenient? Nine o'clock?'

'It's very early,' said Claudia, giggling as if he had made an improper suggestion. '*Very* early. I may still be in bed.'

'Oh, we'd better say yes, Cee. He'll only keep on at us if we don't.'

'Thank you,' Wexford said as Lyn Fancourt came in. 'See Mrs Tredown and Miss Ricardo out, will you?' he said.

Both giggling now, they went. Burden said they were like two schoolgirls who have enjoyed themselves but not quite succeeded in goading their teacher into losing his cool.

'I don't know. It's a bit more sinister than that. They're more like a couple of thoroughly nasty participants in a witches' sabbath.'

'Most of it was done to annoy. No doubt, they don't have enough to do. Maybe Tredown sends them out of the house so that he can work in peace. But was it done to distract?'

'Distract from what, Mike?'

'Well, obviously something they don't want us to know about. One thing they did tell us, though. I know you noticed, I could tell by the way you suddenly looked disgusted.'

Wexford nodded. 'You mean her reference to "that retarded boy", as Claudia so charmingly called him? That's obviously Charlie Cummings. Mike, I think that should have occurred to us. Is the body in the cellar Charlie Cummings?'

'He disappeared three years before the man in the cellar died.'

'Even so it's possible,' said Wexford.

D oris Lomax, who had lived next door to Charlie Cummings and his mother, was a very old woman by this time. In the eleven years and more which had passed she had gradually lost her sight and was now registered as blind. Hannah Goldsmith, who could be tough and unrelenting with men and particularly with the young vigorous sort, was understanding with her own sex, reserving a particular tenderness and sympathy for old women whom she judged victims of a hard life and male oppression. She spoke with extreme gentleness to Doris Lomax in a voice Wexford would barely have recognised.

The little stuffy room in which they sat was insufferably hot, for, though the day was mild for the time of year, Mrs Lomax had her gas fire full on. The windows looked as if they had never been opened and now had seized up through disuse. Hannah gave no sign of discomfort, in spite of the sweat starting in her armpits, a physical manifestation she most disliked.

'Not cold, are you, dear?' were almost the first words Mrs Lomax uttered.

'Not a bit, Mrs Lomax, thank you. Now I quite understand you're unable to read the newspaper. Let me say I really don't think you miss much. But it did mean you weren't able to see the picture of the clothes Charlie was wearing, didn't it?'

'I do have a carer comes in a lot, dear, and she's ever so kind.

She reads bits of the local paper to me but she never read that bit. What did you say he was wearing?'

'A t-shirt, Mrs Lomax.' Hannah could tell she didn't know what this was. 'A thing – a garment – something like a jumper, only cotton. It's white and it's got a scorpion printed on it.'

'A what, dear?'

Describing a scorpion is surprisingly difficult. 'A black thing,' Hannah began. Was it a reptile? An insect? An arachnid? 'A bit like a sort of spider with a long tail—'

Doris Lomax cut her short. 'Oh, no dear. I knitted a jumper for him but it was plain blue. Maybe he had a thing like that but I don't know.' An unwelcome possibility occurred to her. 'You don't mean, oh, you can't mean you've found—'

'We're not sure yet, Mrs Lomax. We really can't tell but it's possible.' She had to say that.

'Oh, poor Charlie, poor Charlie. He wasn't quite right in his head you know, but such a nice boy. A *good* boy.' Another unhappy idea occurred to her. 'You don't want me to come and look at him, do you? I can see a bit – well, sort of shapes, but I wouldn't – I couldn't . . .'

'No, of course not,' Hannah said. 'Of course not.' She didn't add that there was nothing to see but the basic structure of a man, common to all men. 'One more thing – can you tell me what colour Charlie's hair was?'

'His mother had fair hair, dear, but all the Cummingses was dark. Charlie was quite dark.' She looked gravely at Hannah. 'Not quite as dark as you, dear, but getting on that way.'

Hannah was finding she desperately didn't want the body in Grimble's cellar to be Charlie Cummings. It was very unlike her, she thought, but she didn't want this old woman to suffer further hurt. Inspiration came to her. 'How tall was Charlie, Mrs Lomax?'

'Not very tall for a man, dear. Maybe five feet five or six.'

Hannah's relieved expression wouldn't have been visible but the little sigh she gave reached Mrs Lomax. 'Thank you, Mrs Lomax.

You've been very helpful. I think you can be sure this isn't Charlie Cummings.'

'Can I, dear? But he's still dead somewhere, isn't he?'

A Passage to India was darkish and cool. A ceiling fan, not too aggressive, blew the air about and faintly agitated the coloured streamers, figured in red and blue and gold, which hung against the walls. It was hard to tell if these were Indian decor or early Christmas decorations. Wexford and Burden were shown to what Rao the proprietor was starting to call 'their' table.

Burden wore his silk suit. It was very discreet, charcoal grey with knife-edge creases to the trousers and long lapels to the jacket. But still it *was* silk and Wexford thought it a bit much, though he kept this to himself. Burden's shirt was plain white and his tie light grey with a single slightly off-centre vertical stripe in black, as if he was trying to play down the effect of the suit which he too perhaps knew was over the top. Matea, the beautiful Somali girl, brought menus and asked them in her heavily accented soft voice what they would like to drink. Water, of course, it would have to be water. She seemed to sense their reluctance and she smiled. Wexford asked her if they could have the fan off and she said she'd tell Rao.

When she had disappeared behind the bead curtain, he said to Burden, 'If I didn't know you for an uxorious man, I'd suspect all this sartorial elegance being designed to impress or better still attract Matea.'

'Utter nonsense.' Burden never blushed. His face retained its even biscuit colour through all embarrassments. 'When I got dressed this morning I didn't even know we'd come here. It was your idea if you remember. Since we're in the long words department, my attitude to Matea is paternal or maybe avuncular.'

'Really? I hope you don't go telling people that old one about her being your niece. With your colouring no one would believe you.'

Burden laughed. 'You were wrong about the body in the cellar being Charlie Cummings. He was far too tall.'

'Yes.' Wexford hesitated. 'God knows who it is. We know the remains are those of a man and he was between forty and fifty when he died. Carina's now saying he's been dead eight years. We've run out of possible people he might be.'

'Could we try the National DNA Database?'

'Try it with what, Mike? The man in the cellar's DNA won't be on it, he died too long ago.'

Matea came back with a large jug of iced water and took their order. The long black hair which had hung loose when Wexford saw her at the inaugural meeting of KAAM had been wound up on to the top of her head and secured there with long jewel-headed pins. It struck him that she didn't wear the hijab. It would have been a shame if she had, he thought, the scarf covering her crowning glory. Perhaps she was one of those modern progressive Moslems who had broken with the old traditions or maybe she wasn't a Moslem at all. Some Somalis were Christians, he had heard, some animists. Her hairstyle gave Matea a regal look. With her head held high and her back plumb-line straight, she walked, as Burden remarked, like some African queen.

'Seen many, have you?' Wexford made a face. 'All we really know is that the clothes in the kitchen belonged to the man in the cellar. We don't know why he took them off or why, wearing only a vest and pants, he went down into that filthy cellar. Or was he killed elsewhere? There were no keys, no identification. Did his killer take those things?'

Wexford broke off as sweet-scented spicy dishes were brought, a large bowl of fragrant rice, little stone pots of green and scarlet pickles, a basket of naan. Matea asked if everything was all right.

'Excellent, thank you,' said Burden. 'Delicious.'

But it was Wexford that she glanced at, did more than glance, let her eyes rest on him for a few seconds, hesitating as if there was something she wanted to say. But she said nothing, half-smiled a little shyly, the first sign of awkwardness they had seen her give, and walked quickly away.

'Those Tredown women,' Burden said, 'that was all a bit odd. I said it was done to distract us. I think they made two attempts, the first one being when they thought we were still interested in Douglas Chadwick and they tried to make us believe he'd been having an affair with Louise Axall. Very clumsy, that. The woman wasn't even living there then.'

'And then they moved on to Irene McNeil. Again a vague insinuation. Mrs McNeil went in and out of Grimble's house. When that didn't seem to impress us they said she stole things, removed things from the house. You could tell it was an afterthought. But why, Mike? Why all this?'

'As I said, to distract us from something they don't want looked into.'

'Yes, but what? There is one thing or rather one person they might want to deflect us from, the one person among all the people in that corner of Flagford we haven't questioned, we haven't even seen.'

'Tredown,' said Burden.

'Exactly. The great author. There he is, shut up in his ivory tower, writing for all he's worth to keep those two in comfort, his nose apparently kept to the grindstone by them but protected by them as well. Interesting, don't you think?'

Matea brought the bill and Wexford gave her his credit card. Burden went off to the men's room and was still there when she came back. She said in her low sweet voice, 'Mr Wexford?'

How did she know his name? From the card, of course, or because she remembered it from the meeting. He smiled at her.

'I want to ask—'

The sentence was cut off by Rao the proprietor coming up to her and asking her to show two more customers to a table. Burden came back and asked what she had said to him. 'She wanted to ask me something but she didn't say what.'

'Perhaps some question of asylum or immigration or whatever.'

'Perhaps,' said Wexford.

*　*　*

I t was Hallowe'en, a celebration he disliked. Every window he passed on his way home, or every window behind which children lived, had a skeleton mobile dancing on strings or a pumpkin with a grinning mouth cut out. Guy Fawkes Night wasn't among his favourite festivals but it was an improvement on this. Was it on its way out, soon to be superseded by this dumbed-down black magic? At the corner of his own road he passed a group of sub-teenagers dressed in black and gathered under a street lamp, the chemical light showing up their painted cheeks and foreheads, blotched in green and purple but for one whose face was made-up to look like a skull. Their demand that he choose trick or treat failed to break his silence and he passed them without another glance.

Dora was out. She had driven herself over to Sylvia's to babysit Mary and the house was empty. He poured himself a glass of claret, stood at one of the front windows eyeing the street until his presence attracted first one group of trick-or-treaters, then two boys, combining Hallowe'en with Guy Fawkes Night and wheeling up his path a home-made skeleton in a pushchair. He drew the curtains and retreated as fireworks were set off in one of the neighbouring gardens, a series of explosions, then the whistle and scream of a rocket. His next-door neighbours' dog began to howl.

He went into the kitchen, took out of the oven the lasagne Dora had left for him and sat down to eat it at the kitchen table. The doorbell rang and someone pounded on the knocker. He took no notice. When he had finished his meal, he poured a second glass of wine and went to stand at the small window to the right of the front door. From there, with no lights on, he could watch the street unseen. Dora would be back soon. The moment she turned the car into their own drive she would be mobbed by the trick or treat throng if he wasn't there to stop them.

The phone ringing called him away. It was Sheila, wanting to talk about plans for *The First Heaven* film. Fireworks were deafening, both here and outside her Hampstead home. He was saying, 'Sorry, my dear, we'll have to carry on with this conversation another time,' when another machine-gun rattle from firecrackers made further speech impossible. Immediately after the explosions, as he put the phone down, there came another knock at the front door. Repeated knocks, in fact, echoing the fireworks' chatter, as if his caller had previously tried the doorbell in vain.

Of course he wasn't going to answer it. It might be an innocent and harmless Hallowe'ener, surfing the place on his own, someone who didn't know that no householder in his street was imprudent enough to open a front door on 31 October, but still he wasn't going to answer it. Very softly he made his way back to the little window in the dark. The doorbell rang but it was a rather timid, diffident summons this time. He hadn't realised that only the side wall of the porch was visible from this point and he was on the point of giving up, was walking away, when he turned his head.

The caller who had knocked and rung had made her final attempt and was just closing his gate behind her. Not a teenage boy or girl but a woman. Her head was covered and she was wrapped in a thick dark coat. Could it be Matea? There was nothing to tell him if it was, only the woman's upright carriage and light step. A firework, exploding next door without warning, temporarily blinded him, and when he could see again the woman had disappeared.

It took him a moment to find his keys. He fished them out of his raincoat pocket, shut the door behind him and ran after her up the street but she had taken a left or a right turning and there was no sign of her.

CHAPTER ELEVEN

Though it was a sunny morning, the weather forecast predicted heavy showers. Barry Vine hadn't taken his raincoat off its peg since he brought it home from Wales. Unlike most of his contemporaries who preferred various types of waterproof jacket, he possessed a raincoat because he thought it lent him dignity. It made him look like a detective, the sort of detective you saw in films from the forties. It was the belt which did it, an adjunct he thought suited him because it hid his thickening waistline. Getting into his car, he felt in the pocket, found only a sheet of folded newspaper and remembered his keys were in his trousers pocket.

He nearly threw the paper away. He would have done if he could have found a recycling bin. Instead he put it, unfolded, on his desk in the office he shared with Hannah Goldsmith and Damon Coleman. Why had he wanted to read it in the first place? Because that uncouth woman Dilys Hughes had been reading it? Surely not. He had just glanced at the headline: *Gone Without Trace: The Lost Father* by Selina Hexham, Part One, when he was summoned to Wexford's morning conference. It must have been those words 'gone without trace' and that word 'lost' which attracted his attention. Everyone at the conference lived, ate, drank and slept with those words on the tip of their tongues but so far it hadn't got them far.

* * *

W exford cancelled the appointment he had made with Maeve Tredown and Claudia Ricardo and instead of making a new one, decided to surprise the occupants of Athelstan House. As he said to Burden, he had no grounds on which to question Tredown, certainly none on which to arrest him and therefore take him to the police station. All he had was an inner conviction which refused to go away, that Tredown was being protected, hidden, by Claudia and Maeve who apparently ruled him.

He and Burden had chosen mid-afternoon for their call. 'He can't be hard at work all the time,' Wexford said. 'If he writes every morning and part of the afternoon, he must have some sort of respite. About now might be a good time.'

They expected they would have to infiltrate the women's defences. Maeve would open the door, Claudia would be a few yards inside, and together they would offer one excuse after another why Tredown couldn't be seen. He was resting, he was asleep, he was back at his writing, and it would all be delivered in that jokey way they had, a mixture of zaniness and giggles, apparent frankness and apparent stupidity. Plus a lot of what Burden called off-colour remarks from Claudia. Things turned out differently.

The predicted heavy showers had never come. It was one of those early November days when the sky is blue, the sun brilliant and visibility nearly perfect. From the Kingsmarkham to Flagford road you could see Cheriton Forest spread out, still leafy in colours varying from dark green to pale yellow, and in the pure clarity of the air, the Downs rose smooth but distinct against the mistless horizon. Donaldson drove into the village byway of the road that led past Morella's fruit farm and the church and the long row of Flagford's picturesque but grotesquely uncomfortable cottages. All right if you were no more than five feet three, Wexford remarked to Burden, but the ceilings were far too low for modern man, as he knew to his cost.

In the clear bright light, even Athelstan House seemed attractive, a multicoloured Victorian curiosity. As they approached up the drive Wexford spotted a tall, rather stooped figure, walking along the side of the house towards the rear. He told Donaldson to stop where they were and park there. He and Burden would follow the man. He must surely be Owen Tredown. The sun was low in the sky, offering dazzling glimpses of itself through trees which looked black against it. A blackbird sang in one of those trees, sweet as a nightingale. There was so little wind that the leaf fall seemed suspended until a single one, fan-shaped from a chestnut tree, floated gently down past Burden's face.

Tredown it was. They could see him clearly now and Wexford recognised the writer from a photograph on a book jacket. He had crossed the wide lawn and sat down on a wooden seat at the edge of a shrubbery in which rowans and dogwoods were shimmering red amongst the fading greens. It was a largely uncultivated place where nothing had been pruned and nothing planted. Only the grass had been tended and closely mown. Lengthening shadows stretched out across the lawn, among them those of the two policemen which Tredown must have seen, for he turned to watch them approach. He seemed unsurprised. He smiled.

Without asking who they were – could he tell by looking at them? – he said in one of the most mellifluous voices Wexford had ever heard, 'You see me, like the Lord God, walking in the garden in the cool of the day.'

He was smoking a pipe, a habit Wexford hadn't seen anyone indulge in for a long time. The smell was pungent. It wasn't tobacco, but something herbal, something *culinary*.

He introduced himself and Burden. Without getting up, Tredown shook hands, an action Wexford rather disliked in these circumstances. You never knew how the relationship might deteriorate and in the not too far distant future. It was awkward to find yourself arresting and cautioning someone with whom you had been on matey terms. 'What can I do for you gentlemen?'

'Perhaps we could sit down?'

'Of course.' Tredown shifted along the seat. 'How remiss of me. I hope you don't mind my smoking.'

'Not at all,' said Wexford. 'But I'd like to know what it is. It smells like sage.'

'Sage it is. *Salvia divinorum*, a powerful hallucinogenic.' Tredown looked from one to the other of them, perhaps expecting a reaction and met impassivity. 'This is my second pipe of the day, so I had my out-of-body experience this morning. This one expands my mind and makes me sweat but that is all.'

'Your out-of-body experience?' Wexford's eyebrows went up.

'Oh, yes. Does that surprise you? Sage brings transcendence, not to say hallucinations of the most interesting kind.'

Owen Tredown was even taller than Wexford and a great deal thinner, almost cadaverous, and he remembered that the man had cancer. His skin was greenish yellow. His was one of those concave faces, the brow high, the nose short, the chin prominent and the mouth an almost lipless line. The hair, which had once been flaxen, was still abundant, a streaky brownish-grey, falling across his sallow forehead and pushed back behind his ears. He was dressed in baggy khaki trousers and an open-necked denim shirt. On the third finger of each long bony hand was a plain gold ring. One for each wife? Wexford wondered briefly about that before he spoke.

'We found, Mr Tredown, that we had talked to everyone who lives in this immediate neighbourhood except you. That seemed an omission that should be remedied.'

'I doubt if I can tell you much.' He spoke like someone coming out of a dream. The pipe held at arm's length now, he seemed to be addressing it rather than the two policemen. 'The elder Mr Grimble I can't recall ever speaking to. Of course, we were far from happy at the younger Mr Grimble's plans to build four houses next door to us. As you see,' he said to the pipe, 'we are not at all overlooked at present. But I expect my wife and Miss Ricardo have told you that.'

So that was how he dealt with the two-wives problem. Come to that, how else could he have dealt with it?

'In fact, I expect they have told you everything we know, the digging of the trench, for instance, and the burglary we had about that time and – oh, the necessary filling in of the trench when planning permission was refused. They do like to save me trouble, you know. They protect me from the wickedness of the world.'

Tredown laughed. It was an unexpected sound, a high-pitched neighing, in contrast to the soft honeyed voice. They let him have his laugh out, listened indulgently, though nothing in the least amusing had been said, only a confirmation of what Wexford had suspected. He glanced at Burden and Burden said, 'What burglary was that, Mr Tredown?'

Tredown took the pipe between his lips and drew on it, shivering a little. 'Oh, didn't they tell you? Nothing much was taken. As a matter of fact I heard none of it. I was asleep in bed. It was quite some time before Miss Ricardo told me there *had* been a break-in. She and my wife are so kind. They always want to save me anxiety.'

'Exactly when was this, sir?' Wexford asked.

'Let me see. I'd say it was sometime in the weeks between the elder Mr Grimble's death and the younger Mr Grimble digging his trench. But my wife and Miss Ricardo would know.'

Burden asked what had been taken.

'Oh, only some cutlery, nothing valuable, not even silver, and, rather oddly, I thought, some bedlinen.'

Something made Wexford glance towards the French windows. On a sunny day – the sun hadn't yet set – it is impossible to see much through glass of what lies behind it. He could just make out two figures watching them and then one of them moved away.

'Here comes Miss Ricardo now,' said Tredown. 'She can tell you better than I can.'

Claudia was crossing the lawn, her long lacy black skirt sweeping the grass. Which ring on those long fingers was for her? Or had neither any connection with those two women?

'I think you've met these gentlemen, Cee. I was telling them about our burglary.'

'Burglary? I thought you had to break a window to qualify as a burglar. Some homeless person got in – I'd left a downstairs window on the catch. He took some knives and forks and a sheet.'

'Would that have been a purple-coloured sheet, Miss Ricardo?'

'How could you possibly know?' Her voice rose an octave. 'How clever of you! It was mine actually. When I came to live here I brought some of my old bedlinen. I'd been a hippie, you know, I'm sure you can believe it, I'm still a bit of a one now. All that lovely sexual free-for-all. I put myself about a bit, as you can imagine.' She seemed to recall that a question had been asked. 'Oh, yes, we had stuff like that, black and red and purple sheets, quite mad.'

'You don't read the papers then?' said Burden.

'No, indeed. They're always full of horrors. Wars and murders and torture – oh, and rapes, of course.' Uttering this catalogue of human suffering brought on a fit of the giggles. 'Oh, do excuse me. It's not funny, is it?'

'I asked,' said Burden, in his best dull, humourless and plod-ding way, a manner he adopted to hide his anger, 'because we appealed for people to identify a purple sheet.'

Soundlessly, not apparently disturbing the still air, Maeve had arrived. Turning his head, Wexford saw her standing just behind him, uncomfortably close behind him, the dying sun shining on her yellow hair. She smelt of vanilla, a perfume strong enough to fight with and conquer the lingering aroma of sage. 'Still cross with us, Chief Inspector?' she whispered almost into his ear.

He ignored her. 'Did you report this break-in to the police? No? I must tell you that a purple sheet was wrapped round the body in the trench.'

Claudia gave a shriek, loud enough to cause the blackbird to take flight. 'How dreadful. My old sheet used as a shroud!'

'We'll leave you now, Mr Tredown,' Wexford said. 'Tell me, are you writing anything at the moment?'

Claudia answered for him. 'Not at the *moment*, as you can see. At the *moment* he's sitting here, smoking *Salvia*.' She began to laugh again. 'Aren't you shocked? It may be a psychoactive substance but it's perfectly legal. A bit naughty but legal.'

For the first time her ex-husband seemed embarrassed by her. He said, 'Now, Cee, come along,' in a feeble way, then to Wexford, 'As a matter of fact I'm back at my old theme for a change, using the rich seam of Bible history for my source. Have you read any of my books?'

'I've read *The Queen of Babylon*.' Please don't ask me if I enjoyed it.

He didn't ask. 'Ah, yes, Esther, she who was responsible for hanging Haman high. This time I am using the story of Judith and Holofernes.'

He got up, staggered a little, put one hand to his back. Was this the cancer or the sage? Wexford wondered. They accompanied him back to the house and the women followed them, giggling together. Wexford, saying goodbye to Maeve Tredown, had never before thought it possible he would see something sinister about a small fair-haired woman in jumper and skirt. They walked to the car.

'Are they all mad?' Burden said.

'God knows. At least he's civil. He doesn't snigger at every word one utters. Do they grow the sage? Or do they buy it? Is it effective against pain? Claudia is right about it being perfectly legal.'

Burden avoided the *Salvia* question. 'He looks to me like he's dying. You're the reader. You can tell me. Do people really read books – novels – about Bible stories? I mean, would they be popular?'

'I wouldn't think so. I didn't much care for that Babylon one. I didn't finish it. But the one they're making the play about, the thing Sheila's going to be in, that's not about the Bible. That's fantasy, ancient gods and goddesses, fabulous animals, heaven and hell. It was a tremendous bestseller.'

'I shall never understand that sort of thing,' said Burden.

Wexford was telling his conference about the purple sheet. 'However, the burglary wasn't reported. I doubt if we'd still have a record of it if it had been. Any questions?'

Hannah's hand was up. 'Are we thinking the burglar was our perpetrator, guv?'

'It's possible. Maeve Tredown would like us to think that way.'

'But it's crazy, guv. Some villain steals a sheet on purpose to have a shroud all ready to wrap a body in? And he steals it from the house next door? Is he trying to incriminate the Tredowns? Does he *know* the Tredowns?'

'I don't know, Hannah. When you come up with some answers, I'll be interested to hear them.'

Damon Coleman had nothing to contribute. It was Friday and he and Burden were off to speak to Irene McNeil and then to revisit the house in Grimble's Field. Barry was on the point of saying something about the extract he had read in the *Sunday Times* but he thought better of it, it was too thin, too distant and remote. He folded up the newspaper page once more and put it in his jacket pocket.

Mrs McNeil's cleaner showed them in. Her employer sat in an armchair with her feet up on a footstool, her swollen ankles bulging over the sides and tops of her shoes. They looked as if they must cause her pain as well as discomfort.

'We want to ask you a little more about your visits to Mr Grimble's house, Mrs McNeil,' Burden said, keeping his eyes away from those ankles.

Irene McNeil said rather too quickly, 'I never went into the house. What gave you that idea?'

'Never? Not even, for instance, after Mr Grimble was dead? I wondered if his son asked you to have a look round the place, you or your husband, and choose some little thing of Mr Grimble's as a memento. You'd been neighbours for a long while, after all.'

'Grimble ask me that?' She sounded genuinely indignant. 'The man's a complete boor. He'd no more offer me something like that than he'd have a courteous word for me. I told you I never entered that house and I meant it. I'm extremely tired. I hope all this arguing isn't going to go on much longer.'

Burden said, 'I'm sorry you see it as arguing, Mrs McNeil. We simply want to get to the truth of the matter and to do that I'm afraid we have to question you. We'll try not to pressurise you.'

'Then I think you ought to believe me when I say I never went into that house. I hadn't any call to go in there. It wouldn't have crossed my mind to go in there. I hadn't got a key, had I? What would I go in there for?'

She was protesting too much, Burden noted. 'Mrs McNeil, what would you say if I were to tell you that you were seen going into that house?'

'I'd say that whoever told you that was a liar.' She had reared her heavy bulk up in her chair in order to say this and the effort exhausted her. She collapsed back, said, 'I don't feel at all well. Please give me some water.'

Damon poured water from a carafe on a side table and handed it to her. She didn't thank him but stared as if they had never met before. The cleaner came in, appointed herself Mrs McNeil's carer and bustled about, feeling her employer's forehead, announcing that she would get fresh water, and glaring horribly at the two policemen. They left.

'I wonder what she went in there *for*.' Burden looked back at the house as if it might answer him.

'If she went in, sir,' said Damon.

'She went in all right.'

Vincenzo Bellini, called one of the four great figures of Italian opera, was preferred by Barry Vine over all others. He often wondered what beautiful music was lost to the world by the composer's dying of gastroenteritis at the age of thirty-three. On Saturday evening, his wife having gone to see her parents, he was indulging himself by listening to *I puritani*. But when its sweet pathos drew to a close and a pardon had been issued to Riccardo, he remembered the piece of newsprint he had put into his desk and suddenly it no longer seemed to him – what were the words he had used of it? Remote? Distant? – anything but urgent. How could he have neglected it for so long, nearly a week? Was he that irresponsible?

His parents-in-law lived only in the next street and his wife hadn't taken the car. Thank God. Without the means of getting down to the police station he'd have laid awake all night worrying about *Gone Without Trace*. It was with a sense of enormous relief that he found the piece of paper where he had left it and he settled down there and then in the empty office to read.

CHAPTER TWELVE

The *Sunday Times*, News Review, 29 October 2006
Gone Without Trace: The Lost Father

The day he went away remains very clearly in my mind and not just because it was the day I lost my father. It was also the day that drew a line between my happy and untroubled childhood and the rest of my life, a precise line coming halfway along. I was twelve and now I'm twenty-three. That's why I'm writing this, because of that halfway mark, and because, wherever he is now and whatever has happened to him, I think he deserves a memorial.

When you are twelve you've reached an age when you can make a fairly accurate assessment of other people's state of mind, of how happy or unhappy they are. My parents were happy together. They showed it. They were 'touchers' and demonstrative. When Dad came home from school – he was a teacher in a comprehensive school – he always kissed my mother and sometimes, if he'd had a specially good day, I suppose, or had that sort of all's-right-with-the-world feeling, he'd put his arms round her and hug her. Or maybe it was just because he loved her. He talked to my sister and me. If that seems obvious it's not really. My friends' dads didn't really talk to them. I'd been in their houses and seen how their dads were kind and pleasant and all that sort of thing but mostly what they said to their kids was 'Yes, all right, but not while I'm watching this', or 'I've had a hard day and I just want to relax, right?' My dad seemed to like answering our questions, especially the ones about animals and natural history and evolution. He had a degree in biology and while other people's fathers were crazy about this or that footballer or the Rolling Stones or some politician, his hero was Charles Darwin. At the weekends he took us out and that's why, when I reached that fateful halfway mark, the Natural History and Science museums were as familiar to me as sports grounds were to some people.

He used to tell us stories too. Not read, tell. And I mean he still did, even though we were ten and twelve. The stories were a long way from his science and evolution and animal behaviour. I suppose you could say they were the Greek myths retold, tales of the whole pantheon of the Greek gods, most of them, as I later found out, from Ovid. But the one I liked best was about the Trojan War, starting with the beauty contest that Paris judged, his winning Helen as his reward and how the war broke out because Helen was Menelaus's wife and he resented her being stolen from him. Ever since then, whenever I hear about that war or the name Homer or Achilles and most of all Helen, I think of my dad and wish he'd never gone away and left us. Or whatever he really did.

We respected each other in our house. My sister Vivien and I had been brought up like that, to understand that Mum and Dad respected our privacy and our right to be listened to and to accord them the same attention. If I have to find faults in my parents, and they had their failings like everyone else, I'd say Mum was a bit too house-proud and fussy and a bit too in the way of 'keeping herself to herself', reserved really to the point of shyness. As for my dad, maybe he did rather stuff us full of knowledge, more perhaps than we could handle, and he was a secretive person. I don't know if that's the right way to put it but what I mean is that he would withdraw himself from the rest of us sometimes, go to the little room that was his study and work at – something. Not at the weekends. Those were ours. At mealtimes he liked us all to engage in conversation – quite intellectual talk, considering our ages. He was there to help us with our homework and did so in the best possible way. But when we went to bed he went to his study and stayed in there till midnight.

I still don't really know what he did. 'He's working for a master's degree,' my mother said and then, later, that he was researching for a thesis. We had to accept. So many people we know were somehow involved with academia on one level or another. But every night? Not at the weekends but in the week, two or three hours every night? What I'm going to say now will make me look like a very selfish little girl and my sister another, for Vivien felt the same as I did. Our house was a three-bedroomed end-of-terrace, one bedroom for Mum and Dad, one to be shared by Vivien and me, the third my dad's study. We couldn't see why he needed it. Why couldn't he do whatever it was he did in our living room (sitting room and dining room converted into one) or in his own bedroom? Then I could keep our bedroom and Vivien, as the younger of us, could have the study. We asked, we even nagged a bit, but Dad was adamant and Mum, of course, backed him up. To do him justice – and I'm always willing to do that – he bore it patiently for a long time until one day he said in his quiet firm way that couldn't be defied, 'That's enough, you two. I don't want to hear any more of it. All over, finished, right?'

Vivien argued a bit. I think she'd agree that she whined. Dad meted out the only punishment we ever had. 'All right, Vivien, go to the bedroom you so inconveniently have to share with Selina and stay there till I say you can come down.' And that was the end of it. He can't have got as far as submitting his thesis because if he'd been awarded a master's we would have heard about it, no doubt we would all have celebrated it. I mention all this because we never did find out exactly what he did in that study, but we all believed it had something to do with the reason for his departure, though no else did, not the police who weren't interested anyway or his friends or our grandparents. They all thought what we knew to be impossible, that he'd gone off with another woman.

It was Thursday 15 June, 1995, and his school was to be used as a polling station in the local elections and was therefore closed. It happened to be the day the funeral was to take place of an old friend of my father's and the closing of his school meant that he could attend it which he very much wanted to do. Mum would have gone with him but there was no question of that with the two of us arriving home at three-thirty. Mine wasn't the sort of mother who left her daughters, aged ten and twelve, to come home to an empty house.

The funeral was in Lewes in Sussex which is on the Brighton line. I said I remember the day clearly and I do, that it was a wet morning, exceptionally dark at 8 a.m. and as a result Vivien and I overslept. Mum had to come in twice to get us up and when we finally did we had to rush. Rushing was something she hated in her ordered and organised way and I remember she was rather testy at breakfast, telling us it was ridiculous to insist on second pieces of toast when we'd already had Weetabix and orange juice. Did we think we were going to be malnourished if for once we went without a slice of brown bread and marmalade? Dad ate nothing. I remember this because it was so unusual. He never ate between meals but he never missed a meal either. He did that morning, just drinking a cup of coffee. Mum said later, when the terror started, that she thought he was too upset about Maurice Davidson's funeral to eat anything.

The boys next door, Martin and Mark Saunders, called for us as they always did and we were bundled off to school. We both kissed Dad which was something we didn't always do and prob- ably wouldn't have if he hadn't made a point of coming up to each of us in turn while the boys waited and putting his arms round us. To this day I remember the feel of his hands holding my shoul- ders and his lips on my cheek. That brief precious contact, the last, will be with me for ever and Vivien says it is the same for her, the touch of our beloved father who we were never to see again.

Maths for me that morning, followed by music, then PE. A double science period in the afternoon and we had a test. I know I was able to answer most of the questions correctly because of the conversations we'd had at teatime with Dad and our visits to the Natural History Museum. But then it's because of those things that I'm a biologist now. We went home. Not with the boys this time but in a crowd until we reached the corner of our street where the others all went off in different directions. It had been raining most of the day but now it had cleared up and a weak sun was shining between the heavy clouds. Mum was at the gate to meet us as she often was. She said she had come out to see if the rain had stopped but I think it was really to see us coming.

Dad wasn't expected home until early evening. The children of a male teacher are used to having their father home at teatime if he doesn't work too far away. We missed him. I remember how much I wanted to tell him about my biology test and that I thought I'd done well. Isn't it funny how I remember what we had for tea? Bread and butter and Marmite and home-made scones and a Kit-Kat each. Families don't eat together any more, or so I'm told, but we did all the time. I suppose we were old-fashioned.

Mobile phones were getting quite common even then but Dad didn't have one so my mother wasn't expecting him to call her. Even so, she started getting a bit anxious when it got to half-past six. We had the television on because by then she thought there might be something on the news about a hold-up on the Brighton line. There wasn't and it got to seven, to seven-fifteen, to seven-thirty . . . The rain had begun again and it was coming down in sheets. At eight o'clock Mum phoned Carol Davidson, Maurice's widow in Lewes. She didn't want to, she said it was awful phoning a widow whose husband would never come home again about your husband who was just a bit late home. Little did she know. Carol Davidson was very nice. She just said she appreciated Dad coming 'all this way' and they'd had a lovely talk about Maurice and old times. Dad had stayed and had something to eat but he'd left at about two. She asked Carol if Dad had been all right when he left and Carol said yes, he'd been fine. Of course he'd been upset but that was natural.

That was six hours before and it was then that Mum started getting really worried. She thought he must have had an accident and be in hospital somewhere and it would have to have been a serious accident, he'd have had to be unconscious, otherwise he'd have phoned or got someone else to phone. After another half-hour had gone by she phoned the police. They were very nice and they wanted to know if she'd like to report him as a missing person, go down to the station and fill in a form. But they said it was very soon to do that and the chances were that by the time she had filled in the form he'd be back. The policeman she spoke to gave her the number of two hospitals in the Brighton area and suggested she phoned them and enquire, which she did but Dad wasn't in either of them. Once she'd started she wanted to go on and by ten she'd phoned all the hospitals down there that she could find.

There was no question of Vivien and me going to bed. We stayed up with Mum, waiting and hoping and sometimes doing that ridiculous thing of running to the front door and out to the gate to look up and down our street. Viv and I did it four or five times and then Mum said to stop because it was raining so hard and we came in soaked. She kept saying, 'I wish the rain would stop, I wish it would stop,' as if it made things worse, Dad being out in the rain.

Eventually, we went to bed but we couldn't sleep and we heard Mum go downstairs and walk about and come back up again and go down again. She came into our room in the morning and said we had to go to school, it would turn out that there was some simple explanation for Dad not coming home, but we could tell she didn't believe this and after a while she said we need not go. It was better for us to be here with her, she needed us here. And then she gave an awful sort of sob as if her heart would break.

She went to the police station at about nine and we went with her. It was true what she'd said, she didn't want to be anywhere without us. She filled in the missing-person form and the policeman who was looking after us said she wasn't to worry as he was sure to be back that day. In fact, he said, the police didn't search seriously if fit healthy men of his age – he was forty-four – went missing. It wasn't like children and young girls or old people. Most men of his age, 'the vast majority' he said, came back within seventy-two hours. My mother thanked him and said he was very kind but even then, at that early stage, she knew my dad hadn't done any of the things other people suggested, gone off with another woman, gone away to start a new life somewhere, been on a binge, wakened in a strange bed and been afraid to go home. Even then, she was saying he must be dead.

Next week: Selina tries to discover the secrets in the life of her father, Alan Hexham. These extracts are from Gone Without Trace: The Lost Father *by Selina Hexham, to be published by Lawrence Busoni Hill in January 2007.*

CHAPTER THIRTEEN

D amon Coleman had interviewed her and later so had Burden. Both had reported her as difficult, prickly and old-fashioned. Wexford's experience of Mrs Irene McNeil consisted of the letter she had written him, and that had led him to expect a deeply conservative woman, a snob, her ethos centred in another, long-past age. Still, he thought he would be talking to someone with more sense and more dignity than the Tredown women.

What he didn't expect was that he would feel sorry for her. It wasn't her great lumbering girth and the fact that she had to use a stick – would soon need two sticks – which provoked his pity. It wasn't her apparent distress at coping with disability or the pain in her arthritic limbs but, rather, something in her eyes, a bewilderment at finding herself ending up alone here in a house which, though she had been there for nearly eight years, was still new and alien to her, without child or friend or companion. He told himself that whatever she told him, whatever he and Burden found out from her, he must be gentle and considerate.

The house which she and her husband had bought because it was near the shops and on a bus route – the bus went just twice a day – and 'easy to run' had evidently been designed for a young couple out at work all day. Its interior was stark, lined with built-in cupboards, ceiling eyelet lighting, hardwood laminate floors. There was something pathetic about Mrs McNeil's padded, buttoned velvet furniture in this minimalist setting, her footstools and cushions and ornaments crowded together and seeming to jostle one another.

Her husband had had his first stroke eight years before and had died six months after they moved in, when they were still at the stage, Mrs McNeil said, of saying to each other that they would settle down, they would get used to it. She had had to get used to it alone. Wexford's recalling her mind to Flagford Hall, the house which she had left behind, let forth a flood of reminiscence. Mrs McNeil spoke in a steady complaining whine, the voice of a woman who has left all life's pleasures in the past and to whom the present is all labour and sorrow.

'Even with that dreadful man Grimble living opposite, we were comfortable and peaceful there.' Sweat trickled down her cheeks. 'It was my husband's family home. You could call it his ancestral home. His family had lived there for generations. The house is perfect Queen Anne, you know, and the gardens are gorgeous – or they were, I don't suppose they are now. As for this place, you wouldn't believe the noise there is at night here, louts and young girls drunk and screaming in the street. Even on the day Mr Grimble turned that young man out, when he put his furniture out into the front garden, there was nothing like I get here.'

'Let me take you back to that time, Mrs McNeil.'

'I wish you could,' said Mrs McNeil bitterly.

'I believe you kept watch on the house that had belonged to Mr Grimble after he was dead and it belonged to his son. Nothing wrong in that. In fact, very commendable – we might well call it neighbourhood watch.' Wexford avoided Burden's satirical eye. 'Did you see many people go in there, apart of course from Mr John Grimble himself?'

'He never went in there much. He wasn't interested. He told Mrs Hunter and Mrs Hunter told me it was a load of old junk – those were his very words. It was only fit to be burnt and that was what he intended to do once he got his planning permission. Have a bonfire of the lot, he said, and then demolish the place. An old white elephant, he called it. We're opposing his planning application, Mrs Hunter said, and I said so were we.'

Old and lonely, she was relishing pouring out her memories to a sympathetic ear. There could be, when he chose, something in Wexford's manner that invited confidences from those who had little opportunity to air their miseries and their grievances. During a quarrel over their respective lifestyles, his daughter Sylvia had said to him. 'You ought to have been a bloody psychotherapist.'

'Well, it looks as if you were successful as permission was refused,' he said. 'Did anyone else go in there? I don't just mean immediately after Mr Grimble senior was dead but in the months and even years to come. I'm sure you didn't relax your surveillance.'

'Oh, no. I kept up my neighbourhood watch, as you called it.' She seemed well contented to see herself in the role of local special constable. 'As to your question, several people went in there. One evening I saw a woman who used to work in the chemist's shop go in there with a man I'd never seen before. You could guess what they were up to.' When Wexford made no comment, she went on, 'My husband saw Mrs Tredown go in there one day. I mean the *second* Mrs Tredown, the one with the yellow hair. Of course none of these people went in by the front door. Mr Grimble had boarded up the front door. All of them sneaked round the back.'

'Mrs McNeil, you're being very helpful.' Wexford knew she was lying. He could tell by her tone rather than her body language. Of that she had none, for she remained in the only position possible to her, a heavy slumping among cushions and shawls. She was one of those rare people who allow their hands to rest quite still while they talk. 'Can you tell me how these people got into the house? They can't all have had a key, can they?'

Falsehood promptly became truth. 'Oh, he always kept his back-door key under a lump of stone outside the back door.'

'And people knew that? All these people?' This was Burden. Wexford wished he hadn't intervened. His voice was abrupt and incredulous and Mrs McNeil plainly resented it.

'I don't like your tone, whoever you are.' She seemed to have forgotten she had seen him before. 'I was talking to this gentleman.' She turned back to Wexford. 'They must have known, mustn't they?' she said like the little girl she had been so long ago. 'I expect they told each other. Yes, that would be it.'

She had become pathetic again, desperate to bolster up her lies. Wexford of course knew what it all meant, that she had discovered the hiding place of the key herself and had divulged it to no one except perhaps her husband. He had to ask, but would the result of his questioning be to make her clam up, take refuge in offended silence?

'Mrs McNeil,' he said in a pleasant and interested tone, the kind a scholar might use when enquiring of an expert in his field, 'knowing where the key was, were you never tempted just to have a look round in there yourself? I mean, as part of your surveillance system? I imagine you may well have wanted to check that no damage had been done to Mr John Grimble's property.'

She smiled. It was the first time. 'Well, of course, you're perfectly right. That was exactly how I did feel. I did go in and my husband did. I didn't say so before because people always put the worst possible construction on that sort of thing. My husband and I – we even considered removing the key into our own safe keeping but, on careful consideration, we decided that would be taking good neighbourliness too far.'

He had to ask her about the cellar. But more flattery first. There are some people who can take any amount of flattery and politicians are said to be among them; rural gentry too, particularly those who have lost the position in the county their forebears enjoyed, have no position at all except the dubious one of clinging to the rim of an upper middle class. He thought he could flatter Irene McNeil a little more without arousing her suspicions and he ignored Burden's stare. 'It's unusual to meet with this sort of rectitude in these unregenerate days, Mrs McNeil. Did you ever find anything in that house which made you feel your – er, investigations were justified?'

This was a thrust, albeit a very gentle one, which had gone

home. He saw he was approaching the crux. Irene McNeil said, 'Would you mind fetching me a glass of water?'

They both left her and went out into the snow-and-ice-coloured operating theatre of a kitchen. Once in there, you could believe Irene McNeil never ate anything cooked. A gas hob still looked the way it must have done in the showroom. Burden ran the tap, filled a glass.

'Leave us, would you, Mike?' Wexford said. 'No reflection on you but I may get somewhere if it's just me with her.'

'It'll be a pleasure. Shall I stay in the house?'

'You may as well.'

Wexford took the glass back and handed it to her. He noticed that the big arthritic hand shook as she took it. 'Mrs McNeil, did you happen to go down to the cellar?' How that 'happen' softened the question, making it a casual enquiry.

She was prickly with guilt. 'Is there any reason why I shouldn't have?'

Only that you shouldn't have been in the house at all. 'I simply wondered why you shut the door to the cellar.'

'Because I was . . .' She realised she had admitted it, clapped one hand over her mouth and after staring at him aghast for a moment, broke into wild weeping. Her body heaved with sobs. At last she moved her hands, holding them up like someone pleading for mercy.

He held the water to her lips but she pushed it away violently, the way an angry child might, soaking his jacket and shirt. With an effort at control, he gave no sign of the shock the icy water had been. 'Mrs McNeil,' he said, 'there is no need for this. There's nothing for you to distress yourself about.' But perhaps there was. How could he tell if this was hysteria or a heartbroken confession? He could find no tissues in that kitchen, brought her instead a drying-up cloth her cleaner must have laundered. She buried her face in it. No more than a minute later she sat up, was more erect than she had been for the whole of the interview, her face patted dry, reminding him that she, after all, belonged to what her kind called 'the old school'. Still she didn't speak.

He prompted her. 'Because you were what, Mrs McNeil?' Inspired, he guessed. 'Because you were frightened?'

'Yes!'

'What frightened you? Mrs McNeil, nothing will happen to you' – could he be sure of that? – 'if you tell me the truth.'

S he came out with the whole story. Once she had begun it seemed there was no stopping her. The floodgates had opened and words cascaded. Even so, Burden dared not take notes. He had come back into the room but sat a little way away from Wexford and her. He could see that whatever she might think of him, she had made of Wexford a sympathetic friend.

'The man, I don't know what he died of,' she began. 'Perhaps it was his heart. Ronald, my husband, went into the house – oh, it was eight years ago, in September – he went in because he could see something moving about, I mean see it through the front window. That window was never boarded up, I don't know why not. We'd both seen it, a figure moving about. I remember it like it was yesterday. It was a man wearing a red coat – well, orange – and he was tall. He had to bend his head to get through a doorway. Ronald said he was going to see what was going on. Children, he thought, we sometimes saw children go in there, but this man was much too tall to be a child. Ronald wouldn't let me go with him.

'He was gone a long time. It was late afternoon – well, evening, but still quite light. It was evening by the time he came back.' The flood waters trickled now, then stopped. There was a sob in her voice when she spoke again and though the tears had ceased, sweat now broke out on her face and neck. 'He came into the house and he was so white I thought he was ill. Well, he was ill, he was. I cried out to him, "What's the matter, what's wrong?" and he said, he said it in a voice I didn't recognise, "Reeny, there's a man in there and he's dead. Can you come, please?"

'I went across the road with him. It was light enough to see by.

There was no electricity on in the house. We went in the back door.' She looked up into Wexford's face. 'I wasn't so heavy as I am now. I could move faster and I was quite strong. I had to be.' She reached for the water but most of it she had spilt over Wexford. Burden refilled the glass and she drank from it. 'We went into the bathroom. *He* was in there, the man. He was lying on the floor and there was – blood.'

At this point Wexford had to interrupt her, trying to keep the sternness out of his voice, 'Mrs McNeil, think what you are saying. You told us you thought this man might have died of a heart attack.'

'No, he didn't. I shouldn't have said that. Ronald – oh, it was so terrible, he had a gun. He had a licence for it, it was all above board. He took his shotgun with him when he went into the house.'

Wexford stopped her. His voice had become very grave.

'Are you saying your husband shot this man? That's a very serious accusation, Mrs McNeil.'

'I said to him, "Did you shoot him?" and Ronald said, "He came at me with a knife. I backed away and he came after me, I had to defend myself."'

'All right. What happened then?'

'My husband said that we must move him, we couldn't leave him there. You see, Ronald had shot him. No one would have believed it was in self-defence.'

You might have put it to the test, Wexford thought. You might just have decided late in the day that honesty was the best policy. What a catalogue of folly all this was – yet he believed it. These two self-appointed vigilantes had somehow convinced themselves that it was their job to police that house. Or had it all been a simple but voracious curiosity? A need in their dull lives to trespass and transgress in ways more suited to the pranks of children?

'You moved him?' he said.

'Ronald couldn't have done it alone. He needed me to help.' She seemed pathetically proud of it. 'We dared not leave him there, not with all those other people coming in.'

'So you took him down to the cellar?' said Burden.

'He wasn't wearing any clothes – well, just his underclothes. That's why he went into the bathroom, Ronald said. He thought perhaps he could have a bath or just wash himself.'

Ghoulishly, she began to giggle, a sound not unlike her sobs, quite different from the Tredown women's cackling. 'We wrapped him up in newspaper to take him downstairs. There was newspaper in the cellar. I went down and fetched the paper and we wrapped him in that. We put him in the cellar and my husband piled logs on top of him and boards and boxes and we left him. Ronald said that would have to do until he could think of some way to get rid of him. Burn him perhaps or bury him but he didn't know where.'

'But you never did?'

'No, we never did.' She lifted to them a woebegone face. 'Ronald had his first stroke the next day. He couldn't have burnt or buried anyone after that.'

'Mrs McNeil, did you shut the cellar door when you left?'

She shook her head. 'Not then. I did when I went back.'

T he heart of Kingsmarkham was no place to be on a Saturday evening, especially if you were over forty. It had once been a quiet country town, sleepy and peaceful, but now you might as well have been in Piccadilly Circus. The binge drinkers were out in force, spilling out of the pubs and clubs on to the pavement because this was an exceptionally warm November. Wexford told Donaldson to drive them to the little pub on the Kingsbrook called the Gooseberry Bush and not to wait for them, they would walk home from there. The place wasn't crowded but it wasn't exactly deserted either. Young people without cars disliked the half-hour walk from the town along footpaths bordering water meadows. The car park was full of the transport used by the middle-aged. If you turned your back to it, as Wexford said, if you pretended it wasn't there, you could look instead from your table at a clear starry sky and a moon shedding its pale light on to meadows bisected by dark hedges, willows fringing the Kingsbrook.

'That was awful,' he said flatly. 'I should have been tougher but I felt so sorry for her.'

'Did she say any more after I'd gone?' Burden had left the house and gone outside to sit in the car.

'Only that they'd never moved the body. I mean they'd never done what she says they intended, that is burn it or bury it. Well, we know they didn't. They moved house, leaving the body in there, covered by all the logs.'

Burden ordered drinks for them without asking Wexford what he wanted. He knew. 'That's how it was when Damon and I found it.'

'Her husband died. I suppose the shock of knowing he'd killed a man caused his first stroke. She kept thinking she would go back into the bungalow and take a look, see if it could remain there, but she didn't. Not till two years ago. Mrs Pickford asked her to tea. She says she went over there on the bus and got there a bit early. Grimble's key was still under the stone by the back door. She went in and down the stairs.'

'The place must have stunk.'

'I know. All she said was that there was a faint smell of decay in the cellar. Of "something gone bad" was the way she put it. She pulled off some of the logs – God knows what she thought that would achieve – and when she saw what was underneath – well, you know what it must have been two years ago – she just fled. "It frightened me," she said. "I was so frightened." She ran out, lumbered out, I suppose, poor old thing, slamming the door behind her.'

'No doubt that's why I had a job getting it open.'

'She staggered up the stairs, went home and tried to forget about it, I suppose.' Wexford lifted his glass, savoured the claret which filled it and sighed a little. 'I'm going back tomorrow.'

'Tomorrow's Sunday.'

'Can't be helped. The better the day, the better the deed, as my grandad said, or if he didn't he should have.'

'Are we going to charge her at least with concealing a death?'

'I don't know if I'd have the heart,' said Wexford, 'but I must eventually. I showed her the photo of the t-shirt but it was plain she didn't recognise it. All she'd seen of him through the window was the orange anorak.'

'What became of the knife?' Burden asked.

T he lost father couldn't be the man they were looking for, could he? The time was right, eleven years ago, disappeared in June, a male, the right sort of age as far as Carina Laxton could tell the age. If the DNA, that ultimate certain proof, was right ... Two people were alive to provide it, those two daughters. Barry Vine's first thought when he had read the piece in the News Review was that he must immediately tell Wexford but it was Saturday night and next day part two of Selina Hexham's memoir would appear. There might be something in tomorrow's instalment to make it impossible for Alan Hexham to be their man.

He drove home and read it again. Nowhere did the writer say she positively knew her father was dead and knew how he died; nowhere did she say whether she and her sister had ever heard from him in the intervening years. She might say so in the next instalment. Would he be justified in showing it to Wexford at this hour when he didn't know if the whole thing would turn out to make it impossible that Alan Hexham's was the body in Grimble's trench? Selina might write that her father had phoned home a year later without saying where he was or that they had had a postcard from Australia. His imagination working away, Barry forgot for a moment that whatever might appear tomorrow, Selina Hexham had already written it, perhaps a year ago, and wasn't feverishly penning her memories now for a newspaper due to publish them in a few hours' time. Then he remembered, told himself not to be ridiculous, to wait till tomorrow and settled down to his Linda di Chamonix CD.

CHAPTER FOURTEEN

The *Sunday Times*, News Review, 5 November 2006
Part Two of *Gone Without Trace: The Lost Father*

My mother knew he was dead. She knew it from that first day, the day we all went to the police together. She didn't say that to the police or to us, of course she didn't, but years later she told me she had known it from the first. There was no other explanation for his staying away for twenty-four hours without getting in touch with her. She knew when she was loved and she knew herself to be a sensitive, perceptive woman who would quickly have been able to tell if her husband was seeing another woman. It was this self-knowledge which perhaps made it worse when the rumour spread round our neighbourhood, at our school, even at the church where Mum sometimes went, that Dad had run off with Denise Cole. There were other theories for his disappearance, of course: he was heavily in debt (he who had never owed anyone a penny), he was depressed because he felt himself a failure as a teacher (he who was a brilliant teacher and immensely popular), he had met someone in Lewes (at a funeral!) who had offered him a wonderful job at twice his present salary if he would leave at once, but the favourite one was that of his elopement.

Denise Cole isn't her real name. It would be unfair to give it. I'm sure she was quite innocent either of having designs on my father or of fostering the rumour. She was about twenty-five years old, rented a room in the next street to us and was a checkout supervisor in a supermarket in Leyton High Road. She had left school at sixteen after getting half a dozen rather good O levels. Now she wanted to go to university and study for a psychology degree so that she could go into social work. Whether she ever got her degree and became a social worker I don't know, but I do know that she is married and living up in the North somewhere.

Dad used to coach her. She mostly came to our house for her coaching in biology but sometimes they went to her room where she always had a friend of hers present. There wasn't so much danger then for a teacher to be accused of molesting a student he was alone with, but I suppose Denise and my dad thought it best to be on the safe side. The friend was also sitting for A levels, so Dad had two students to teach. No one ever suggested he was involved with Megan Lloyd. It was always Denise because it so happened that she had gone missing two days before he did.

I remember him going round to the house where she had a room and coming back rather cross to say that one of the other tenants had told him she'd done 'a moonlight flit'. Megan hadn't been there either but there was no question of her being missing. She just hadn't turned up because Denise had told her she owed £3,000 on her Visa card and meant to go off somewhere for a while 'until it had all blown over', whatever that meant.

Everyone began to believe that my dad and Denise Cole had gone off together. Well, not us and our friends, we didn't believe it. Even if Dad had been the sort of man who'd be unfaithful to his wife with a girl nearly twenty years his junior, we knew he'd never even been alone with her. Mum and Vivien and I were always in the house and Megan was always there when he went round to Denise's.

Did the rumour – and it grew into more than a rumour – influence the police not to look for him? Maybe they wouldn't have done anyway. Maybe he just didn't come into their category of vulnerable people. Up to a point we looked for him. Mum phoned every relative we had and wrote to those whose addresses we had but her heart wasn't in it. As I've said, she knew he was dead. It was the only possible explanation.

But the insurance company didn't know. The building society with whom they'd got one of those arrangements that ensure that on a partner's death the other one gets possession of the property absolutely, they didn't know. Our house was only ours if Mum managed to go on paying the mortgage. Dad's pension was only hers if she could prove he was dead. Of course she could have gone on the benefit but she wouldn't do that. She'd been a librarian before she married Dad and she managed to get a job working in a bookshop.

This was all months later and during that time we were living on what was in their joint account and her own savings. She knew it would be a good idea to sell our house and buy a flat which would be big enough for the three of us. But she couldn't sell the house. It didn't belong to her or, rather, it belonged to her and Dad, and Dad wasn't there to agree to the sale. To help make ends meet she let out one of the upstairs rooms, her own bedroom. We kept our room and she moved into Dad's study.

Before that happened it had to be cleared of what was in it. I ought to make it plain how dreadful all this was for her, how painful for all of us but specially horrible for her. To leave their bedroom to a stranger was bad enough but to go into Dad's study which she always looked on as somehow sacred to him, inviolable and absolutely private, to take it apart and empty it, that was agony to her, the ultimate sacrilege. But she did, she had to and we went with her. It wasn't that we asked to be there but that she asked *us*. I think she didn't want to be alone in there or she was afraid she might collapse in uncontrollable tears.

It sounds strange to say this but we'd never been in that room before. I mean Vivien and I hadn't. Mum had, of course she had, probably when we were little and she and Dad were getting it ready to be his sort of sanctum. Later on we'd seen into it on our way to bed, for instance, when Dad had come out to say good-night and left the door open. The fact was we hadn't been all that interested. It was just an ordinary little room, the kind of place which in houses like ours was called the box room – because when the houses were first built and space wasn't at a premium people kept bags and suitcases in there? We looked in and saw a place not much bigger than a cupboard with a desk in it and a chair, a filing cabinet, bookshelves full of books and an awful lot of paper. That's all there was room for. When we went in for the first time, six months after we lost our father and Mum her husband, there was only just room for us all to get in there and then it was only possible because we were small thin people.

There wasn't a computer. Vivien and I had got used to computers, we had them at school, though neither of us then possessed one, and we'd never before seen an electric typewriter. Mum had to tell us what it was. It seemed to us as ancient, as *antediluvian*, as a fountain pen or a pound note. What did Dad use it for? we wanted to know. 'Working for his postgraduate degree,' was the only answer she could come up with and then she said, 'Researching. Writing his thesis.' If this was true, what happened to the thesis? Had he started it? Was it half-completed?

Whatever it had been, there was no trace of it remaining. For all we found, he might have sat up here reading and rereading the books on the shelves. Those books themselves gave no clue. There was the *Shorter Oxford Dictionary*, *Roget's Thesaurus* and *Brewer's Dictionary of Phrase and Fable*, a Classical dictionary, Ovid's *Metamorphoses* in a new translation, Icelandic sagas, novels by J. R. R. Tolkien and Ursula Le Guin and Terry Pratchett, Darwin's *Origin of Species* and his *Voyage of the Beagle*, books by Stephen Jay Gould and Richard Dawkins.

We took the books downstairs and stacked them on top of the bookcase. There was no other space. The papers we put up in the loft and the blank sheets we kept to use for writing letters on. But we hardly wrote any letters, we had no one to write to, and the sheets of paper are still in the house where I have lived alone since Mum died. We found only one piece of paper which might have given us some hint as to where Dad went when he left Maurice Davidson's funeral, but it didn't. I don't really know why I thought it might. Maybe because it was the only thing we found in there in Dad's handwriting. Oh, there were cheque stubs, of course – he attended to business in that room, paying bills, completing forms and that sort of thing – but this scrap of paper, half an A4 sheet, was the only thing he left behind that he'd written by hand. It was hard to escape the conclusion that he'd deliberately cleared the place of anything which might have provided a clue to where he was going and what he intended to do. I actually said this to Mum but she wasn't having any of it. 'He didn't know he was going to die,' she said, 'and I know he's dead. I just know it.'

And the scrap of paper that was the only thing in his handwriting? It was a list of names of contemporary authors, mostly science-fiction writers, all of them still alive, along with a list of publishers. Underneath he had written 'Fact-finding? Proofreading? Editing?'

Mum said it wouldn't help us find where he had gone that afternoon. Years before, she remembered, when they were short of money and she couldn't take a job because they had us, Dad had considered trying to get work as a publisher's reader. He knew such a thing was possible because publishers employed people to read manuscripts. But he never did. The pay would have been too little to make it worth his while. We actually phoned the publishing houses on the list but none of them had ever heard of him. So that was no use. Don't they call it a red herring?

Meanwhile his study was cleared – he had been gone for over a year by then – and Mum moved in, leaving her bedroom for the lodger. Vera was a quiet tidy sort of woman but Vivien and I never liked her. We resented having to share a bathroom with her, though we had never minded sharing with Dad. It must have been much more of a hardship for her sharing with us. We were coming up to the age when girls take over a bathroom, dropping towels on the floor and leaving mess behind them. She fried most of what she ate and our kitchen always reeked of chip fat. Mum minded that more than almost anything, more than sleeping in that tiny room, which, after all, must hourly have reminded her of Dad sitting in there in happy silence, more than having to sell the car and forgo summer holidays.

You can get used to anything, can't you? Our lives were utterly changed but we still had school, which we both loved, and our friends and the grandparents who were unendingly good to us. We didn't know it at the time, children aren't interested, but Mum told us later that Dad's mother and father paid the mortgage for two years and all the services bills. Our gran died when I was fifteen and Vivien was thirteen and Grandad moved in with us. That was the end of Vera with her chip pan and the stink of cheap perfume she left in the bathroom, the end too of watching everything we spent and denying ourselves anything new. It was three years since my mother had even bought herself a sweater, still less a pair of shoes. Things were different with Grandad there. He had sold his own house for what Mum said was an amazing amount of money, he had a very good pension as well and he brought his car with him.

We both loved Grandad. He was generous and easy-going and never intrusive but I think the best thing about him was that he reminded us of Dad. This must have been painful for Mum but it wasn't for me and I don't think it was for Vivien. His voice sounded like Dad's. He had the same build as Dad, though Dad was a bit taller, and he hadn't lost his hair which was still quite dark. Sometimes I'd come home from school and go into our living room and Grandad would be there, sitting in an armchair reading. He was a great reader – like Dad. He'd turn to say hallo, put out a hand and kiss me, and then for a moment it was my dad, the same feel of the hand, the same dry firm lips.

So things got better for us. Or for Vivien and me they did. Mum had got very thin and the sadness in her face was permanent. She was in perpetual mourning. One evening, after Grandad had gone to bed and Vivien was in our room doing her homework, Mum said in a matter-of-fact way, 'I would quite like to die.' No doubt she shouldn't have said that to a child of sixteen but I suppose she felt she had to say it to someone. I think she put in that 'quite' to soften things a bit. 'I've lived without him for four years,' she said, 'and it hasn't got any better. If I'm in a crowd of people I see him, for a moment I know it's him but of course it isn't. I was in the Tube station the other day and I saw him coming down the escalator. I see him in photos in the paper and crowds on the television. I'd like to die so that that doesn't happen any more.'

I didn't know what to say. It made me cry but she didn't cry. She just sat there gazing in an empty sort of way across the room. 'I haven't minded much about selling the car and having to have Vera and getting a job and all that. That was nothing compared to losing him.'

It was then I asked her if it would be easier for her if we knew what had happened to Dad but she just said she didn't think it would. She had always known he was dead. I wanted to ask her how she thought he could have died, I mean what could have caused his death, if she was so certain, but I dared not say anything which might have hurt her more. Vivien and I had our own ideas of what might have happened to him. She favoured drowning because Lewes isn't far from the South Coast and her idea was that he had gone to Brighton or somewhere down there where all those white cliffs are and fallen into the sea. Considering it had been pouring with torrential rain that day I couldn't see why anyone would choose to go to the seaside. My idea was that Dad had had a heart attack in some lonely spot while walking to the station after Maurice Davidson's funeral. If he had been walking through a wood and died there his body might never have been found.

We had plans to go to Lewes, go to Carol Davidson's house and follow the route Dad would have taken to the station. We never did. It was more a fantasy and a dream than a practicality. And things were different for us than for Mum. I had my A levels and Vivien her GCSEs. I had a boyfriend. Vivien was in the school tennis six and played the violin in the orchestra. Our lives began to be crammed with interests. We both worked hard at school, harder I think than we might have done if Dad had still been with us. We knew we'd need to get good jobs one day and we'd have to go to university first.

We always felt the loss of Dad, sometimes very painfully, but it wasn't like it was for Mum. When he went everything that meant anything to her went out of her life. Well, she had us and I think that was a comfort to her but not really a consolation. She said a deep sense of loneliness was with her all the time. I was eighteen and in my first year at the University of York when she became ill. I'd noticed how thin she'd got and she couldn't really afford to lose weight. When I came home for the holidays I told her she should go to her GP, it wasn't natural to be so emaciated, but she said she was fine apart from a bit of backache. I went back to York in October but came home for a weekend in the following month after a panicky phone call from Vivien. Mum had been diagnosed with breast cancer which had spread into the spine.

She hadn't gone to her doctor when I'd suggested she should and eventually when she had gone because the pain was so bad, they started chemo immediately. They told me at the hospital that it was too late and all they could do for her now was palliative care to keep the pain away. She was so thin that her rings dropped off her fingers. Smiling her death's head smile, she handed me the wedding and engagement rings and told me to keep them safe, one for me and one for Vivien to wear one day if we wanted to. She knew there was no hope for her. 'Dad's wedding ring was the same as mine,' she said, 'with the same engraving inside.'

I didn't say anything. I just sat there, holding her ringless hand.

'I think about him all the time,' she said. 'I wish I believed we'll meet again, but I don't, I really don't.'

When I got home I read the inscription inside the wedding ring. It was a gold ring. Chased with leaves, and with *For Ever* inside. Well, it did last for ever, their for ever. Mum died in the middle of January of the following year. I went home whenever I could but Vivien was there with her all the time in her last months and saw her every day. 'She knew what was wrong with her,' she said to me. 'I know she did, though she never said. She'd found a lump in the left breast all of a year ago but she didn't do anything about it. She only went to the doctor when the pain in her back got unbearable.'

I asked her what Mum was afraid of.

'Nothing,' she said. 'She wasn't afraid of anything except of going on living. She did nothing about the lump because she wanted to die. She wouldn't kill herself but she knew this would kill her and that was what she wanted.'

So we lived on alone there with Grandad who had lost his wife and his only child. He too died a couple of years later but at eighty-two which isn't a tragic age to die at, not like forty-four and forty-nine, though the loss of him was just someone else for us to miss. Grandad left us everything he had, enough to pay off the mortgage and have quite a bit for each of us. I bought Vivien out because she wanted to live in a flat with her boyfriend and now I live in the house alone. But I won't sell it. I'm not like Mum, I don't think Dad is dead. One day he'll come back and I'll be here waiting for him. With all I have that was once his: the wedding ring he gave Mum and a scrap of paper with his writing on it. All that I have left of him.

Selina Hexham's memoir of her father, Gone Without Trace: The Lost Father *will be published in January 2007 by Lawrence Busoni Hill at £19.99.*

Barry put the sheets of newsprint, these and the ones from the previous Sunday, into an envelope and drove over to Kingsmarkham with them. He had put in a covering note in case Wexford wasn't in, saying the cuttings were from him and out of the *Sunday Times* but nothing more. Wexford would know. His daughter Sheila answered the door, a baby in her arms. She didn't know Barry but he of course knew her the way everyone did. Her face was one of those familiar to all television viewers and newspaper readers. She said her father was out, she didn't know where, but wouldn't he come in? They were just having coffee.

Barry said no, thanks, but it was very kind of her. Suppose this man Hexham was the body in the trench, he thought as he drove back to Stowerton, and he had found him? That would be something. He was angry too, in the way he thought Wexford might be. Someone, maybe one of those people he had talked to, maybe not, had killed this man and thrown his body into a trench, like they buried cattle dead of some disease. Barry thought of those girls and their mother and her parents. Not only had they a much-loved man to mourn for but privation to face, the hardship which comes when a death can't be presumed. One of those people had caused all this and probably for no other motive than gain or cowardice.

If it was Hexham.

CHAPTER FIFTEEN

'Should I have my solicitor here?'

He was surprised she knew of such a requirement. Then he remembered all the law and police programmes on television that the housebound watch. He shook his head, thought of saying, 'Not yet,' but said nothing. Was he eventually going to arrest her?

This Sunday morning she was no less pathetic. She hadn't been alone when he left her the evening before. He had insisted on her having someone with her before he went and she had phoned her cleaner who agreed to come. It seemed to him dreadful that the only companion she could find was a woman not particularly sympathetic to her whom she would have to pay. She wouldn't, of course, have said why she wanted the cleaner but only that she wasn't feeling well and was nervous about being alone.

She reclined on the bulbous buttoned sofa, her swollen legs up on a cushion. Her face was caked with white powder and in the heat from the radiators, unnecessary and unwanted, she fanned herself with a brochure out of some newspaper. He had angry helpless feelings that something should be done about people like her, something to help them, ameliorate their lot, but he didn't know what that something could be. She wasn't poor, she wasn't in want, she was like that woman in the poem: 'O why do you walk through the fields in gloves . . . O fat white woman whom nobody loves'. No doubt, it was her own fault that no one loved her but it was too late for that now.

'Do you have any idea who this man was?' he asked her.

'Of course I don't,' she answered rather too quickly. 'I don't know those sorts of people. I know I'd never seen him before.'

'There were some clothes in the house, Mrs McNeil,' he began, 'in the kitchen. They were his.'

'I said I saw him through the window and that orange thing he was wearing. I never saw him again till he was dead.'

Till after your husband had shot him. Wexford made the correction silently. The man went across the road carrying a shotgun in broad daylight. But why not? Who would remark on that? Who would be perturbed if they heard the shots? Rabbits and pigeons were shot around here at any time. There was no closed season.

'And a cupboardful in the bedroom,' she said. 'All old Mr Grimble's clothes. The son never removed them, left them all hanging there. People have no respect these days. I'm glad I had no children.'

He forbore to say that if she had, they would now be approaching sixty. 'Did you see the clothes on the kitchen counter?'

'They were his, the man who came at Ronald with a knife. He took them off when he went to the bathroom.'

'Now Mrs McNeil, I want you to think carefully before you answer. Did you and your husband take anything from the clothes in the kitchen after the man was – was dead?'

Instead of thinking carefully, she answered at once.

'What sort of thing?'

The things he must have had, Wexford thought, the things everyone has, no matter how poor. 'Small change, a driving licence, keys?'

A look that was part scorn, part impatience crossed her face. It was one that Wexford knew well, expressing as it did dismissal of the kind of people Mrs McNeil's parents would have said kept the coal in the bath, and she herself that the only reason they no longer did so was because the council supplied them with central heating.

'A person like that doesn't have that sort of thing,' she said.

'A person like what, Mrs McNeil?'

'A working-class person. Not that they work much.'

Wexford had to hold on hard to the pity he felt for her before it slipped away. 'Not even a key?'

She hesitated. She looked about her, to the right and to the left, as if for a way of escape. 'My husband looked through the clothes.' Her lips compressed, she paused, then said very carefully, 'There was some money.'

A new expression had come into her eyes, one Wexford hadn't seen there before. Self-righteousness? Murder, or at any rate manslaughter, concealing a death, trespass, none of those had been able to evoke it, but property, possession, money, were different. Being deprived of those or depriving another of those was the ultimate crime.

'Where was it?'

'In the pocket of those trousers they all wear. Blue things.'

'How much money, Mrs McNeil?'

'A great deal. I don't know. I didn't count it.' Indignation spread across her face. 'Are you suggesting we stole it? How dare you! Stealing is *wrong*.'

'I know very well you didn't, Mrs McNeil.'

'Then what more do you want? I told you the man was dead. My husband shot him in self-defence.'

At a range of – what? Ten feet? Twelve?

The cleaner arrived, offered to prepare lunch for Irene McNeil, and to sit with her throughout the afternoon. If she had ever had friends they must all be dead by now. She had no one – but Wexford's sympathy was all gone. According to Maeve Tredown and, more reliably, the cleaner, Irene McNeil was eighty-four. Was he going to take it upon himself to charge a woman of her age with anything? Maybe he would have to. He asked her again about the shooting and the knife.

'I wasn't there.' She was on the verge of whimpering. 'I didn't see it. Ronald said he came at him with a knife and Ronald would never tell a lie.'

'Did you see the knife?'

'I don't know. I think I did, I don't remember. It was a shock when Ronald came back and said he'd killed a man. Even though it was self-defence. I was upset, I didn't ask him a lot of questions.'

'Mrs McNeil, are you saying that when this man went into the bathroom, wearing nothing but his underwear, leaving his clothes behind in the kitchen, he took a knife with him?'

'I don't know,' she said. 'My husband said he did. Ronald never lied.'

'The knife would still be there, wouldn't it? This man would have dropped it and it would still be there in the bathroom.'

'I don't know. I don't remember. I'm so tired.' She began to cry. 'I don't know what to do.'

The cleaner was a fierce-looking woman with a stare. She said, 'You've upset her properly. I hope you're satisfied.'

Dora and Sheila and the little girls had all had their lunch. Paul was coming for Sheila later in the afternoon. Wexford ate the food they had left for him, cold chicken and salad, not his favourite meal; with sparkling water and cranberry juice to choose from, he drank nothing but listened to his wife and daughter discussing Sheila's forthcoming wedding. Dora was so relieved Sheila was actually getting married at last, that she put up no objections to the plans for having the ceremony on one of the beaches of an island off the West Coast of Scotland. Only the proposal to have Amulet and Anoushka as bridesmaids aroused her to protest. Wexford thought he might quite enjoy it, especially as, unlike her first wedding at St Peter's, Kingsmarkham, he wouldn't be expected to foot the bill.

An envelope addressed to him had been placed beside his plate. When he had finished the chicken and eaten enough of the salad to placate his wife, he opened it. In the list he kept in his head, Wexford's Seventh Law was that while women like cold food and loved raw food, men do not. He unfolded two newspaper cuttings, one dated today. He read them, moving into an armchair before starting on the second. Sheila came over and sat beside him, Anoushka on her knee.

'Are you tired, Pop? You look a bit tired.'

'I suppose I am.' He was having a lot of practice lately at reading expressions. 'I see you want something. What is it?'

'While you were out Mrs Dirir came round to see me. She knew I'd be here, Mum told her. She wanted to know if she could see you this evening. There's someone – a girl – she wants to bring round to see you.'

He gave a little groan. It sounded absurdly plaintive in his own ears. 'It's Sunday, Sheila.' Why did he bother? That wasn't an excuse which carried any weight with her generation and those younger. Sunday was no longer a day of rest, no longer a day when shops were closed and entertainments shut, no longer a time when people stayed at home in peace and quiet.

'I think it's important, Pop. It's something to do with genital mutilation.'

'When is she coming?'

She smiled. She knew he had given in.

'About seven, she said.'

When Paul had come and taken her and his small daughters away, Wexford reread the extracts Barry Vine had sent him. It was possible, he thought. Perhaps more than that. The dates were right, Thursday 15 June, 1995, the day Hexham disappeared, two days before the trench in Grimble's Field was finally filled in. The man's age was right. Between forty and fifty, Carina Laxton had said, and Alan Hexham's age had been forty-four. Throughout the investigation into this murder, it had been suggested that this first unidentified man must have been a visitor to the place. If nothing in this account indicated that Hexham had ever gone near Kingsmarkham or visited Flagford, there was nothing to disprove it or even make it unlikely. He had been in Lewes until two o'clock and after that he seemed to have vanished off the face of the earth. He might have taken the train to Kingsmarkham just as he might have gone to Brighton or returned to London and taken another train or a bus elsewhere.

Of course it would have to be investigated. This young woman, Selina Hexham, must be interviewed and he would have to do it himself. One thing was certain, it couldn't just be put on the back burner. Thinking this way made him wonder about back burners – was the heat generated by them, whether its source was gas or electricity, necessarily less than that on the front ones? He thought not. In a moment he would go and check in his own kitchen but as he pondered the question he fell asleep.

The girl who came with Iman Dirir was Matea. So this was why she had wanted to speak to him the last time he and Burden had been to A Passage to India. This was why she had come to his front door on Hallowe'en.

She wore the kind of clothes which are equally Western and Eastern, loose cotton trousers and a long-sleeved tunic, embroidered and sequinned, as fashionable in London as in Amman or Mogadishu. Wexford thought she looked like a girl out of *Omar Khayyam* that any man would choose to sit with in the wilderness alongside a loaf of bread and a cup of wine. Her long black hair was a river flowing down her back. They sat in front of a log fire Dora had just lit, believing immigrants from warm places must be perpetually cold in their adopted country.

Outside, fallen leaves covered everything so that not a square inch of green grass showed in the light that fell on the lawn from the French windows. The only thing which moved was a squirrel nosing methodically through the yellow carpet. The wind had dropped. Matea sat as still as the air, her hands folded in her lap. Mrs Dirir, who was so like Matea that she might have been her mother, said quietly to Wexford, 'This is something we are brought up not to talk about in our community. It would be better if we talked about it but no one does. The nearest we ever get is if one girl asks another, "Are you cut?"'

Wexford saw the girl tremble. It was a very slight movement, less than a shiver. The other woman went on, 'They say you only become a woman after it is done. It is a – a sign of – what is the word I want? – of status.'

Dora said quickly, 'Yes, I see.' She got up and drew the curtains as if to shut out ugly menacing things.

'You know that my husband and I brought our daughters here to save them from that,' Iman Dirir said to Wexford. She put out a hand to the girl in a graceful gesture. 'Matea hasn't been saved. It has already happened to her. She was cut when she was very young.'

The girl blushed a painful red. 'I was three years old.'

'It's hard for her to speak about it, Mr Wexford. She has never before spoken about it except to me and to one or two others who are – are against it.'

'I know,' he said. 'Or rather I can imagine.' He heard Dora beside him make a little sound of distress.

'She has told me it was not so bad for her as for some,' said Mrs Dirir. Matea nodded vigorously. 'She has not many problems. Not like many others who have cysts and fistulas and cannot – all right, Matea, I won't go on.'

'How about the men?' Dora asked. 'What do they feel about it? The husbands and fathers, I mean.'

'They say it is woman's business. Not for them to interfere but there are some who say it is good because it keeps women – I think I am trying to say "pure". Would that be the right word?'

'Pure, chaste, something like that,' Wexford said.

'A woman who has been cut, they say, will not be unfaithful.' A dark red flush mounted in Iman Dirir's face. 'I find this hard to say. I will try. Women who have been circumcised don't like what men and women do – can you understand what I mean?'

'Of course,' Wexford said. 'Of course we can.'

Iman Dirir paused and her face gradually returned to its dark cream colour. 'It's not for herself that Matea has come to you. For her it's too late. It's for her sister's sake she has come.'

Matea's English had improved. She spoke with a strong accent but improved fluency. 'It is for my sister Shamis. She is five years old but not yet in school. My mother and father go home to Somalia for vacation soon. They take with them my brother Adel and my sister.'

Wexford decided to help her. 'You're afraid your parents intend to have your sister circumcised while they are in Somalia?'

'I know it,' Matea said.

'It's against the law,' he said, knowing this to be a useless remark. Taking a female out of the country for the purpose of having her genitally mutilated had been a crime punishable by up to fourteen years' imprisonment for four years now, but there had been no prosecutions. The reason for this Mrs Dirir had already outlined. A blanket of silence was maintained amongst these people on the subject. No one would 'betray' a lawbreaker to the authorities, no one would go to the police or the medical profession. 'You should tell your parents of the penalty – I mean, that they could go to prison for a long time.'

She shook her head. 'Mrs Dirir has done that. They say – they say on and on – we go only for vacation.'

'I will have someone speak to them,' he said, thinking of Karen Malahyde, the Child Protection Officer. 'I'll do my best.'

'Thank you,' Matea said and he could see a leap of hope in her eyes.

He slept badly that night. In sleeping dreams and the waking kind, he kept seeing a five-year-old held down on the ground amid a ring of watching women, held by her spread legs and her struggling arms, while another cut into her flesh with a sharpened stone. He would do his best. Would it be enough to prevent an outrage being perpetrated on a helpless child, not yet at primary school?

CHAPTER SIXTEEN

elina Hexham might have made the whole thing up. *Gone Without Trace* sounded factual, but perhaps it was a work of fiction. Thinking this way after his disturbed night, Wexford had Hannah check the weather on 15 June, 1995, with the Weather Centre, formerly the Meteorological Office, and the trains on that day between London and Lewes and Lewes and Kingsmarkham. She found that, as Selina Hexham had said, it rained all that day. A train from London to Lewes had left Victoria at 9.25 a.m. and reached Lewes at 10.12, while in the afternoon the 2.20 from Lewes had arrived in Kingsmarkham at 2.42.

The third Carol Davidson Hannah tried was the right one. She was still a widow but she had moved from Lewes to Uckfield. Hannah had difficulties with her. She hadn't seen the *Sunday Times*, neither yesterday's nor the previous Sunday's, and the result of enlightening her was at first to arouse indignation. Hannah knew that this was the reaction of most people when they hear they have been mentioned in a newspaper without being asked for their permission. Carol Davidson assumed that something derogatory must have been written about her and her late husband. If this was paranoia it was very common and Hannah let her vent her anger for a full minute. At the end of it she assured her that Selina Hexham had written nothing but pleasant things about her parents' friendship with the Davidsons and gradually Carol Davidson grew calmer.

'What did you phone me *for*?' she asked in a sullen tone. 'Apart from thoroughly upsetting me?'

'I'm very sorry about that, Mrs Davidson.' Hannah particularly disliked addressing a woman by her wifely style and she disliked apologising almost as much, but she gritted her teeth. 'All I want is to confirm a few details with you.'

'Yes, well, he disappeared. I mean, Alan Hexham did. People said he went off with another woman, though it doesn't sound much like him. But you never can tell. I don't suppose Selina has anything to say about that.'

'She does, as a matter of fact. May I ask you for a few details?'

'I suppose so. Go ahead.'

'Mr Hexham appears to have left your house at 2 p.m. Is that correct?'

'I can't tell you to the minute. It was something like that. It was the day of my husband's funeral – you want to remember that.'

Hannah controlled her rage. That husband had been dead eleven years and no doubt, like most if not absolutely all marriages, theirs hadn't been a bed of roses. 'Can you tell me how far your house was from Lewes train station?'

'I really do resent the way we have to talk about train stations these days. "Railway station" used to be the expression. How far was it? Not far. Ten minutes' walk?'

'Did Mr Hexham walk?'

'I really don't remember. It's a long time ago. I do know he was going to the station.'

'There was a train at 2.20.'

'Well, if you know, why ask me? He didn't tell me where he was going. Home, I imagine.'

Hannah had nothing more to ask. Consulting a street plan online, she found that the Davidsons' house was very near Lewes station. It would hardly have taken twenty minutes to get there but Hannah knew very well that some people like to be on the platform with plenty of time to spare before their train is due. Her mother was such a one, and as a child, Hannah had several times found herself and her parents waiting for three empty tedious hours in airport lounges. If Hexham's destination had been important to him, or rather what was to happen when he got there was important, he would have been very anxious not to miss that train.

Wexford phoned the *Sunday Times* himself. The literary editor referred him to Selina Hexham's publishers, Lawrence Busoni Hill, at an address in West London. He spoke to her editor who hesitated when he asked her for Miss Hexham's address or phone number. It wasn't their policy to disclose addresses. Not even to the police? he asked. That would be all right, she said, if she could check and call him back. He hadn't much faith in her promise but she did call him back and he found himself in possession of a phone number and an email address.

An answering machine responded. Selina – she gave no surname – wasn't available to speak to him now but if it was important she could be called on her mobile. A number followed. He supposed she was at work, a lab somewhere. He hesitated about calling that number but it was nearly one o'clock and perhaps she would be having lunch. Again she wasn't available but on his third attempt she answered.

'Selina speaking. Will you hold please?' He held. Surnames were on the way out, he thought. Soon it would be like it had been in mediaeval times and people would be called John of London or Jane of the Green. And because it would be so hard to know whom you were referring to, in order to distinguish one person from another given names might become more and more outlandish and strange and . . . She came back on the line. 'I'm sorry about that. What can I do for you?'

He explained who he was.

'You've found my dad?' She was quickly excited.

'No, no, Miss Hexham. Not that. I read the extracts from your book. I'd like to talk to you. I can't say more than that at the moment. Perhaps I could come and see you?'

'I'll come to you,' she said. 'I can't believe it. They said if I wrote about what happened and it was in a newspaper it was a way of finding him but I didn't believe it. When shall I come?'

That afternoon if possible, he said. Of course she would. She could take time off and she didn't want to wait. She wouldn't sleep if she left it overnight. All right, he said, any time you like, there are three trains an hour from Victoria. But he was appalled. In her book she had said she feared her father might be dead, her mother had known he was dead, yet here she was thrilled, jubilant, like a child looking forward to a promised treat.

Once upon a time, every town in Britain had among its streets one or perhaps two looked upon as the least desirable in which to live by those whose homes were in more salubrious parts. Just as they also had one or perhaps two which were the most desirable and vulgarly known as 'millionaire's row'. This has changed now as housing estates have been built and new terraces and little detached boxes proliferate, but the worst and the best still remain tucked in amongst them and they are still the same best and worst. In Kingsmarkham the best had always been Ploughman's Lane – incongruous, Wexford sometimes said, that the most humble of rustic labourers should have given the name of his calling to an avenue of elegant and almost noble mansions, affordable only by the very rich – and the worst Glebe Road. Still, Glebe Road had been gentrified in parts and elevated, in more senses than one, by a couple of not very high tower blocks, cut off at ten floors, as if the architect had lost his nerve.

In the more attractive of these blocks lived Matea's parents, the Imrans, in one of a number of flats alloted five years before to successful asylum seekers. Karen almost felt her heart fail her as she and Lyn climbed the stairs, the Cremorne House lift being out of order. She had no problem with a rigid political correctness but delicacy was a subtly different matter and was what would be needed here. Of that she hadn't much experience. The door was answered by a middle-aged woman wearing a long black gown and a hastily donned headscarf which she removed immediately Karen and Lyn were inside. It had been worn, presumably, lest a man was at the door. Mrs Imran looked carefully at their identification, then indicated with a graceful gesture of her right hand that they should come into the living room.

On the tenth floor – Kingsmarkham Council dared to call it a penthouse, Karen had once noticed – a magnificent view of downs and meadows and Cheriton Forest presented itself beyond an inadequate window. On a sofa with a boy of about ten beside him, Rashid Imran sat playing Monopoly with his son and a small girl who knelt on the floor.

As a general rule, Karen disliked children. She had been told this was because they frightened her, but Wexford believed this indifference was an advantage. It meant she could be detached and not become emotionally involved. Lyn, on the other hand, loved children, wanted to get married so that she could have half a dozen – well, three. She immediately squatted down beside the little girl and asked if she might play. It was apparent that Mrs Imran had very little English, if any. But her husband spoke it well and his son had apparently learnt it at school. The child Shamis had enough to say to Lyn, 'Sit, please. You play.'

Adel Imran answered her in the same language and Karen saw that they had gatecrashed an English lesson. This was something of which she hardly knew whether she should approve or not. A past Home Secretary had said that it was necessary for all immigrants to speak English and at first she had agreed with this but then she had wondered. Would making this a requirement of residency be to endanger people's human rights? She looked at Lyn who was already getting on famously with the children and said to their father, 'Do you think DC Fancourt could take the children into another room for a while? There's something I want to say to you and your wife.'

Immediately Mrs Imran began hustling the little boy and girl. Lyn said, 'We could take the Monopoly with us and I'll play instead of your dad. How about that?'

Karen, who sometimes prided herself on her stony heart, came close to being moved by the sight of Shamis looking up into Lyn's face and shyly taking her hand. Appreciative of beauty, she thought she had seldom seen a lovelier child, her golden skin a little darker than her brother's, her eyes black as basalt. When Mrs Imran had closed the door after them, she began. It was about to be the hardest encounter with the public she had had for a long time and she heartily wished herself out of it but she could see why she, a woman, had to do it and not Barry Vine or Damon.

'Mr Imran, I am sure you and your wife would not wish to break the laws of this country now it's your home.' Was that racist? Surely not. Karen would have been happier and have thought herself more politically correct to address the man's wife but what was the use of that when Mrs Imran's English was so limited? 'The trouble is, isn't it, that we don't always know what the law is. Now we have a law in Britain that makes it an offence, a very serious offence, to circumcise a woman or a girl. To cut her, I mean. Do you understand me?'

The woman turned to her a blank face, obviously uncomprehending. Her husband, who had cast down his eyes, began speaking to her in his own language, a language Karen was ashamed to confess she couldn't identify. Was there one actually called Somali? Mrs Imran nodded, said nothing.

'Do you understand me, Mr Imran?'

'Of course. But why come to us?'

'Mr Imran, we have reason to believe you plan to go on holiday to Somalia and while you are there to have Shamis – er, cut.'

'Oh, no,' he said very quickly. Too quickly. 'We go on vacation only.' Again he whispered to his wife and this time she shook her head.

'No, no. This is vacation.' She stumbled a little at the word. 'Children to see aunties.'

Karen nearly shuddered, seeing old women with razors in their hands, or broken glass or stones. 'You must believe I don't want to frighten you or distress you.' Was that patronising? 'But I have to tell you that the maximum penalty . . .' They wouldn't understand that, they wouldn't have the faintest idea. 'The biggest punishment – do you understand? – is fourteen years in prison for a person who breaks this law.'

They were silent. From the next room came a sudden peal of child's laughter. Rashid Imran lifted his eyes, said, 'We cannot speak of this. It is not right to speak of it. You must know that we take the children just on vacation, nothing else. You should go now.'

She had no choice. Shamis came to the door with her to see them out. Lyn bent down and kissed her. 'Well?' she said when they were on the stairs. Karen shrugged.

'I don't know. They didn't say a word about being against female genital mutilation but they didn't say they were for it either. I'll have to see what the guv says.'

She tried it on him when they got back. 'We could have Shamis examined before they go and again when they come back.'

Wexford shook his head. 'You know it's not as simple as that, Karen. On what grounds would we have her examined? We've no grounds except her older sister's *opinion*. Is she being ill-treated, abused? Absolutely not. It seems like a happy home, good attentive parents, happy children. There's a risk she will be very seriously ill-treated in the future but no threat has been made and we've no proof.'

'And when they bring her back and she's been – mutilated? I won't say "circumcised". It makes it sound like what's done to baby boys and it's *not*.'

'Karen,' he said, talking to her as if she were one of his own daughters, 'I'm very sorry to have to say this to you. Believe me, I hate this business as much as you do. But it's only if the child comes back here very obviously mutilated, if the parents have to take her to hospital because she's bleeding or she's got septicaemia, it's only then that we can act.'

'And if she's not? If they get her done under hygienic conditions, then what?'

'Nothing. We won't know.'

'Matea will tell us,' said Karen.

'Will she? If telling us means one or both her parents go to jail for up to fourteen years? It was one thing to say what she said when it was only a threat but it'll be very different when the child's been mutilated and nothing can change it. All we can do now is wait and see.'

The sister Vivien came too. They were so alike that they might have been twins, tallish slender young women, their faces bare of make-up, their fingernails trimmed closely, but Selina with her dark brown hair in a bob with a fringe, Vivien's long and tightly coiled on the back of her head. Selina was in jeans and a shirt, Vivien in a long skirt and silk jacket. They sat down in the two chairs which had been placed to face him on the other side of his desk and he sent for tea.

'It's good of you to come,' he said.

'Oh, no, not good at all,' Selina said. Her voice was low and sweet. 'I can't tell you how wonderful it is to find our father.'

He was aghast but did his best not to show it. To make this assumption she had taken a great leap over a dozen obstacles and traps. 'Miss Hexham, you mustn't take it for granted this is your father. We have very little to go on as yet. All we have is that we have found the body of a man of your father's sort of age who seems to have died on or around 15 or 16 June, 1995. You're here to help us find the truth.'

'Please call me Selina,' she said, not at all downcast.

'Vivien,' said Vivien.

'We would like one of you to provide us with a DNA sample. That's a very simple procedure, involving taking a swab from the inside of your mouth. Only one of you need do it.'

'And you'll know at once?'

'I'm afraid not, Vivien. It will take a few days. We should also like to know the name of your father's dentist if you can tell us that. Eleven years is rather a long time and you may not know.'

'Yes, we do,' Selina said eagerly. 'She's still in Barnes. That's where we live, Barnes. I don't think I told you that. We still go to her.'

She wrote down the name and address of this dentist in a strong upright hand. The tea came, a pot and three cups, brought in by Bal Bhattacharya's replacement, a pink-faced young man called Adam Thayer. Though perfectly respectful, he eyed both girls with a kind of greedy hopefulness. As he poured the tea, Wexford reflected that he had better teach him about custody of the eyes. Neither Selina nor Vivien took milk, an almost universal departure from custom in the young, he had noticed, and Vivien looked at the liquid in her cup as if she intended to drink it for politeness's sake but would infinitely have preferred rooibos or maté.

'I've brought you a proof copy of my book,' Selina said. 'That is, if you'd like to read the rest of it. Those were very short extracts in the *Sunday Times*. I was very glad to have it, of course – well, I was over the moon. It's marvellous advance publicity for my book.'

She handed Wexford a proof copy of *Gone Without Trace* across the desk. He would have to make time to read it even if, he thought with an inner sigh, that meant sitting up to do so at night. 'There are one or two things I'd like to ask you before that,' he said. 'Do you feel up to that now?'

'Of course,' Vivien said. 'Of *course*. We want to help all we can.'

'Then, to begin with, do you, over the lapse of years, have any more idea what it was your father occupied himself with in his study? You mention it quite briefly in the extracts but you don't come to a conclusion. Perhaps there's more about it in the rest of your book?'

'No, there isn't,' said Selina. 'Not really. We tried to find him, that is we tried to find what had happened to him – that's what a large part of the rest of my book is about – we talked to everyone he'd known, all the teachers at his school, the ones that were willing to talk to us, I mean. Not all of them were. We even talked to some of the kids he'd taught. They were – well, contemporaries of ours. So they didn't mind talking to us as much as they might have done to older people. Nobody could tell us much, only that they thought he was studying for a postgraduate degree. This is all in my book.'

'Yes, but in the part I haven't yet read.'

'Right. Sorry. If he was he'd have had to been in an MA or MSc programme at a university. We went into all that but we couldn't find anywhere. It's possible he was doing it only by correspondence but we found nothing to support that idea. He hadn't access to the Internet at home, only at school, and it was what he was doing at home we wanted to know about. One of the students in his A-levels group suggested he might have been conducting – well, some sort of biological experiments, but he hadn't seen the size of the room. And, you know, biology, experiments in it would involve living things, only plants maybe, but they'd take up space and they'd need water and – well, there was absolutely nothing like that. Dad was crazy about Darwin. He was utterly opposed to these fundamentalists who believe Genesis and God creating the world in six days and all that sh— all that rubbish.'

'Could he have been writing something?' Wexford watched their faces but they showed nothing but their eagerness to know. 'Could he, for instance, have been writing a life of Darwin?'

'If he was,' said Vivien, 'he'd have had books about Darwin, lots of books, previous biographies, but he didn't. He just had *Origin of Species*.'

'He had an electric typewriter. It was outdated even at the time of his – disappearance. I don't know why he didn't use a computer but it can't be relevant, can it?'

Wexford was beginning to realise he was learning nothing new and very likely there was nothing new to learn. He sat thinking, said, 'Which of you would like to provide us with the DNA?'

'Me, please,' said Selina.

'DC Thayer will drive you to the Princess Diana Hospital to have the swab taken.'

When she had gone, escorted by Adam Thayer who looked as if he couldn't believe his luck, Vivien said, 'I've brought Mum's wedding ring. They had identical rings, you know, both with the same message in them.'

It was in a small polythene resealable pack, a gold ring chased with a leaf pattern and *For Ever* engraved inside.

'Your father was wearing his, of course?'

'Oh, yes. I don't think they ever took them off, not even to have showers or wash their hands.'

The remains in the trench had worn no ring. It could have fallen off into the soil, he thought, as the flesh decayed from the bones of the third finger of his left hand, but the earth had been sifted very thoroughly when the body was removed. He remembered watching the masked white-coated men working on it with sieves. Vivien seemed to read his thoughts.

'We'd like to see the – the body. Can we?'

He nearly shuddered. 'I don't think so, Miss – er, Vivien. If you wish to I can't stop you but I don't advise it. What remains' – he had to say this – 'isn't much more than a skeleton.'

Her face had whitened. 'All right. I see.'

She didn't. Of course she didn't. 'I think that if you were to see it, the sight might remain with you always, and there would be no point, there would be nothing to help you identify your father. This DNA test will do that but you must remember it may not be him. Please don't go away from here in the belief that your father has been found.'

Vivien got up. 'Shall I wait here for my sister?'

'We can give you somewhere more comfortable to wait. At a later date I may need to borrow the ring. Would that be all right?'

'Of course.'

He would have many more questions if the identification was positive.

CHAPTER SEVENTEEN

That night he began to read *Gone Without Trace*. Selina had been correct when she summarised its contents, telling him of interviews she and Vivien had conducted with fellow teachers of Alan Hexham's and with students in his A-levels group, their careful search of everything in his study, their speculations as to the postgraduate degree he might have been studying for. Also in her book were some factual details from the transcript of her recorded interview with Denise Cole, and her investigation into the suggestion that her father had been in debt. As he read on, tired now but far from dropping off to sleep, he began to see that their detective work had been exhaustive. Professionals could hardly have done better, yet what it all amounted to was that they had found – nothing.

He finished the book at ten minutes to one but had been too stimulated by it to fall asleep for some time. When he did it was to dream, not that a middle-aged man but a little Somali girl had disappeared, while her family and friends denied she had ever existed. In the morning he found that Alan Hexham and his daughters had receded from the forefront of his mind and Irene McNeil stepped or tottered in to take their place. While he slept he had come to a decision. Old and incapacitated as she was, he was going to have to arrest Irene McNeil, question her at the police station and charge her with what? Concealing a death, certainly. He reflected that Ronald McNeil, trigger-happy Lord of the Manor, had neatly slipped out of any responsibility by dying.

Kingsmarkham police station had once had a single prison cell in its basement. Now there were two. But serious as the offences were, expecting Mrs McNeil to occupy it, for even one night, was unthinkable. She must be arrested and charged and allowed to return home. She came meekly enough to the police station with Wexford in his car, driven by Donaldson. When he interviewed her, her solicitor and Burden also being present, she gave much the same answers as she had in her own home. Apparently, she had expected to see the senior partner in the old-established Kingsmarkham law firm who had represented her and her husband for forty years, but he had retired some time before and the solicitor who arrived was a young woman. Mrs McNeil refused to take any advice Helen Parker gave her and chose to ignore her when she said her client wasn't obliged to answer this or that.

Wexford asked her insistently about the knife she said the intruder had produced to threaten her husband. 'But you weren't there, Mrs McNeil, were you?' he said, only to be told that Ronald never lied. He asked again and again which caused Helen Parker to say that her client had already told him she was not. This inflamed Mrs McNeil, not with anger against Wexford, but against 'this presumptuous girl' who had no business, she said, to be there at all. When Wexford questioned her as to how she could account for a man carrying a knife while in his underwear and Helen Parker told her client not to answer, Mrs McNeil shouted at her to keep out of it. Helen Parker gathered up her jacket and briefcase and walked out.

In the end Mrs McNeil collapsed in tears. It was impossible to continue that day and while Adam Thayer drove her home, Wexford came to a decision. He wouldn't charge her yet. Once he had done so he wouldn't be allowed to go on questioning her. There was talk of the law being changed but it hadn't been changed yet.

His mind made-up, he contemplated the list of missing persons which went back just eight years and Peach's list of the missing that extended much further than that. Ronald McNeil had shot the man in Grimble's house in September 1998 but, according to both lists, although an eighteen-year-old girl had disappeared in that month (and been found two weeks later), no man had gone missing between June 1998 and the following January. There was one group they hadn't yet checked on – the itinerant farm workers.

They had camped on Grimble's Field in June 1995 but, three years later in September, on a field set aside for them by the farmer on the other side of Flagford. Such people had once been called 'gypsies' whether they were Romany or not. They possibly had settled homes in the winter months but in the warmer weather they moved from county to county, camping where they could, offering themselves as unskilled farm workers where fruit or vege- tables were to be harvested. These days things had changed and they had been replaced by asylum seekers or simply by visitors from Eastern Europe who came to work and raise money to take home when the season ended.

When Burden came in he asked him what he made of his theory that the man Ronald McNeil had shot was one of them.

'£1,000 is a big sum of money for someone like that to be carrying about with him,' Burden said.

'Yes, he wouldn't accumulate that picking apples at the rates these fruit farmers pay. But when we talked of this before, you said one of the itinerants might have come back for the purposes of blackmail. How about that?'

'You mean he'd been here three years earlier, found out some- thing a Flagford citizen wouldn't want made public, and, when he came back, extracted money from them for his silence? OK, I can see that. Why take the money into Grimble's house? Why go there at all? Presumably he came in a caravan or mobile home. Why not go back to it?'

'Suppose he no longer intended to pick fruit, now he'd got the money? He went into Grimble's house where very likely he had been before – it was easy enough to get in. The entire population of Flagford seems to have been in and out. I don't know why he couldn't have washed himself in his mobile home or, come to that, in a shower provided on the site. But the only evidence we have that he was ever in that bathroom comes from Mrs McNeil. He may have been, he may have thought there would have been plenty of water on tap and he wanted to wash himself properly. The clothes he took off had almost reached the rags stage. I think he planned on taking clothes out of old Grimble's wardrobe.'

Burden seemed taken with this theory. 'What, a suit maybe, or more likely trousers and that sports jacket we saw in there?'

'Probably. But before he could do that, before he's even had his wash, in comes Colonel Blimp, aka Ronald McNeil, with a gun.'

'And no one on that campsite missed him?'

'It all depends on what he intended to do. He may have told his fellow workers that he didn't mean to stay there any longer. He'd got some money – he needn't have said how or where from – he'd found a way of acquiring some decent clothes and once he'd got them he'd be off.'

'Wouldn't they notice he'd left his mobile home or maybe his car behind?'

Wexford shook his head. 'Not necessarily. These people don't each have a car and some sort of trailer. Sometimes there'll be three or four in each car. They might have noticed he'd left, say, a backpack behind with some probably valueless stuff inside. They wouldn't report someone as missing because most of them don't have any fixed abode. I think it was one of those fruit-pickers, Mike, and we can proceed on that assumption.'

On his way home he called in on Iman Dirir. He knew she was at home because he saw her dimly through the front window. For a moment he had thought she was her own daughter, for the woman he had glimpsed had long black hair hanging over her shoulders to the middle of her back. She took so long answering the door that he was on the point of ringing the bell again when it opened. She was in the uniform which could be Western or Eastern dress, black trousers and a long shirt. They went into her living room which was exactly as it might have been if she and her husband had been middle-aged professionals born in Tunbridge Wells, even to the white walls, chintz furniture and well-stocked bookcase. The plasma television would have been the envy of John Grimble.

'Can I offer you anything? A glass of wine? We don't drink but we have wine for friends.'

He smiled. 'Thank you but I can't stop. I came to tell you that my Child Protection Officer, a woman who's very good at her job, has been to see Matea's parents and cautioned them about taking their five-year-old girl home. She was tactful. She simply told them that to take a child abroad and have her circumcised was an offence punishable by a maximum of fourteen years' imprisonment.'

'I suppose they denied it,' Iman Dirir said.

'They said they were going for a holiday. How well do you know them?'

'Well enough to call and talk to them. Do you want me to do that?'

'I do,' he said. 'Very much. And it should be soon. They leave in a few days' time.'

She put out one long pale brown hand, the nails painted dark red, and took his. It wasn't a simple handshake but rather a gesture of promise or undertaking. 'I'll do my best,' she said.

A once-white t-shirt with a scorpion printed on it and the name 'Sam'. Memorable enough, Damon Coleman thought. Not the kind of thing he would ever consider wearing himself even if he were called Sam and liked scorpions. His taste ran to the colours which suited black skin, those which perhaps only a black man could successfully wear: red, orange, yellow, bright green. Black was a no-no. Apart from all that, as he hawked the t-shirt around Pickfords, Hunters, Louise Axall and Theodore Borodin, he marvelled that none of them gave a sign of recognising it. 'It's a long time ago' was the phrase most often used as they shook their heads. He had little hope and, after enduring abuse from Grimble, nearly gave up on Bill Runge. The man was out, anyway. Was it worth coming back later? He was walking back to the gate from the front door of Runge's cottage when he met the man coming down the road with a carrier bag. From the smell it evidently contained fish and chips and when Damon asked if he could have a word, Runge said only if he didn't mind talking while he ate his dinner before it got cold.

The fish and chips, when released from their greaseproof paper, looked inviting. Damon, who had a big, tall man's appetite, averted his eyes and wished he could also turn aside his nostrils. One thing was for sure, once he was out of here, he'd go straight to that fish and chip shop on the corner and buy his own lunch.

The t-shirt was produced and, instead of shaking his head and saying it was a long time ago, Bill Runge said with his mouth full that he thought he'd seen it before. 'Just let me think,' he said, pouring tomato ketchup over his fillet of cod as if it was a brain food indispensable when memory had to be summoned.

'Eight years ago in September?' Damon tried to prompt him.

'Might have been. I was in Flagford a lot when I was digging that ditch for my pal Grimble but it wasn't then, it wasn't that long ago. I mean, normally I've no call to go there.'

'Would you ever have gone to the fruit farm? Morella's, that is?'

'That's it! I drove the wife to Morella's shop. She never fancies fruit from them supermarkets. It was a Saturday, must have been. I never go to the shops on weekdays. And you're right about eight years ago. That's when it was. We had our girl with us and she was fifteen then. Funny I remember that, but I do because of her being fussy about her food, like they are when they're in their teens, and going on an apple diet. That's all she'd eat, apples and that stuff they call muesli.

'Them fruit-pickers was on the field. This chap was driving the truck what fetched the boxes off the field and brought them to the shop. He come in carrying a box of apples and he was wearing that t-shirt. My daughter said, "Look at what he's wearing, Dad. Look at that picture, that's a scorpion. I wouldn't wear a thing like that," she said. "It's gross." Young chap – well, he was then. My daughter'd seen a programme on the telly about scorpions, she'd seen the name.'

'You're a marvel, Mr Runge,' said Damon. 'You've missed your vocation. You ought to be in the Force.'

He was almost satisfied. But should they have confirmation? In the shop Runge had just come from, he bought cod and chips and a pickled gherkin and ate them in the car. Maybe he should try asking at shops in Flagford where just two remained of the ten which had once been there. At the grocer's which called itself a supermarket and incorporated the post office, he showed the photograph to the man dispensing stamps and the woman at the checkout, but although both of them had been in the same jobs eight years before, no one recognised the scorpion t-shirt. The other shop was one of those where passers-by always speculate as to how it can possibly make any sort of living. It sold or tried to sell maternity wear and baby clothes. A very old woman behind the counter smiled hopefully at him but seemed incapable of understanding what he asked her. Repeatedly she said her shop stocked nothing like the garment in his photograph and never had. It was ugly, she said, it wouldn't appeal to customers.

He gave up and turned his attention to the last people on his list, the Tredowns. They were the nearest to Grimble's Field. It would be visible from every upstairs window in Athelstan House on the western side. As he drove back to Flagford, he thought about what Bill Runge had seen and what it meant. The man in the cellar had worn that t-shirt, and therefore it was almost certain that the man in the cellar had been an itinerant farm worker seen in Flagford just a little before that. Only almost? A second sighting was essential. He drove up to Owen Tredown's house and parked outside the front door.

Burden and Lyn Fancourt were in the bungalow called Sunnybank. They had gone into the bedroom and were contemplating the inside of the wardrobe. Lyn took down one garment after another and laid them on the bed. When she came to the sports jacket, brown tweed with leather patches on the elbows, Burden stopped her. He put a glove on his right hand and, feeling in the pockets, brought out a watch, white metal with a worn leather strap, an equally worn wallet and two keys on a ring.

'So that's why those McNeils found nothing when they searched his clothes,' said Burden.

'Only £1,000, sir.'

'Yes, in the pocket of his jeans. It looks as if he'd just received it and stuffed it in his jeans pocket. Maybe he thought it was safer there, close to his body, than in the pockets of that anorak which is where he must have carried the wallet and the keys.'

'But why put all that stuff in someone else's jacket?'

'He planned to wash himself, didn't he? That's why he took off his watch. This is what I think happened. He stripped down to his underclothes, left his jeans with the £1,000 – did he temporarily *forget* it was there? – his anorak, the t-shirt and his trainers on the kitchen counter. Then he took his wallet – where perhaps he thought he'd put the money – and his keys into the bedroom, opened the wardrobe and found the only garment he fancied wearing, the sports jacket, though I suspect everything in here was in better nick than what he'd had on. Maybe he'd have taken a raincoat as well. He took off his watch, put it with the wallet and the keys into one of the sports jacket's pockets in preparation for putting it on after he'd had his wash. Probably he meant to put the t-shirt back on and no doubt the jeans with the money in. Old Grimble's trousers would have been too short for him. Before he could do that along comes the gallant McNeil and shoots him.'

'No knife, sir.'

'No knife,' Burden repeated.

A dmitted to the house by Owen Tredown himself, Damon thought he had never seen anyone look as ill as this man did and still be on his feet. He was a wraith, a depleted creature with half his substance gone, skeletally thin, his ribs outlined through the thin shirt he wore and his face the colour of old yellowed paper. A bird's-claw hand was put into Damon's.

'I am a sight, aren't I?' Tredown said to this man he had never met before. 'If you met me on a dark night you'd run like hell.'

Damon nodded, tried to smile. 'You don't seem very well, sir.' Could there be a greater understatement? 'Shouldn't you be sitting down?'

'I will in a minute. I don't want to give up before I have to.' They went into a large shabby room where the long brown velvet window curtains had been flung back wildly as if by a frenzied hand. 'I've had to stop writing,' Tredown said. 'It's the worst thing. If I can't write I might as well be dead.'

Damon didn't know what to say. A voice coming from behind the high back of a sofa made him jump. 'How you do exaggerate, Owen,' it said and a long-fingered beringed hand appeared from where the voice had come from and gave a fluttering wave.

Tredown had seated himself in an armchair and motioned Damon to another before the owner of the voice appeared, a tall woman with a girl's long dark hair and an old woman's lined face. She looked him up and down. 'Hallo. We haven't met. I'm Claudia Ricardo. Do you find it difficult being black in a place like this?'

'Don't, Claudia,' said Tredown mildly.

Damon didn't answer her. He wasn't going to answer her, he thought, even if it cost him his job. He was taking the photograph of the t-shirt out of his briefcase when a small, round woman in a grey wool dress came into the room. She stopped when she saw the photograph – because she recognised it?

'What a ghastly thing,' she said in a contemptuous tone.

The other woman, barely suppressing giggles, said, 'This is my wife-in-law, Maeve. The *present* Mrs Tredown,' as if there might be some possibility of the fragile wreck in the other armchair remarrying. 'He's a policeman, though you wouldn't think it to look at him, would you?'

'Have any of you seen this garment before?' He was losing the will to be polite.

'What is it?' This was Claudia Ricardo. 'Would anyone in their right mind actually wear a thing like that.'

'Someone with no taste might,' said Maeve Tredown.

Damon thought this a bit rich, coming as it did from a woman responsible for furnishing this bleak room in the browns and reds of gravy, ketchup and bolognese sauce. 'Have you seen it before?'

'Where might we have seen it?' Tredown asked politely. 'Perhaps you could jog our memories.'

This, of course, was something Damon was unwilling to do but he went so far as to say that they might have seen someone wearing it in Grimble's Field. 'Several years ago,' he said.

He watched the women's faces and thought he saw scorn in Claudia's and caution in Maeve's but this was only conjecture or less than that, no more than guesswork. He must have been mistaken when he thought he had seen recognition in Maeve Tredown's eyes as she entered the room. There was nothing to be gained by staying here, he was thinking, when Tredown surprised him. 'I may have seen it before,' he said. 'Yes, I think I have. It's quite unusual, isn't it? Let me see. Eight or nine years ago. I was working upstairs. I saw this man from the window. In the road, I think, or maybe in our garden.'

'You cannot possibly remember that far back. You know your memory's gone to pieces. It's laughable.' Claudia Ricardo cast on him a look of glacial scorn.

'Perhaps I can't,' he said. 'I don't know. I'm so damned tired.' He closed his eyes and to Damon he looked already dead, his face waxen like a dead face. 'They tell me I shall have to go into the hospice at Pomfret to die there,' he said without opening his eyes.

The two women stood silent, apparently unmoved.

CHAPTER EIGHTEEN

Wexford chose his words carefully. 'I was going to say, prepare yourself. But I'm not sure there's any preparation for this. The dead man I told you about was your father.' His eyes met hers. 'I'm very sorry. I can't tell you much more, only that his body was buried in a field in a village called Flagford, a pleasant quiet place, if that is any comfort to you.'

Selina Hexham gave a little cry, the sound someone might make when stung. They were sitting in the living room of her house in Barnes, the house which had been her childhood home and the home of her parents. He guessed or intuited that it was exactly as it had been when her mother died, furnished with an eye to comfort and the solace of the mind, books, a music player, small surely original paintings, rather than style.

'How did he die?'

'We don't know. It may be we never shall know.'

'Could it be – is it possible – I mean, is it absolutely certain it was a – a *violent* death? Could it have been a heart attack? Could he have just fallen down dead in that field?'

Wexford sighed. 'You don't know how much I would like to let you believe that, Selina, but I can't. His body had been buried. Why would it have been buried if he had died a natural death?'

'No, I see.'

'I know you're upset. You would be a very unnatural daughter if you weren't. If you like I can say that will do for now and I can leave you alone to tell your sister and I can come back tomorrow or the next day. But I have some questions I need to ask you now we have identified your father's body. The sooner I ask them the sooner we shall find whoever – how your father came to die.'

'Of course you must ask me. Vivien won't be here till five. We'll have the evening together.'

'Then first, if I may,' said Wexford, 'I should like to see the room that was his study.'

They went upstairs. He had been in many houses like this one in the course of his work, semi-detached, the two ground floor rooms usually made into one, two sizeable bedrooms and a 'box room'. They had sprung up all over England before and just after the Second World War, comfortable, once affordable, modest houses designed for a couple and two children. The box room here was tinier than usual. It was still as it must have been when Diana Hexham occupied it. Her single bed was still there, a long mirror on the wall, a narrow wardrobe barely a foot deep. That was all there was room for apart from a row of books on the windowsill, held in place by wooden bookends, a complete set of Jane Austen in paperback, *To Kill a Mockingbird*, *Madame Bovary* in translation, the poems of Wilfred Owen.

'Your father had a desk in here and an electric typewriter?' he asked.

'And the chair he sat in and a lot of books.'

'Yes. What happened to them?'

'His books? We kept them all together when Mum moved in here. They're downstairs.'

He had another look round the tiny room but nothing was to be learnt there. Back in the living room where they had sat, she led him to the bookshelves which had been built in to the corner on the left of the French windows and which extended along most of the adjacent wall.

'The ones that are in that section are the ones that were in his study,' Selina said. 'Oh, except for the *Oxford Dictionary* and *Brewer's*

Dictionary of Phrase and Fable. They're with the other dictionaries over there.'

He read the titles. Darwin's *Origin of Species* and The *Voyage of the Beagle*, *Roget's Thesaurus*, Ovid's *Metamorphoses*, *The Greek Myths* by Robert Graves, a collection of Icelandic sagas, half a dozen books by Stephen Jay Gould and Richard Dawkins. It seemed a wild idea now that he might find some link between them to help him find what work Alan Hexham had been doing in that minuscule room.

'Do they help?' Selina asked.

'I don't think so.'

He looked along the other shelves, saw novels by various authors who had been well known a dozen years before and were still well known. Among them were Owen Tredown's *The Son of Nun* and *The Queen of Babylon*.

'The half-sheet of A4 paper you mention in your book,' he said, 'with a list on it in your father's handwriting, may I see it?'

'Of course,' she said, but as she opened a drawer under the bookshelves and handed him an envelope, he saw there were tears in her eyes.

Hexham had been one of those rare people, growing rarer, whose handwriting was beautiful, a fine calligraphy but plain and without flourishes. He had listed seven authors of science fiction and two of historical novels, several of them, Wexford believed, no longer well known. Alongside the names he had written, in two cases, what were probably phone numbers, and underneath these: 'Factfinding? Proofreading? Editing?'

'Mr Wexford,' Selina said as they returned to the seats they had had earlier, 'I don't really care if you find the – the person who did whatever he did to my father. It doesn't matter now, does it?'

He shook his head. 'You're wrong there. It matters. We haven't put it into words yet but I will now. Someone killed your father and it would be wrong for that person to get away with it, to have profited from his crime. I have to believe that if I am to be in this business I'm in. For one thing, he might do it again, and for another, killing is the worst thing anyone can do and society needs to punish the perpetrator of such a crime for its own – its own well-being.'

'I suppose you're right. What did you want to ask me?'

'First of all, can you think why your father would have gone to Flagford? Did he know anyone there?'

'The only place he ever went to in Sussex – apart from when we all went to Worthing once on holiday – was Lewes. That was because of Maurice Davidson. They'd been friends at university, though Mr Davidson was a mature student, he was much older than Dad. They didn't see a great deal of each other. I think they met mainly when Mr Davidson came up to London. We all went there once for lunch. It was summer and I think it was for a picnic. I don't remember much about it. I was only about four.'

'Lewes is quite a long way from Flagford,' Wexford said. 'I'm going to say some names to you and ask you to tell me if your father ever mentioned them. If you think you can remember.'

'I'd remember.'

'All right.' He enunciated the names slowly, pausing between each one and watching her face. 'McNeil. Hunter. Pickford. Grimble. Tredown.'

'Tredown,' she said. 'That's the name of the writer who wrote *The First Heaven*.'

'One and the same,' Wexford said. 'His name's not on this list. Your father never spoke of him?'

'I don't think *The First Heaven* had been published by then.'

'I noticed two of his earlier books on your shelves. Were they your father's?'

'I suppose so. Or my mother's.'

'And no bells are rung by McNeil, Grimble, Pickford or Hunter? Louise Axall? Theodore Borodin?'

'I don't think so. I just can't imagine why my dad would have gone to a village in the middle of Sussex. Is there a train station?'

'Not at Flagford. There's one a few miles away at Kingsmarkham. Anyone heading for Flagford would have to take a taxi unless he was very keen on walking. Was he?'

'It was pouring with rain, Mr Wexford. I don't think he'd have tried walking.'

Wexford pondered. 'Did he take anything with him? I realise a child doesn't take too much notice of that sort of thing.'

'Vivien and I left for school before he left.' Her voice trembled a little and she coughed to clear her throat. 'But he already had his raincoat on. He didn't have an umbrella, he never carried one. I know he meant to take his briefcase because he had it open and was looking inside a few minutes before. I never thought much about it at the time but it was rather odd, wasn't it, taking a brief-case to a funeral?'

'Not so odd perhaps. He was a reading man so he'd have had a book with him to read in the train. A magazine? A newspaper? Maybe something of Mr Davidson's to give his widow as a memento, something he'd had since university?'

'You're right. I suppose it could have been any of those things. I wish I could be more help.'

He wondered if what he had said had made her change her mind about wanting her father's murderer brought to justice. Perhaps. He said goodbye, that he would need to see her again, and left for his own walk to the station. Coming along the street he met Vivien Hexham.

'Your sister will tell you about it,' he said, 'better than I can.'

Having lunch with Burden in A Passage to India, he was approached rather shyly by Matea who told him her parents had gone on holiday to Mogadishu, taking Adel and Shamis with them.

'I cannot make them not go,' she said.

Wexford shook his head. 'Unfortunately, nor can I.'

Following her with his eyes as she disappeared through the bead curtain, Burden said, 'Isn't she stunning? Just so perfect.'

Rage welled up in Wexford. 'Let me tell you, sex with her wouldn't give you or her much pleasure.'

Burden recoiled, shocked, not so much by the words as where they came from. 'That's a bit near the bone, isn't it?'

'Is it? Well, anger hath a privilege, as someone says in Shakespeare.'

'I take it you're implying she's been circumcised?'

'Genitally mutilated. They all have, all these beautiful women. Ninety-nine per cent of them in Somalia. And now let's talk of something else.' Wexford poured still water for both of them. 'It looks likely that Hexham took the 2.20 train from Lewes which reached Kingsmarkham at 2.42. We know he ended up in Grimble's Field, poor chap, and it seems reasonable to guess that he took one of the station taxis to Flagford, a place where he may never have been before.'

'Why do you say that?'

'Selina Hexham says her parents had been to Sussex only to visit the Davidsons in Lewes and once when they all went on holiday to Worthing Alan Hexham seems to have been rather a secretive man so it may be that he came down here sometimes without telling his wife or children but somehow I don't think so.'

'He was secretive about only one thing – what he did in that study.'

Matea came back with their biryanis, a plate of naan and a dish of spices and relishes. Her hands were the longest and slenderest Wexford had ever seen on a woman but he left it to Burden to comment.

'Her wrists have the span of some women's fingers,' said Burden.

'Do shut up,' Wexford said. 'Now what you said before uttering that sloppy exaggeration is probably true. He seems to have been quite open in other respects, a good father, a good teacher and no doubt a good husband. From what I now know of him I'd be very surprised if there was ever another woman in his life or if he ever looked at one.' This with a pointed glance at Burden.

'Whatever use he put that room to I'm pretty sure it was nothing – dishonourable, if that isn't too outdated a word these days.'

'I'm wondering,' Burden said thoughtfully, 'if it could have been

175

something he was doing or was trying to do that he didn't want his family to know about until he had – well, *succeeded*.'

'Interesting. Go on.'

'Some business he was setting up. Maybe something he'd invented, some small thing, a gadget – he was a scientist, after all.'

'Yes, but a biologist, not some sort of engineer. This, whatever it was, has to have been something that needed very little equipment and presumably entailed very little expense.'

'Was he doing it to make money, d'you think?'

'I don't know,' said Wexford. 'No doubt, they needed money. They could have done with a bigger house but it doesn't seem to me a need for more money loomed very large in his existence. I think doing whatever it was had some particular importance in his life irrespective of what financial gain was involved.'

Fixed on his idea of Hexham as inventor, Burden said, 'You pointed out that he was a biologist, not an engineer. Douglas Chadwick was an engineer and he'd been living in Flagford. More than that, he'd been living in Grimble's house.'

'But he was gone before the summer of 1995, Mike. Still, I like your idea. Hexham might not have known he no longer lived there or that old Grimble was dead. We know Chadwick died two years ago but we don't know where he went when he left Grimble's. He and Hexham may have corresponded. He may have come back to Flagford for the purpose of meeting Hexham there. But it's all speculation, isn't it? And I haven't the faintest idea how we could prove it or what would come out of it if we did.'

'As you say, Hexham must have got to Flagford in a taxi. It was pouring with rain so there's no way he'd have walked, it's much too far.'

'You're saying we can start on the taxi firms or those which were operating eleven years ago?' Wexford almost groaned, remembering past investigations, questioning cab drivers, checking times. 'I suppose Damon could do it or the new chap. But is it likely, is it even possible, any driver would remember that far back? Would you remember the face of a driver who picked you up in a taxi at Kingsmarkham station in 1995?'

'Probably not, but that's rather different. How many people look at taxi drivers' faces? But they look at ours. I think we should try it.'

F lagford was on the edge of the fruit-growing area, for some reason particularly suited to apples, pears, plums and soft fruit, in the midst of dairy farming. Of the two fruit farms, Morella's was the bigger with a thriving farmer's market and a juice-production plant as well as acres of orchards and strawberry fields. In recent years, these last had been covered in glittering polytunnels, which in midsummer looked like sheets of ice melting in the sun but which now were fallow fields where nothing grew. In the orchards all the apples and pears had been picked weeks before. The rows of trees were in the process of being pruned. Damon drove himself and Barry along a lane which led between rows of alders to a building which housed the offices of the chief executive and the administrative staff.

It appeared that Morella's had come a long way since the day Bill Runge had come here with his wife and daughter. The chief executive, a man called Graham Bailey, said they now employed people from Eastern Europe, mostly Romanians and Bulgarians, from June till October, housing them in what he called 'hostels' and pointed out of the window. Six trim buildings now stood on the field where fruit-pickers had once camped, concrete paths linking each one to its neighbour and to the forecourt and shop. Bailey said proudly that every building was equipped with 'bathroom facilities', showers and a self-service laundry.

'Did you ever employ itinerant workers?'

'Gyppos?' said Graham Bailey. 'Not in my time. I've only been here three years. There were some who used to come here and camp over there. That was before we put up the hostels.' He took Barry and Damon into the farmer's market store and called over an assistant who, he said, had worked there for fifteen years, first on the land and later when the store first opened as a small shop.

The shop sold cakes and pies and frozen food, ice cream and elaborate desserts, as well as fruit and vegetables. Everything was pristine and neatly kept. Damon, always hungry, asked if he could buy a blackcurrant pie, a request which earned a frown from Barry and a sharp suggestion that they should move on. They were taken into an administrative office, Bailey telling them with excusable pride that the names of everyone who had ever worked for them were kept on record, names and home addresses even if their homes were (as was the case recently) in Sofia or Krakow or on the Black Sea coast.

One of the women seated at a computer offered to produce a printout of the list of names and addresses for September 1998 and handed Barry a sheet of paper with a formidable catalogue of workers on it. A quick glance told him that none of these people hailed from Eastern Europe. Well, a lot had happened in those intervening eight years.

'A good many of the people here have no home addresses,' he said.

'Well, they wouldn't, would they? Not if they were travellers.'

Barry counted twenty-two names, of whom twelve were women. As far as he could see, there was no way of telling which his man was – even supposing he had worked for Morella's.

'I know this is a question I can't expect you to answer,' Damon said, 'but would any of you remember a man in a t-shirt with a black scorpion and the name "Sam" in red on it?'

'Funny sort of pet,' said the woman who had done the printout, 'but I suppose it takes all sorts to make a world.'

When the laughter had died down, Damon explained that the scorpion wasn't real but printed on the fabric and he showed them the photograph. They all looked at it, Bailey with rather more concentration than the others. But, 'No,' he said for all of them. 'No, it doesn't ring any bells.'

A phone call from his daughter Sheila was what determined Wexford's evening task. 'Have you read that book I gave you yet, Pop?'

'*The First Heaven*? No, I haven't.' He added, like the little boy he had once been, 'Do I have to?'

'Well, I should think you'd want to, considering I'm starring in the film.'

'I'll give it a go,' he said rather disconsolately. It was a funny thing how the time came when your children started talking to you the way your parents had. And you answered them much as you had answered your parents. There was only quite a short gap between acquiescing to the strictures of Mum and Dad and placating and obeying your children. He had hoped to spend this rare free evening sitting beside Dora and watching a DVD of *Don't Look Now*. Instead he helped himself to the essential glass of claret and opened *The First Heaven*.

A man he knew very well without quite being able to call him a friend was Burden's brother-in-law who was a publisher. Or, more correctly, a publisher's editor. Wexford had often thought what a bore and a chore it must be for such people, not to be able to read what they chose, as was the case with him when he had the time, but always to be obliged to read the manuscripts of authors whose books they published. Amyas, Burden's brother-in-law, had told him the only chance he got to reread Anthony Powell, his favourite writer, was when he was away on holiday.

Thinking of Selina Hexham's *Gone Without Trace* which hadn't been his chosen reading matter, he reflected that he was fast going that way himself. He began to read. When he reached the foot of page one he remembered another thing Amyas had said, that an experienced editor could tell from the first page whether a novel was any good or not. Well, he wasn't an experienced editor or any sort of editor at all and he couldn't tell. Perhaps it was only that he didn't care for fantasy. The fantasy here made itself plain from halfway down that first page. And by the time he came to the end of chapter one, Tredown was showing his predilection, if not for characters from Genesis and Kings, for biblical language. There were a great many 'hast thous' and 'whence cometh' and in chapter two even the animals addressed each other in this manner.

He could appreciate some of the descriptions of a prehistoric earth. They were on a grand scale and showed that an exceptionally fertile imagination had been at work. But they went on and on and sometimes in the minutest detail so that he found himself skipping whole paragraphs. When Tredown began describing the appearance of Baal, of Ashtaroth and Dagon, he closed the book, fetched himself another glass of wine and went to find Dora. He had only missed a quarter of an hour of *Don't Look Now*, which mattered hardly at all as he had seen it before.

At about two in the morning he woke up. The germ of an idea had awakened him and now it began to grow and flourish. Suppose it was for Athelstan House that Hexham had been bound that rainy afternoon? Suppose he was on his way to see Tredown to undertake research for him. Tredown wanted someone who could advise him in two areas, mythic deities and prehistoric creatures. Maybe more than that. It should include basic biology and the origin of life.

Wexford had read that note in Hexham's handwriting so many times that now he had it off by heart. 'Fact-finding? Proofreading? Editing?' And above that a list of names of publishers and authors. Tredown hadn't been among them but that meant very little. When Hexham made the list he might never have read anything of Tredown's. But suppose, when he did, that he discovered inaccuracies or anachronisms? He might then have thought that this particular author was in need of advice and have offered his services. The trouble with this theory was that while Hexham was the ideal adviser on the prehistoric fauna and the deities in *The First Heaven*, as far as Wexford knew he wasn't an expert on Bible history. The picture his daughter had presented of him made it extremely unlikely this was the case.

But things would look very different if Hexham had written to Tredown correcting inaccuracies in the writer's description of Baal worship or Dagon rituals, both of which figured in *The Queen of Babylon*, suggesting he needed help in these areas. And Tredown might have replied to this letter, telling Hexham that he planned an ambitious novel, combining the Theory of Evolution with Middle Eastern mythology, and would very much appreciate the services of a researcher. There were holes in this reconstruction but still Wexford liked it. Researching would account for what Hexham was doing in that tiny box room if not for the secrecy. But some people simply were secretive, though it was difficult to justify keeping such an innocent occupation from a beloved wife.

Selina or Vivien might have the answers.

CHAPTER NINETEEN

Everyone has a phone, Lyn told herself. Whatever they lack, they have a phone. These days even those who live permanently on caravan sites have mobiles. Seated in front of her computer for long hours – absently helping herself to sugar-free sweets from a pack on her lap – Lyn found only two phone numbers among the men on the list. One was for an address in Stockton-on-Tees, the other in Penzance. Not much to her surprise by this time, a woman answered in each case. In the case of the former man, a William Green, the woman, who sounded very old, was his aunt. Of *course*. These men were permanently on the road or on a caravan site. If they gave addresses they would be those of their relatives and sure to be women, Lyn thought. Men tended to be rovers, wild, not anchored, while women clung to their homes. This wasn't sexist, Lyn had been too thoroughly indoctrinated by Hannah to fall into that trap. It was a good thing, a sane sensible thing, to want to have your own place, your nest, your refuge.

William Green's aunt, his late uncle's widow, also called Green, could tell her very little about her nephew. In her quavering voice she said she hardly ever saw him, she didn't know where 'the lad' was now, the last time she had seen him was six years ago. That was enough for Lyn. The man in Grimble's cellar had been dead two years by then. The other man, Frank Maniora, had given the address of a closer relative, his sister. This time she was surprised. Fernanda Maniora spoke with a Caribbean accent. For some reason she couldn't now account for, Lyn had assumed without thinking much about it, that everyone on the list was white.

Miss Maniora called her 'darling' in every sentence she spoke. She talked at great length about her brother, which was something Lyn could have done without. If the man in the cellar had been black *everyone* in Flagford would have noticed and remembered him. She asked, really for something to say, if Fernanda Maniora had seen her brother lately, to be told that he had dropped in only last week, darling, and what a joy it was to see him.

Might he know something about the other men he had worked with at Morella's? She knew for a fact he had been there eight years before. 'Where is he now, Miss Maniora?'

'He said he'd made a lot of money, darling. God bless him. He was going to Spain for a holiday. He'll be there now, you know.'

'Have you an address?'

But Frank Maniora's sister hadn't.

Still, talking to these women had given Lyn an idea. It was the women workers at Morella's she should be getting in touch with. For one thing, women noticed men and for another, women were simply more observant. Phone numbers for them were much easier to find. As she had thought, some had given mobile numbers. Eight years ago – would they still be the same? She could only try.

E xactly what he had expected had happened. Reading that book he had anticipated a chore, a bit of a bore, a slog, it was so long, more than 500 pages. A slog it was and he put it down, never to take it up again, long before page 516 was reached.

The story he could have summarised if he had to. There was no need to read those last five chapters. *The First Heaven* was about the world before there were people in it. No people, no animals and no birds, only sea creatures and insects, the whole ruled over by gods and goddesses, some with well-known names, some invented, but all with an Old Testament flavour. These deities behaved like human brings in that they loved and hated, committed crimes and performed heroic deeds, but were apparently immortal and therefore could watch the process of evolution, the gradual change of the tiny swimming things into land creatures and flying creatures. As the millennia passed, the gods foresaw the appearance on earth of man by a process of evolution but were powerless to stop it, though they knew it would mean an end to their immortality. It would mean a *Götterdämmerung*.

By this time he had forgotten that he had begun to read Owen Tredown's book to please Sheila. She didn't let him forget and was on the phone early next morning.

'Great, isn't it, Pop?'

'Not in my opinion. I said I wouldn't like it and I didn't. I don't know how many times I've told you I don't care for fantasy.'

'I would never have said you were bigoted. You made up your mind you weren't going to like it so you didn't. That's my last word on the subject.'

'That's a blessing anyway,' said Wexford, 'though I doubt it's true. You know what they say. Good books make bad films and bad books make good films. I expect it will pull millions into the world's cinemas.'

Sheila began listing all the people she knew who had 'adored' *The First Heaven*: Paul, of course, her sister Sylvia, the producer of the forthcoming film, its director. He covered his mouth to silence the sound of his yawn.

When she paused for breath, he said, 'This producer, does he use advisers and researchers?'

'Well, of *course*, Pop.'

So Tredown surely must have. He didn't say this aloud. After she had rung off he fetched *The Son of Nun* – noting that it was overdue at the public library – and *The Queen of Babylon* and leafed through them, looking for points of resemblance, while believing he wouldn't find any. There he was wrong. The subject matter was quite different or so it seemed at first. But it was as he had thought. Tredown appeared very interested in strange gods and their worship, in rituals, in sacrifice, in Baal and Dagon and

Ashtaroth, the deities he mentioned in *The First Heaven*. He recognised that, for those who liked this sort of thing, this book was more exciting and suspenseful than either of the biblical epics Wexford had read but there was a kind of flavour or atmosphere about it that made it recognisable as Tredown's work. Perhaps it was in the sort of phrasing he used, the recurrence of certain favourite words, even the way he chose to describe his leading characters.

'*The First Heaven* was published in the mid-nineties,' he said to Dora. 'Have you read any of his later ones?'

She hadn't. 'I can get one out of the library tomorrow, if you like.'

'I'd just like to know if he reverted to his old favourites or if *The First Heaven* marked a sort of turning point in his career. Are there any sequels, for instance?'

'I'll get you the lot,' Dora said, eyebrows raised.

P rivately, Barry Vine believed putting a name to the body in Grimble's cellar was unimportant. He had been a traveller or gypsy or itinerant, whatever you liked to call him, had trespassed on someone else's property and been shot by some old lunatic. But it was crucial to police work and Wexford thought it of the first importance, which was why Barry and Lyn were off to see a woman in Maidstone who might know a woman whose boyfriend had left her in September 1998 and just might . . .

'It's worth giving it a go, isn't it Sarge?' said Lyn whose researches had found Lily Riley.

'It's my daughter who knew her,' Lily Riley said, bringing them cups of tea the colour of mulligatawny soup in the living room of her little house. 'Her and this Bridget used to go fruit-picking together. Mostly it was up near Colchester but one year they come down here so Michelle could stop with me. Not Bridget, though. She had her own van.'

Looking at her list, Lyn said, 'That would be Bridget Cook and Michelle Riley?'

'That's right, love. Bridget brought her down in her van along with her boyfriend – I mean, Bridget's boyfriend. I only saw him the once. He'd been to Flagford before, Michelle said, three or four years before for the strawberries. This time it was plums they was picking, Victorias.'

'Do you remember his name, Mrs Riley?'

'Dusty, they called him. Well, not Bridget. She had another name for him but I disremember what it was. Them two, Dusty and Bridget, they stopped in the van. Michelle was in here with me.'

'You said you saw him, Mrs Riley. What was he like?'

'Good-looking,' she said. 'Well, I reckon you could call him good-looking. Mind you, he always looked dirty to me but I daresay I'm fussy. Bridget kept on telling him to wash himself. I'll tell you one thing, he was always knocking his head on the ceiling in that caravan, he was so tall, you see.'

M rs Riley insisted on a second round of tea and went to refill their cups.

'It's him, Sarge,' Lyn said excitedly. 'Six feet four, the chap in the cellar was.'

'It looks like it,' said the more cautious Barry, 'but let's not jump to conclusions yet awhile.'

The tray once more set down on the table, Lily Riley began getting into her stride. 'Him and Bridget was talking of getting married. What I do remember was Bridget saying to Michelle as he was too young for her really, being only forty and her getting on for fifty. A funny thing was she said he wrote poems to her. It was romantic, she said. Anyway, they stopped a couple of days and then they went off to this Flagford, all three of them.'

Lyn was suspicious. 'How come you remember all this, Mrs Riley?'

Lily Riley spoke huffily. There had been an imputation in Lyn's tone she hadn't liked. 'I'll tell you *how come*. He left Bridget, this Dusty did. They was going to get married, the date was fixed and all. They said to me, you've got to come to our wedding, Lily, and I said OK, I would.

'Well, they'd been picking plums all day at Morella's, Michelle said, and they come home to the van and Dusty said he had to go out, he'd be gone an hour at the most and off he went but *he never come back*. That's how I remember it. Michelle was that upset. She's got a soft heart, my girl, and she was in tears. He broke poor Bridget's heart, that man.'

Barry came to the crucial question. 'Do you know his other name, Mrs Riley? Could it have been Sam?'

'Dusty, they called him. I don't know what else. I never heard it. I know he come from somewhere in London. Same with Bridget, somewhere in London.'

'That wasn't much help, Sarge,' Lyn said when they were outside.

'You've done a good job finding that Mrs Riley, Lyn,' said Barry, 'but that's where you're wrong. When they call a man Dusty it's because his surname's Miller. Like a man called Grey is Smoky and a man called White is Chalky or Snowy but someone called Miller is always Dusty. So now you know.'

'If you say so, Sarge. I thought it might be because he looked dirty like Mrs Riley said.'

The Family Records Centre showed a large number of Millers but, because this man had been forty, it was possible to narrow it down to those born in the late fifties and early sixties.

'I suppose I can put each one of these into the web,' Lyn said, 'and get a search engine to track him down. But if he's who we think he is, our man's *dead*. He's been dead eight years and he won't be on an electoral register any more. Maybe it would be better to find dead Millers.'

'A re we looking for a connection between these two men?' Burden asked. 'I mean, are we working on the premise that the chap in the cellar wasn't the only one Ronald McNeil killed? That he also shot Alan Hexham?'

'That's why I'm going to see Irene McNeil again now that she's home,' said Wexford. 'But I don't think so, do you? There's no question of Hexham trespassing anywhere.'

'Adam's talked to all the taxi firms who were here eleven years ago, he's been very thorough, I must say. But it was always a hopeless task. What kind of a miraculous memory would someone have to have to remember that far back?'

'I don't know. I don't see how there can be a connection, yet if there's not it's too much of a coincidence. But I'm sure Hexham came here and came to see Tredown. I think he came to do research for Tredown's book *The First Heaven*. I've left a message on Selina Hexham's voicemail' – Wexford was proud of himself for knowing the term and bringing it out with such ease – 'but she hasn't called me back yet.'

Irene McNeil had spent two days in a private nursing home since what she called her 'ordeal' at Kingsmarkham police station. Since her return home, showing she wasn't always the helpless creature, prone to tears, she seemed to be, she had engaged a full-time carer. This was a young man of daunting efficiency who had transformed the soulless cupboard-lined house with bowls of flowers and jardinières of houseplants. The place smelt of lemon air freshener. A boy in jeans and t-shirt was the last kind of person Wexford supposed Mrs McNeil would find to tend on her but he began to see that his analysis of her character had been wide of the mark. She might be old-fashioned and prudish, a stickler for manners and a snob, but she was very much an upper-middle-class woman of her generation too, one who had always had a man about the house – first her father, then her husband – and who bitterly missed the masculine presence. No doubt, also, whatever she said, she would have liked a son. Greg the carer answered a deeply felt need. Wexford suspected it was he who had painted her fingernails a silvery rose-pink but it still amazed him that Mrs McNeil let him call her 'Reeny'.

She still had her feet up but now she was reclining on a sofa, her legs discreetly covered with a blanket. Rather to his surprise she made no reference to their previous meetings but instead was fervent on the subject of Greg, his excellences and his charm.

'Of course, having him here wouldn't have done at all when I was young,' she said. 'I may be older than he' – as if there was any doubt about it – 'but that would have made no difference. If one was a woman alone one simply could not have a man staying overnight and that was all there was to it. It would have caused talk. Oh, thank you so much, Greg.'

The carer had brought not tea but a glass of what looked like iced coffee and a plate of the kind of biscuits you can only buy in delicatessens. 'And what can I get you, sir?'

Wexford thought it might have been the first time in his life – at any rate for a long time – that anyone but the members of his team had called him sir, and even they now mostly called him 'guv', thanks to Hannah. 'A cup of tea would be good,' he said, thinking Greg would be more likely to understand 'good' than 'nice'.

'Isn't he perfect?' Like a woman in love, Mrs McNeil watched Greg depart for the kitchen, closing the door quietly behind him. In more mundane accents she asked Wexford what she could do for him. 'Can I update you?' wasn't the kind of question she would have asked before the advent of Greg.

'The man your husband shot—' he began but Irene McNeil interrupted him.

'In self-defence!'

'Yes, well – you must have got a good look at him.'

'After he was dead. I didn't look too closely, I can tell you. He wasn't a pretty sight.'

'Mrs McNeil, what exactly do you mean by that? Do you mean he was dirty or injured in some other way?'

'I don't know. He wasn't old, I can tell you that. Not much older than Greg, probably, only Greg's always so spotlessly clean and neat.'

'If I told you this man's age was forty, would that be about right?'

Before she could reply, Greg came back with Wexford's tea. The biscuits provided were of a slightly lower standard than those on Mrs McNeil's plate. Greg flashed his employer so dazzling a smile that Wexford found himself wondering in exactly what way he was on the make.

'About forty, Mrs McNeil?'

'No, no, Greg is just forty – oh, you meant that creature who was trespassing in Mr Grimble's house? I don't know. Possibly. I suppose he was about that.'

Next he asked her about the knife her husband had said was about to be used to attack him. This prompted Irene McNeil into an angry diatribe against Helen Parker, the young solicitor. He steered her back to the knife.

'There was no knife in the house, Mrs McNeil, that's the difficulty.'

'John Grimble took things away, you know. You shouldn't believe him when he says he didn't take a thing, just left everything there.'

Wexford gently reminded her that whatever John Grimble had removed from his father's house, he had taken eleven years before, not eight. 'Could your husband have brought the knife back home with him?'

A flash of alarm showed in her eyes. 'Why would he do that?'

It was hardly for Wexford to find explanations for the behaviour of a man like Ronald McNeil. 'Your husband might have told you if he disposed of the knife.'

'Or I might have.' She spoke carefully. 'I might have given it away. He might have brought it back home. I mean, when we lived at the Hall.'

'Is that what happened, Mrs McNeil?'

'Will I get into trouble?' She spoke like a little girl who has been disobedient. 'It wouldn't be very wrong, would it, to get rid of a knife? It wasn't mine, you see. Would it be stealing? It wasn't mine, it was that man's.'

Wexford was almost at a loss. He seemed to have strayed into the country of the mad. He was seeing what happens to people –

women, mostly – who have been sheltered and protected all their lives and suddenly find themselves alone.

'Did you get rid of it, Mrs McNeil?'

'It was stolen,' she said. 'The cleaner I had stole it.' She stared at him. 'I'm telling you the absolute truth.'

It was very nearly too much for him. He changed the subject.

'Had you ever seen this man before, Mrs McNeil? Think carefully before you answer.'

'I know I'd never seen him before.'

'His name may have been Miller. He was called Dusty.'

This time she did ponder on the name. 'The Tredowns once had a – well, a handyman they called Dusty. He used to drive their car sometimes too. I never saw him. That Ricardo woman told me.'

'When was this?'

'Oh, my goodness, how you expect me to remember things like this I really don't know.'

'You're doing very well,' he said eagerly.

This seemed to please her. She was susceptible to flattery and she smiled, though this may have been due to the reappearance of Greg with a tray on which was a rolled-up hot towel of the kind they give you in Chinese restaurants, a bottle of violet-scented toilet water and a tube of hand cream.

'He's so thoughtful,' she said when she had anointed her hands. 'I can't imagine now how I got on without him. When was it this Dusty was with them? Oh, at least ten years ago, maybe more like twelve.' She became almost chatty. 'Mr Tredown can drive but he doesn't. Apparently he once caused an awful accident, someone was killed and he's never driven since. The Ricardo woman can't and Mrs Tredown can but she hadn't passed her test then. She passed it a year or two before we moved. Ronald said she'd no business being on the road when he heard she'd passed.'

All this was interesting enough but it seemed of little use to him. The vital contribution Mrs McNeil had made, perhaps the only contribution of any worth, was that a man called Dusty had worked for the Tredowns. Only they could tell him more now.

'I shall ask you about the knife again,' he said.

She shrugged, made an unusual movement with her hand, an impatient flutter. He was on his way out and Donaldson was waiting when his phone rang. It was Selina Hexham.

CHAPTER TWENTY

He took the call in the car. The answer he expected was a negative one, because now he had less faith in the idea which had come to him in the small hours. Things you think of when you wake in the night often look bizarre or stupid in the morning.

Instead she said, 'That would mean the piece of paper with his writing on it makes sense. But I don't know. One small thing, though. It's so small I didn't think it worth putting in my book. I remember a magazine – well, a journal, I suppose you'd call it – lying on a table in our house. It was called *The Author*. Where it came from I don't know but there were some ads in it from people offering to do research for authors. I don't remember any more except Mum saying that would be a nice job for someone.'

He thanked her and unexpectedly she began to talk about how she'd changed her mind about finding her father's killer. Now she agreed with him. This man should be found but still she was glad capital punishment had gone for ever. Later he wondered how much credence he should put on her remembering *The Author* and her mother's comment. Would anyone's memory be that good? It was more likely, he thought, that Selina had, perhaps unconsciously, invented it in an effort to help him find the perpetrator of a crime.

* * *

They followed her car along the short drive and under the dripping trees. Maeve Tredown wasn't a good driver, uncertain and apparently nervous at the wheel. She came close to scraping the side of the old Volvo against the trunk of a towering conifer and pulled up too sharply outside the front door, setting the car juddering. The curious colours of the house, the jarring yellows and reds, looked brighter when washed by teeming rain. She opened the driver's door and leaned out to see who had come to visit.

'Good morning, Mrs Tredown,' Wexford said. 'Perhaps it would be best if we went straight inside.' He expected some irrational argument but she got quickly out of the car, slamming the door violently, and let them into the house. 'How is your husband?' he asked when they were inside.

'They are taking him into a hospice tomorrow,' she said. 'There isn't any hope.' She said it in the kind of cheerful tone she might have used to say there wasn't anything to fear. 'I thought a hospice was a place monks lived in with St Bernard dogs. But apparently not any more.'

Wexford could smell the vanilla scent she wore as she led them along the dark passage past the haphazardly hung coats and flung footwear, throwing her raincoat on to a peg as she passed. This time they weren't to be received in the gloomy living room. Instead they went into a kind of farmhouse kitchen where, in front of an open fire, Tredown lay in an armchair with his legs up on the seat of another, pipe in mouth. Blankets covered him, though it was insufferably hot. At the other end of the room, the part where cooking was done, Claudia Ricardo stood in front of an Aga, apparently making lemon curd. The whole place smelt of a mixture of lemons and burning sage.

'I believe it's very hot in here,' Tredown said, removing the pipe without lifting his head. 'I'm afraid I always feel cold these days. Perhaps you should take these gentlemen into the drawing room, Em.'

'Please don't worry about the heat, Mr Tredown,' Wexford said. 'We'd like to talk to you as well.'

'You'd better sit down then.' Maeve Tredown was as offhand as her husband was courteous.

'Would you make us some coffee or tea, Cee?' Tredown apparently thought it safer to make this request of his ex-wife than his present one or perhaps he only did so because Claudia was already engaged in cooking. She waved a wooden spoon in a gesture of acquiescence. 'What did you want to ask me, Mr Wexford?'

'I believe you once employed a man who went by the name of Dusty.'

Tredown put the pipe down on a saucer and turned his cadaverous yellow face towards Wexford while holding out his hands to the flames. 'I forget so many things,' he said. 'Let me think. Did we, Em?'

Stony-faced, Maeve Tredown said, 'He asked *you*. Why don't you answer? You know very well we did.'

Speaking very slowly, Tredown said, 'I don't believe I ever saw him.' He managed a smile, a death's head grin. There seemed to be no flesh on his face, only skin stretched over the skull. 'I was always working, you see. Upstairs working.'

'You mean writing, Owen. Why don't you say "writing"?'

'Because it is working. It's what I do.' Wexford couldn't tell if the sound he made was a sigh or an indrawn breath. 'What I used to do.'

The unidentifiable warm drink which Claudia Ricardo brought to them in thick earthenware cups was very different from that provided by Mrs McNeil's Greg. Wexford couldn't tell if it was tea or coffee and, catching sight of Burden's face, saw that he meant to abandon his. Claudia drank hers with apparent pleasure, set down her cup with a loud rattle in its saucer and said, 'I remember Dusty perfectly. He was rather attractive. I really quite fancied him. You're frightfully common, I thought, but I've always liked a bit of rough.'

'Oh, Cee, you are *awful*.' Maeve spluttered into her cup.

Tredown had closed his eyes, whether in weariness or distaste it was impossible to tell. 'You employed him to drive your car?' Wexford persevered.

'Once or twice. Mostly it was to *mend* the car. Poor old car hadn't been driven for yonks – is that still a cool expression? Em couldn't drive then. It was – oh, a long time ago. When did you pass your test, Em?'

'December '97,' said Maeve.

'I've never learnt. My head is always in the clouds, you know, and it wouldn't have done. Owen used to drive, I mean he *can*, but he killed someone in an accident. He turned right without looking and hit someone and the person died. It was while he was married to me, which may have had something to do with it.'

Tredown managed to rear himself up. He managed too a voice loud enough to exhaust him. 'Be quiet, Claudia. If you can't talk sense, go away.' Speaking to her in this way had cost him emotional effort as well. Utterly spent, he lay back, sweat standing in beads on his face.

Burden said coldly, 'Can we return to Dusty? Where did he come from?'

It seemed that Maeve had decided she and Claudia had gone far enough. 'He'd been one of those fruit-pickers that were on Grimble's Field . . .'

'Just a moment, Mrs Tredown,' Wexford said. 'Are we talking about eight years ago or eleven?'

'Eleven, of course. They weren't on the field eight years ago. This was '95. One day Dusty came through our garden when I was out there and asked if I'd any work for him. I said, was he any good as a mechanic because we'd got this car no one had driven for years and could he put it right and drive it for us. Well, he did and we paid him. There, does that satisfy you?'

'Not entirely, Mrs Tredown. You say this was eleven years ago. Was it before Mr Grimble and Mr Runge turned the pickers off the field or afterwards?'

'Afterwards, of course, silly.' Claudia answered for her. 'He wanted a job because he'd lost the one he'd got strawberry-picking. What else?' She returned to her curd-making, reaching the stage of placing a spoonful of the yellow mixture on a saucer to test if it had gelled.

She watched it, sniffed it, nodded, said to Wexford, 'Do you like lemon curd?'

'Very much,' he said, adding quickly, 'but not now. When he'd fixed the car, he drove for you?'

'He took us shopping a few times and he did a bit of gardening. He put a washer on a tap.' Maeve shrugged. 'You can't be interested in all these domestic details. He was only with us two or three weeks.'

'But he came back three years later?'

At last Wexford could see he and Burden had touched a sensitive nerve. Claudia held her spoon in mid-air for a second or two. Maeve, who had been feeling her husband's forehead in an unusual gesture of care, remained utterly still, her hand resting on the damp ochreish skin. It was the ex-wife who recovered first.

'Dusty came over to say hallo, that's all. He said he was getting married to a woman called Bridget.'

Those were perhaps the first serious sentences Wexford had ever heard uttered by Claudia Ricardo. 'Did you give him any money?'

'As a matter of fact, we did.' Maeve took her hand from Tredown's brow. He had fallen asleep. 'Things were very prosperous about then. *The First Heaven* had been a bestseller for a long time. Those were the days.' She glanced at the sleeping man. 'He's never been able to write a sequel to come up to it. God knows why not. I gave Dusty £100 for a wedding present.'

'That was all?'

'I *beg* your pardon? He was bloody lucky to get that.'

'Where did the rest come from?'

Wexford watched the trickles of rain run down the big window in his office. The moving water distorted the trees outside to a melange of gold and brown. The sky was pale, colourless, all cloud. 'She may be lying, Mike, and I wonder why. D'you realise, we don't even know his first name? We *conclude* from his nickname that he was called Miller and from the t-shirt that his first name was Sam. But that's guesswork. We know he's dead and Ronald McNeil killed him. Or to correct that, Irene McNeil says he killed him. We have to see Bridget Cook. Hannah can do that and pick her brains. She may know about the £1,000 and she'll certainly know what Dusty's real name was.'

'I've never thought much of the tea we get in here,' Burden said, and with unusual and almost poetical exaggeration, 'but compared with that muck Claudia gave us, it's the nectar of the gods.' He lifted the cup to his lips and savoured the contents. 'Excellent. A bit brutal what Maeve said about the sequels to that book of Tredown's not being very good.'

'She *is* brutal but I'm afraid she's right.'

Burden raised his eyebrows.

'Dora fetched me two of his books from the public library, the recent ones, I mean. They're not a patch on *The First Heaven*. I didn't like *The First Heaven*, I don't like fantasy, but I could see it was good. I couldn't finish the others. I got halfway through one but couldn't finish it and I only managed one chapter of the other. *The First Heaven* ends with the coming of man to earth, that is man as we know him, not half an ape. In the first sequel – it's called *In His Own Image* and that says it all – he's writing about Adam and Eve and the Garden of Eden and God turning them out of the garden, while the point of *The First Heaven* is that it's about evolution and the death of gods. The man's obsessed with the Bible. That's his trouble.'

The glazed look which usually came over Burden's face when literature was mentioned, masked it now. 'Why's that then? I mean, is that why the others aren't so good?'

'I suppose he couldn't bring himself to leave biblical subjects for long. And biblical subjects don't interest people very much any more. They don't interest me but evolution does and classical mythology does too. His mistake was not just in reverting to his old subject but reverting to one which seems to deny his new subject. Do you see what I mean?'

'I suppose so but it's not something I know anything about. Is it important?'

'I don't know,' Wexford said. 'I don't know what's important in this case and what isn't.'

F inding Bridget Cook wasn't difficult but calling on her in her home was. 'She won't want you seeing her at her place,' Michelle Riley said. 'Her bloke's there all the time and if you say a word about any man she was seeing before him he'll go bananas. And when he does he'll beat her up, that's for sure.'

It was a piece of luck for Hannah that Bridget Cook's partner was out – 'Down the benefit' – when she phoned. 'I can't see you here.' Bridget said. 'Not if you want to talk about Samuel.'

'Who?' said Hannah.

'Samuel. That's his name. Samuel Miller. I never called him Dusty, though all the rest of them did.'

They arranged to meet at a café in Norbury, half a mile from the flat where Hannah lived with Bal Bhattacharya. Hannah's mother had a term she used to describe women whose appearance was less than well-cared for, which she generally applied to those interviewed on television on what she called sink estates or bog-standard schools. 'She looks a bit rough' was the phrase Hannah had grown up with. She had rejected it as unacceptable but it came into her head when Bridget Cook turned up – fifteen minutes late – at La Capuccella café.

She was a big tall woman, one who, it was easy to believe, could have performed heavier and more demanding farm work than picking fruit. Her face had once been lovely, the features having a classical stern beauty, but now it was bruised and marked by time and perhaps by human mistreatment. It was the face of a sculpture from ancient Greece, damaged by long exposure to winds and weather. Hannah thought she looked like a Native American, what her mother had told her would once have been called a Red Indian, and her politically correct soul had shuddered at that.

Bridget Cook was nearing sixty but, in spite of her fading beauty, looked more. Yet this man she lived with, Hannah marvelled, was jealous of a previous lover she hadn't seen for eight years. Rather to Hannah's surprise, she extended her right hand and shook hers, pumping it vigorously. 'Hi. How are you? I'm Bridget Cook – or Williams, as my fellow likes me to say.'

Hannah thought she need not pander to this man's vanity. 'I'd like to talk about Samuel Miller, Miss Cook, if you're happy about that.'

'Sure. Why not? Him and me, we were going to get married but he walked out on me. Got cold feet, I guess. I'd been married before but he never had. Still, it's all water under the bridge now, isn't it?'

Not quite, Hannah thought. 'Before we go any further, Miss Cook, I'd better tell you Samuel Miller is dead. I'm sorry. I hope this won't upset you.'

She was silent. Her strong masculine features remained rigid. She passed one hand over her forehead and said, 'He wrote poems, you know. He'd written a book too. Sam was no fool.'

Hannah noted the diminutive. 'I didn't know.'

'No. People didn't. He wrote a poem for me but Williams found it and tore it up. D'you want a coffee?'

'I'll get it,' Hannah said.

Looking over her shoulder when she was at the counter, she saw the big woman put her head into her hands. A wedding ring was on the third finger of her left hand and Hannah wondered if the jealous lover was resentful of that too. She took the two cups of coffee back to their table.

'Why did he go to see the Tredowns when you were all in Flagford?'

'I don't know. Did he?'

'He'd worked for them three years before, the last time he came fruit-picking in Flagford. A man called Grimble turned the pickers off his field and Samuel Miller went to see the Tredowns and they gave him a job repairing their car and then driving it.'

'D'you mean Tredown the book-writer? The one that did that book called something about heaven? The one they're making a film of?'

'That's the one.'

'He lived in Flagford?'

'Still does,' said Hannah. 'Samuel . . .' The name bothered her, it was inappropriate for what she had supposed Dusty was, not so odd for a writer and a poet. 'Samuel – did he know it was *that* Tredown? I mean, if he was a writer, did he go to see Tredown because *he* was?'

'Don't ask me. I never knew Tredown lived there. Sam never said.'

'I'm wondering if he brought something he'd written with him to show Tredown.'

Bridget plainly wasn't interested. 'If he did I never saw it. How did he die?'

Hannah longed to be able to say this was something Bridget Cook didn't need to know but she couldn't do that. 'I'm afraid he was killed. He was shot.' She said quickly, 'The man who shot him is dead.' She let the words register, sink in, then said, 'Miss Cook, do you know if Sam carried a knife?'

'It was for his own protection. The folks he hung out with – you needed a knife with that lot. He never used it, that I am sure of.'

'The last time you saw him – can you remember that?'

'That's not something you forget,' Bridget Riley said. 'We'd fixed up to get married in three weeks. It wasn't just me, he really wanted it. I'm telling you that because people – well, they used to say things on account of Sam was so much younger than me. Anyway, that day, we'd finished picking for the day. We had a shower in the van but it got broke and Sam was going to mend it but he never did. He come in and said he'd found a place where he could have a bit of a wash. It was an empty house in a field where he'd camped three years ago. When he got back, he said, we'd go down the pub and then he said, here you are, this is for you, and he give me this ring.'

'The ring you're wearing?'

Bridget nodded. 'I'd given him a present too. I'd bought him a t-shirt with his name on.'

At last. Hannah felt the tension in her shoulders relax. She produced the photograph from her bag. 'Was it this one?'

The ravaged face went white. Bridget Cook's reaction was more intense than it had been even to news of Miller's death. 'Oh, my God.' She touched the glossy surface of the photograph with a calloused forefinger.

'I'm sorry if it's been a shock, Miss Cook.'

'No, no. I'm OK. I saw it – the t-shirt with his name on it – in the Oxfam shop in Myringham. Me and Michelle was having a day out. I said to her, "Look at that, I've got to have that for Sam," and she said, "He won't want that thing on it, will he?" She meant the scorpion but I said, "He's got a scorpion tattoo on his shoulder but it's his name he'll like," and I was right, he did. He put it on when he went off to have his wash. I never saw him again.' Keeping herself from crying had made her voice hoarse. She looked down at her left hand. 'Funny he give me this when he was leaving me.' Revelation came to her. 'But he didn't, did he? He got himself killed.' She shook her head. 'Williams thinks it's my wedding ring or he'd have had it off me.'

Hannah went home to Bal, wondering how long this woman would stay with a man who beat her up and destroyed the poem another man had written for her. Then, holding Bal in her arms, she caught sight of the two of them, young and good-looking, in the mirror and thought that circumstances alter cases.

CHAPTER TWENTY-ONE

The hospice which would be Owen Tredown's home until he came to his final resting place was in Pomfret, a purpose-built unit set among trees. In the area between it and Pomfret High Street was a fairly large man-made pond on which were mallards and a couple of moorhens. Bulrushes and hostas with succulent bluish leaves fringed its banks. Donaldson drove past it, turned and parked outside the hospice gates for Wexford to spend five minutes admiring its generous windows, its carefully laid-out garden and all the various kinds of access provided for disabled visitors.

He liked the theory or idea of a hospice. He had looked the word up in the dictionary before coming out and found the first definition given for it was 'a house of rest and entertainment for pilgrims'. Rest was right, but entertainment? Hardly, unless you counted the television sets which he'd heard were provided in every room. He approved but still he asked himself what it must feel like to go into a place you knew you'd never come out of alive. You knew this was it, the last place in the world to lie down in, this was the antechamber to the crematorium. He told Donaldson to drive on.

The newspapers must already have Tredown's obituaries prepared. One or two of them would discard those prewritten epitaphs in favour of a tribute composed by a personal friend. There would be a photograph of Tredown, probably taken some twenty-five years before, when the author was young and hand-some. The last line would be 'he is survived by his wife Maeve.'

The rain had gone and it was another fine day, cold as November must be, but bright and sunny as summer without summer's haze. Greg was in the front garden of Mrs McNeil's house, sweeping leaves from the path. When he saw Wexford arrive he pulled off the jade green latex gloves he was wearing and ran to open the car door. Like a doorman at a luxury hotel, Wexford thought. Greg's t-shirt was white enough for a washing-powder advertisement, dazzling as fresh fallen snow, his jeans so tight as perhaps to ruin for ever his chances of becoming a parent. He ushered the chief inspector into the house with some ceremony, called out, 'Reeny, darling, your guest is here,' and asked Wexford what he would like to drink.

She was a different woman. If he had met her outside her expected environment he wouldn't have recognised her. Though bound to await trial on various serious charges, she looked ten years younger and happier than he had ever seen her. She still had her feet up on a footstool but she had sheer stockings on her legs and those feet encased in court shoes. Her hair had just been done – did Greg's talents extend that far? – and she wore a silk blouse and neat black skirt. She gave Wexford one of the first smiles he had ever had from her and extended a hand with freshly painted nails.

'Mrs McNeil, I want to talk to you again about the – er, intruder in Mr Grimble's house,' he said when Greg had brought tea for him and what might have been water with ice and lemon but was more likely gin and tonic for Irene McNeil. 'We now know his name was Samuel Miller. I want you to cast your mind back to September eight years ago and tell me something. In the days or weeks following the day you and your husband had removed his body from the bathroom to the cellar, did you talk about it? Did you discuss it? Did anyone else in the neighbourhood mention him? Ask about him?'

She picked up a chocolate biscuit off the plate Greg had brought, laid it down again and selected instead one with a crust of coconut icing. 'I didn't talk about it. The less said about it the better, I thought. It was best forgotten.'

He marvelled, not so much at her as at the society she had moved in which bred such dismissive indifference to a man's death. 'Did your husband talk to you about it?'

'Ronald wanted to bury the body. He said it wasn't safe leaving it there. John Grimble or whatever his name is, he might find it. All I said was he shouldn't try to do that on his own, move it and bury it, I mean. He didn't ask me to help again. It was too much to expect of me.'

'Did he try to bury the body?'

'Of course he didn't,' said Mrs McNeil. 'It was in the cellar, wasn't it, when you found it? Ronald wasn't strong enough. He was nearly eighty, he wasn't well. It hurt his back when we had to move the body down those stairs. I shall always say it was that which damaged his hip. I told you it was the day after that he had a stroke and he wasn't strong enough to have a hip replacement. He wouldn't have stood the anaesthetic.'

It was a grotesque and nightmarish picture she had conjured up, these two aged and no doubt misshapen people, limping and short of breath, struggling and gasping as they humped a dead man down a narrow staircase into a subterranean chamber. 'Why do you think Miller was in the house?' Wexford asked.

'Looking for something to steal,' she said promptly. 'And then he went to wash himself. That would be stealing too, wouldn't it, stealing Mr Grimble's water?'

Wexford left her and returned to Flagford. The sun was low in the sky, creating a dazzling glare which the sun visor on the windscreen did little to remedy. Grimble's Field had become a haven for rabbits which scattered for the shelter of the trees when Wexford walked up the path. The bungalow had already been searched twice but he still thought taking a third look might be worth a try. The first thing he did was try the cold taps in the bathroom, one over the bath and one on the washbasin. To his surprise – he had never fully believed in the theory that Miller had gone in there to wash himself or have a bath – water came from both. Not a gush or even a steady stream of water but a good deal more than a trickle. It would have been easy to fill the washbasin and not too unpleasant to wash in it in September. The sliver of soap was still there, cracked and blackened now. The shaving brush and the scrap of grey towelling were still there. But the knife . . . ?

Since they must both have known there was a chance of the body being discovered in the cellar, it would have been very much in Ronald McNeil's interest to place the knife near the body. But was there ever a knife? Bridget Cook had told Hannah he carried one 'for his own protection', an excuse Wexford had heard many times before. In spite of all the searching which had been done, could the knife still be in here? Wexford surveyed the bathroom which must have been a squalid place even while in daily use by old Grimble. Watermarks and rust stains disfigured taps and plug-holes. All the pipework was exposed or wrapped in dirty rags and several tiles had come away from the side of the bath. The floor had been deep in dust but most of that had been swept up by the searchers. He knelt down on the cleanest spot and peered at the floorboards.

Moving his hands through the drifts of powdery yet gritty grey stuff which had accumulated behind the lavatory pan, he pushed his forefinger down a space between the boards. There was nothing to be seen, but his finger encountered some kind of obstruction. What he needed was a knife (a knife!) to slide down into the crack. He went into the kitchen, opened a likely-looking drawer and found a handful of ancient and rusty cutlery. The knives were far too blunt to stab anyone or be, as far as he could see, of any use at all except perhaps the use he had in mind for one of them. He returned to the bathroom, slid the rusty blade down into the crack and pushed until it half-lifted the obstruction, something small and cylindrical. Easing it out, he blew the dust from it and saw that what he had found was a cartridge, probably, almost certainly, from a twelve-bore shotgun.

*   *   *

That, at any rate, proved Mrs McNeil's story. How much now did it matter if the mystery of the knife was never solved? Whether McNeil had killed in self-defence or in malice hardly mattered either. He was dead and the only offence with which his widow could be charged was that of concealing a death. If Grimble ever got his planning permission, would anyone want to live in a house (or two houses or three) built here, where two murders had happened, where two bodies had been hidden? Wexford was thinking about this, imagining himself as a potential buyer, when he heard a door close softly and a footstep in the kitchen.

He turned round, finding himself in the same position as Miller must have been when he was surprised by McNeil entering the house. This intruder, however, wasn't carrying a shotgun. Claudia Ricardo said, without polite preamble, 'I saw your car outside with that driver of yours in it.' Why was 'that driver of yours' so much more offensive than 'your driver'? The words meant the same thing. 'It seemed an opportunity to get some facts out of you.'

He said nothing, waited.

'Is it true that was Dusty's body you found in here?'

'Yes, it's true.'

'And he'd been dead for eight years? Murdered? How funny. And it was eight years in September?'

'It would seem so,' said Wexford.

'If only we'd known,' she said, as if to herself. 'That's why he never came back. I thought he'd come back, I really did.'

The thought came to him then that this woman, attractive in a bizarre way, had been sexually involved with Miller. Not perhaps in 1998 but three years before that. In jeans and clinging red sweater, she looked younger than when she wore her long skirts and 'hippyish' patchwork. She pushed her hands through her hair, the movement lifting her cheeks and giving youth to her face. Silent for a while, apparently speculating, she said, 'What happened to the money?'

'The thousand—' he said deliberately, 'I mean, the £100 wedding present?'

207

She wasn't the kind of woman who blushed but her eyes narrowed.

'I can't tell you that, Miss Ricardo,' he said. 'Now it's your turn to tell me something. When Miller came to you eleven years ago, worked for you as a handyman and drove your car, did he bring you the manuscript of a novel for Mr Tredown to read?'

A strange expression had come into her face, calculating and sly. 'Whatever makes you ask?'

'Perhaps you'd just answer the question.'

'Only if we can go and sit down somewhere. Have a little tête-à-tête? This place is a hole and a dump but it's not as foul as this in the bedroom.'

The stench of old clothes and mothballs was unpleasant. Mice had been eating the old flock mattress. It was strange, Wexford had sometimes thought, how rodents could eat unpalatable, nutrition-free substances and apparently thrive on them. 'Now perhaps you'd answer the question,' he said again.

She shrugged in a way that managed to be offhand and involved at the same time. He noticed how long her neck was, a desirable feature in a woman. 'Yes, well, people were always sending him manuscripts,' she said, contempt in her voice. 'It was him teaching in creative writing schools that did it. They'd go along and sign up or whatever they did, poor deluded creatures, and go to his classes and most of them got crushes on him. He used to be quite good-looking – we were known as a handsome couple – would you believe it?' When she saw Wexford didn't intend to answer her, she shrugged and went on, 'Of course he only did it for the money. He had to. I've never worked – did you know that? Never. Maeve did. She was someone's secretary. But me, I never fancied working, you have to get up so early in the morning, and Owen didn't make much from his books. The people he taught, they'd go home and write something, usually some derivative rubbish or so *boring* you wouldn't believe. They'd send it to him asking for his comments. We got divorced and he married Maeve. She had an income from somewhere, not much, but better than nothing. Those manuscripts,

Maeve and I used to read bits of them out loud and have a laugh, it was most amusing. Owen read them all, he was sorry for the people who wrote them, and he'd spend good money on the return postage.'

'And Miller, did he bring a manuscript?'

'You asked me that before,' she said. 'He may have. How would I know? If he did Owen didn't say anything to me about it. He didn't like us laughing at them, he's got a soft heart, poor old thing, so maybe he kept it dark. He was well then, of course.'

Wexford wondered which piece of information that he had given her or question he had asked was responsible for the huge improvement in her spirits since she first walked into the house. Then she had been tense, anxious, but now as they left, her step was lighter and she looked young. It was no longer too difficult to believe that eleven years ago she had been the lover of a man of thirty-two.

'I'm off to see Owen,' she said conversationally. 'With Maeve, of course. I mean, she'll have to drive me. I'm not prepared to go on the bus. You wouldn't give me a lift, I suppose?'

'I'm afraid not, Miss Ricardo,' he said.

His destination led him in the opposite direction to hers, back into Kingsmarkham. This suburban estate – many like it had sprung up around the town – lay quietly under a mother-of-pearl sky, November's sunset colours. One of the residents daringly mowed his lawn, another was cutting the last roses of the year, the bruised and misshapen flowers of late autumn. Irene McNeil's house had the indefinable look homes have in the daytime when their occupants are asleep. A shuttered silent look, a stillness.

If he hadn't known someone must be at home, Wexford would have given up after the second ring. But he pressed the bell a third time, there was a patter of soft footsteps and Greg opened the door. Five minutes before, Wexford was sure, he had been asleep, had combed his hair on the way to let him in. His face was like the face of an infant who has been wakened too soon. But he wasn't one to lose his cool, as he might have said himself.

'Hi, Mr Wexford, how're you?'

When this vacuous greeting started to become commonplace, Wexford resolved not to answer it in any circumstances. 'I'd like to see Mrs McNeil.'

'Oh, dear, she's fast asleep.'

'You'll do,' Wexford said. 'In fact, you may do even better.'

Greg's smile grew wary as he invited Wexford in. 'My pleasure,' he murmured but looked rather startled when asked for his full name.

'Gregory Brewster-Clark,' he said, and then, 'May I ask why you want to know?'

'Well, yes, you may.' For a moment Wexford considered telling him he might ask but not necessarily get an answer. He relented. 'You may think it outdated of me,' he said, 'but I don't much care to call people I don't know by their given names.'

It was plain that Greg didn't know what a given name was. But he had got his answer and cheered up, skipping into the kitchen and asking if he could get him anything. Wexford thought he was more like a hairdresser than a carer. He could imagine him with scissors in his hand, asking a client if he wanted a teeny fraction more off the back.

'I'd like to see inside the cupboards and drawers,' he said.

Greg seemed to see nothing odd about this request. As far as he was concerned, any visitor male or female must have a burning desire to see his handiwork. Everything was clean and neat, sterile-looking and smelling of chlorine, as if an anaesthetised patient might be brought in at any moment to await surgery. Happily, Greg opened one wall cupboard after another, displaying rows and stacks of matching china and glass. If there was food in this place it must all have been kept inside the fridge. A knife rack caught Wexford's attention but there was nothing of interest to be found in it.

Fortunately, it never seemed to occur to Greg to ask him what right he had to search Mrs McNeil's kitchen. The word 'warrant' would perhaps have been foreign to him. Wexford had expected an argument but, as he told Burden later, all he got was smiling acquiescence and a cup of excellent tea.

'First I had a look at the knife rack but the knives were all the same, with plain black handles. Then I asked to see inside the drawers. Greg showed not the least sign of suspicion. Maybe it's normal in the households where he works for visitors to scrutinise the culinary arrangements. Anyway, no knife. I asked him if there'd been a knife in any of the cupboards or drawers when he first arrived and did all this tidying up but he said no. I said I'd wait for Mrs McNeil to wake up. I wanted to get back to this story of hers about the knife being stolen by the cleaner. For some reason I'd begun to believe it.'

Up till now having looked increasingly bored, Burden brightened. He lifted his beer tankard to his lips as if celebrating.

'Greg gave me tea. He gave me biscuits. He talked to me about all the various jobs he'd had, the hotels he'd worked in, his training as a nurse, as an overnight carer, on and on. I thought she'd never wake up. In the end I got him to wake her and he did – gently yet effectively, I must say.'

Burden nodded. 'What happened?'

'I asked her. It always amazes me, Mike, the way our – er, customers lie and lie and when we finally tell them we know they've lied, we can prove they've lied, their lying is a fact, they're not ashamed, they don't say they're sorry or they feel guilty and what must we think of them, they just say "OK" then or, "Right, so what?"'

Burden was quickly dismissive. 'Well, they're a bunch of villains, aren't they? Low life. And Irene McNeil may be an upper class snob but she's as bad as any of them. What did she say?'

'When she went back to the house two years ago – on her way to have tea with the Pickfords, if you recall – she says she didn't look at the body but she saw the knife lying on the floor of the cellar. She put it in her bag, where it presumably remained during the old ladies' tea party, then took it home with her. At this point she seems to have got confused because instead of seeing it as a useful piece of evidence in Ronald McNeil's defence, she decided it was a dangerous weapon, as indeed it is, and would somehow further implicate her husband and herself. I was angry by this time, Mike. I asked her if she knew wasting police time was an offence and she had recourse to "women's weapons, waterdrops".' Wexford shook his head ruefully. 'Hannah would lose all respect for me if she heard me say that.'

'You mean she cried?'

'That's it. Then she says she had a cleaner at the time – I had to listen to a long catalogue of the woman's shortcomings – and this cleaner found the knife in a drawer somewhere and stole it.'

'And you believed her?'

'Just wait. I got the woman's name out of her and who do you think it is?'

'How should I know, Reg?'

'You're exactly the one who would know. She's called Leeanne Fincher, mother of Darrel Fincher. Remember her? She's the woman who gave her son a knife "for his own protection".'

Burden laughed. 'Amazing. We took the knife off him. We've still got it.'

'Excellent,' said Wexford. 'I may add obstructing the police to the charges she already faces just the same. I've lost patience with Mrs M. She may be old but she's old in sin too. I'm going to show that knife to Bridget Cook, though I'm not at all sure what's the point of it, no pun intended.'

'So Miller did take the knife into the bathroom with him?'

'I don't think so. After McNeil shot Miller I think he searched the clothes in the kitchen, found the £1,000 which of course he was far too upright and honest to touch, but he also found the knife. He put it in the bathroom beside the body and later removed it to the cellar, maybe thinking it would help his cause with his wife if she could be made to believe he'd acted in self-defence.' Wexford cast up his eyes. 'He need not have bothered. She's quite as ruthless as he was.'

CHAPTER TWENTY-TWO

He met Iman Dirir by chance in the High Street as she was coming out of Kingsmarkham's only Asian dress shop. She was carrying one of their black and gold bags.

'They're not supposed to be for Africans but we wear much the same clothes,' she told Wexford. 'I've been buying a salwar kameez for my niece's wedding. She's marrying a very handsome Englishman at St Peter's next Saturday.'

Wexford looked his enquiries.

'She's a Christian, Mr Wexford. You get all sorts in Somalia, animists too.'

As far as he knew, the latter worshipped stones and trees but he might be wrong, so he left it. 'Will the Imrans be there?'

'At the wedding? Oh, no, I doubt it. My sister and her husband hardly know them and my niece doesn't at all.'

'But they'll be back by then?'

'I think so. I think they're expected back on Thursday.'

He walked back to the police station, passing A Passage to India where, behind the glass, the shimmering curtains and the artificial lilies, he glimpsed Matea laying tables. Bridget Cook was expected in his office at two. Williams, the partner apparently without a first name, put up no opposition to her travelling to Kingsmarkham, though Wexford doubted if she had told him the true reason for her journey. As he waited he thought about people who make prisons for themselves where none need exist. This woman had landed herself with a man who was a jealous jailer, simply to avoid being alone. Tredown, who evidently cared very little for either of them, had been put under house arrest by two wives who wanted him only as a slave to labour for their keep. Now that *The First Heaven* was to be a film, for which Tredown had no doubt been liberally paid and from which his widow and ex-wife would enjoy the royalties, they were indifferent to his life or death.

Hannah brought Bridget into the office. An old-fashioned expression came into his mind when he saw her: 'raw-boned'. A description everyone understood but which seemed meaningless. She wasn't thin yet the bones seemed to protrude through her skin. Her hands were like a man's and the ring on the left one, with its delicate tracery of leaves, looked incongruous. She sat down heavily but flinched a little when Wexford showed her the knife.

'I don't know,' she said. 'I only saw it the once. It was the guys he hung out with, a rough lot, they were. He said he needed it for his own protection. He never used it, though. I'm sure he never did.'

'You said he was a poet. He wrote poetry to you.' Wexford was conscious of how absurd this would sound and look to an unseen observer, the human fly on the wall. This woman and poetry could hardly be set side by side without raising a raucous laugh. Yet love, he knew, is no respector of beauty or grace. Like the wind which blows where it lists, it can strike almost anyone for almost anyone else. People have no need of love potions in order to fall in love with the ass's ears. He noted the serious nod she gave, the acceptance that she was worthy of verses dedicated to her. 'Did he write anything else?' he asked. 'A play? A piece of fiction?'

'I don't know. Maybe. He wasn't educated but he told me he'd written a book once. Poems and a sort of diary, he said it was.'

'When did you first meet Samuel Miller, Miss Cook?'

'Sometime in '98, it would have been. He moved in with me like in the winter. We was on a site near Southend then. He'd go away a bit but he always came back. We went strawberry-picking up near Hereford in the June and he said they wanted pickers at Morella's in Flagford in the September. That was when he said we'd best get married. I said I was years older than him but he said, so what? He'd always fancied older women.'

Claudia Ricardo, Wexford thought. 'He'd been to Flagford three years before?'

'That's right. Morella's had got a proper campsite, not like the field they had to camp on when he was there before and two guys went after them with guns.'

'Guns?'

'That's what he said.'

Adam Thayer brought the tea in. It was scalding hot but Bridget Cook drank hers greedily. 'Go on, Miss Cook.'

'He wanted to look up old pals while he was there, he said. Them was his words, "old pals". There might be some money in it. They owed him. The day after he'd fixed up our wedding we went picking – it was Victorias – and when we got back he said he was off to see his pals and then have a bit of a wash in a house that was empty on account of our shower going wrong. I waited and waited for him but when it got to midnight I just knew he wasn't coming back. I just knew, I don't know how. It was a funny thing because I thought he really liked me. Maybe it's just that men are a funny lot – sorry, I didn't mean you.'

Wexford assured her he hadn't taken it personally. That made two women who waited for their men to come back and waited in vain, one eleven years before, the other three years after that. He still couldn't tell if there was any connection between the two men but nor could he believe in so great a coincidence.

Sheila was with her mother on the following evening. She had left the children at home with their father and the nanny while she attended the second meeting of the African Women's Health Action Group. Wexford thought of telling her about the Imrans taking their five-year-old daughter home to Somalia and

215

his questioning of their motives. He thought of it and dismissed it. She would launch into one of her impassioned speeches, a denunciation of injustice, wanton cruelty, child abuse and, most telling for him, a catalogue of instructions as to what violent action he ought to take, and take within the next couple of hours. Instead he asked her about the film. Had shooting started yet?

'It won't for ages, Pop. Months.'

'I hope they're paying you well, though I don't suppose it's Hollywood sort of money.'

'Well, no,' she said, 'but it's not bad. Did you know the author's very ill? He's not expected to live to see the film. Isn't that sad?'

'They must have paid him a lot for the rights.'

'You're untypically interested in money today, Pop.'

He laughed. 'I've met him, you know. I could say I know him. I suppose it will all go to his wife.'

'Who else?' said Sheila and she went off to get ready for her meeting.

Dora went with her in the black Mercedes with the handsome driver but Wexford sat on, watching rain, then hailstones, lash the French windows, waiting for Burden to come and share his red-wine ration. No doubt the inspector would defer leaving his house until the rain, forecast as only a shower, passed away over the horizon. He turned his thoughts towards Tredown in the Pomfret hospice. Lord, let me know mine end and the number of my days. Where did that come from? The funeral service, he thought. It was only those with a terminal illness who knew these things and then not accurately. Tredown could only say, I have sixty days at most and (for example) twenty days at least. Did he look back on his life and think it had been good? A wife he had divorced, a second wife whom it was hard to believe anyone could love, those dull Bible-based novels, that one good enduring book he had written . . . If he had written it.

The doorbell ringing made Wexford jump. He got up to let Burden in. The inspector was rather wet, his hair plastered down, raindrops on his face like tears except that he was smiling. 'I got caught in it, stood under a tree till it stopped. Don't say I might have been struck by lightning, I know that already.'

'There wasn't any lightning, was there?'

'According to my wife, there's always lightning when there are hailstones.'

Wexford poured two large glasses of claret. 'I was thinking about Tredown.' He raised his glass, said, 'Owen Tredown. May he have a peaceful end, and soon.'

Burden raised his eyebrows. 'Tredown by all means,' he said, 'but why now?'

'He can't live long. I suppose I pity him. I may be wrong but I imagine him lying in that place – that very nice place, I'm sure – regretting what he's done, regretting that he stole Samuel Miller's manuscript. Because I think it was Miller's. I think Miller wrote *The First Heaven*, or at any rate wrote an outline for it or a draft.'

'That roughneck? That knife-carrying lowlife?' Wexford had never seen such a look of distaste mixed with incredulity on his friend's face. 'Claudia Ricardo told you he was always getting manuscripts sent him by people he'd taught in creative writing classes. Why not one of them?'

'Look at the facts, Mike. Eleven years ago Tredown and the two women were scraping along on what Tredown was making out of those books of his. That and the little bit he got from teaching. And it would have been a little bit. There aren't that many creative writing courses in this country and the ones there are don't pay generously. Neither of the women worked, remember. Claudia boasted that she'd never worked in her life.

'Then along comes Samuel Miller. A roughneck, a lowlife, as you put it, but have we any reason to believe great artists – for the author of *The First Heaven* is or was a great *popular* artist – have we any reason to believe such people are all respectable middle class law-abiding citizens? Genet spent most of his life in prison, Marlowe died in a tavern brawl, Baudelaire was a syphilitic drug addict – no, that argument doesn't work.'

'You're saying Miller brought this manuscript with him on a

couple of weeks of fruit-picking in Flagford? Would he have known Tredown lived here?'

'Why not? He may have attended one of Tredown's classes. The fact that Bridget Cook doesn't know it means nothing. This would have been three years before Bridget met him. Even if he hadn't been Tredown's student, pupil or whatever, the location of Tredown's home if not his actual address appears on the jackets of his books. Can't you imagine him finding out fruit-pickers were wanted in a Sussex village called Flagford and that name resonating with him?' He could see he had awakened Burden's interest – more than that, his enthusiasm. Burden's face wore that narrow-eyed speculative look which commanded his features when he was on the verge of excitement. He had drawn his brows together. 'Go on,' Wexford said. 'You take it from there.'

Burden nodded. 'OK. So he's written this book or done this plan and draft or whatever they do and he takes it with him to Flagford in the hope he may find a way of seeing Tredown. Probably he doesn't know the field they set up camp on is next door to Tredown's house but he soon finds out. They haven't been camped there that long when Grimble junior and his pal Bill Runge turn up and drive them off the land with sticks . . .'

'Or guns.'

'Or guns. The fruit-picking's done or at an end anyway, Miller makes his way into Tredown's garden, offers his services as gardener and handyman and at some point while he's working there tells Tredown he has this manuscript with him and would Tredown take a look at it. How's that?'

'Much what I'd have said myself,' said Wexford.

'It's not so easy after that, though, is it? I mean, does Tredown just say yes, fine, I'd love to, there's nothing I'd like better than wasting a week reading your rubbish? I don't think so.'

Wexford laughed. 'I don't think so either. But remember, I've read *The First Heaven*. I didn't much fancy reading it, I thought I might manage a chapter or two, but once I'd started I recognised it was good. I didn't enjoy it, it's not the kind of thing I like, but I could see others might, thousands of others might.'

Burden was looking at him in a kind of wonder, with that look on his face a man might wear when he hears that an acquaintance has an obsession for some esoteric pursuit, learning Farsi, for instance, or studying sea anemones. But he tried. He concentrated. 'You mean,' he struggled, 'Tredown might have sort of glanced at it not to be – well, not to be rude. He's a very courteous man, don't you think? And then he went on, rather like you, he had a job to put it down and he sort of read to the end and . . .'

'And wondered how he could get hold of it for himself,' Wexford said. 'How he did I can't quite see but somehow he did. Did he buy it from Miller? Or steal it? I could believe one or both of those women somehow cheated Miller out of it.'

'Then Tredown needed to check accuracy and invited Hexham down. I don't like that much, Reg. Why didn't Hexham tell his wife he was going to call on Tredown after he'd been to that funeral?'

'Come to that,' said Wexford, 'why didn't he tell his wife anything about where he was going after the funeral, whether it was to visit Tredown or anything else? He didn't, that's all. But he went somewhere and ended up in that trench in Grimble's Field. Did he somehow find out that Tredown intended to pass off someone else's work as his own? He may have threatened to make what he knew public and was killed for it. We don't know what happened to Miller either, except that he left Tredown and went home, wherever home was at that time. Three years later he came back.'

'And blackmailed Tredown over that book. Maeve or Claudia gave him £1,000 to keep him quiet, not £100 for a wedding present. If he hadn't gone into Grimble's house and got himself shot by Ronald McNeil, I wonder how long it would have been before one of those women killed him.'

'I think you're right, Mike,' Wexford said as he heard his front door open and close again. Dora came into the room with Sheila and Sylvia behind her, said hallo to Burden.

'Why are you two sitting in the dark?'

'I hadn't noticed we were. How was your meeting?'

Sheila put her arms round him and kissed him. 'I can't stop, Pop. It'll take an hour for Clive to drive me home as it is. By the way, Matea Imran was there. She said her parents are back from Somalia and Shamis is all right. Syl will tell you all about it.'

The Imrans had returned home the day before. Of the family, only Matea had been at the meeting. 'She made a point of coming up to me,' Sylvia said, 'and telling me her sister hadn't been circumcised. She'd been mistaken about that.'

'Really?' Wexford saw Burden out, given a lift home in Sheila's car. 'I wouldn't believe a word that girl says,' he said to Sylvia.

She was shocked. 'Dad! I thought you liked her.'

'Liking doesn't come into it. In the circumstances I don't trust her. This is her family, Sylvia. Whatever she may have said at first, coming here and telling me what she was afraid of. Now she knows a bit more about it.'

Dora laid her hand on his arm. 'I can understand,' she said. 'Even if they'd done that awful thing to her sister she won't want her parents sent to prison. She won't do what she'd think of as betraying them.'

'Quite,' he said. 'I couldn't have put it so well myself.'

'Then what are you going to do, Dad?'

'I'm going to bed,' said Wexford, 'and tomorrow I shall have a word with Dr Akande.'

Raymond Akande was Nigerian and a doctor of medicine, his wife Laurette, a sister tutor at the Princess Diana Hospital in Stowerton, from Sierra Leone. Soon after Dr Akande became his GP, Wexford identified a murder victim as their missing daughter Melanie. On the grounds only, as he harshly put it to himself later, that both the living and the dead were black. Akande forgave him quickly; with Laurette it took a little longer but they were friends now.

'The family are on my list,' Akande said when Wexford told him his suspicions about the Imrans, 'but that doesn't mean I can march in there and demand to examine a little girl's vulva.'

'You'd need a court order, I suppose.'

'I'd have to apply to the court for an order. I'm not at all sure I'd get one. On what grounds? Your suspicion? Mine? As far as I know, the home is happy and stable. The children are healthy. The sister denies that anything has been done to the child. Social Services would have to be brought in. They'd have to have a medical review of the case.'

Laurette had come in with coffee on a tray. 'They'll never have had cause to visit the Imrans. I know Shamis. Her parents adore her and it shows. Not that that would stop them having her genitally mutilated. There are plenty of parents would think that a duty to their daughter, a kindness. Without that, how will she ever find a good husband? That's the way they think. I was lucky,' she said, 'not to be done myself. I would have been if my parents hadn't both been killed. I was brought up in an orphanage and somehow got overlooked.'

'So there's nothing to be done?'

'I don't say that,' Akande said quickly. 'Social Services should certainly be alerted. I can do that – maybe we can both do it, Reg. Next time the Imrans come to the surgery or one of them comes I can ask them tactfully about their – well, their attitude to female circumcision.'

Laurette said bitterly, 'They don't need to take her to Africa, you have to realise that. There are plenty of people here who are willing to do it.'

An invitation to Athelstan House was unexpected and unprecedented. Without prior notice, the wife and ex-wife of Owen Tredown had visited Wexford in his own office but even then had shown no particular desire to tell him anything. Their purpose, then and on receiving him subsequently at Athelstan House, seemed to have been only to score off him and Burden and to – well, 'tease' was the word, he thought. Tease, provoke, annoy and show ill will.

Lacking Tredown, the house felt different, colder, busier, and in a way, brighter. Perhaps it was only that the long brown velvet curtains in the drawing room had been drawn back to their fullest extent and tied, not with cords or sashes but with ordinary household string. The bright daylight, which formerly would have revealed dust and dirt and cobwebs, showed that cleaning had been done on a grand scale, an autumn spring-cleaning in fact. The chandelier, washed and polished, now looked more like a light fitting than copulating squids. Clouds of dust no longer puffed out of the sofa cushions when he seated himself. Tredown was gone and, as if he had been a dirty and troublesome pet, his owners had cleaned up after him.

At first neither tea nor coffee were offered Wexford. He sat down because he wanted to, not because he was asked. Claudia Ricardo sat close beside him, too close, and he was overwhelmed by the scent she wore, something he thought might be patchouli. She spread her long embroidered skirt over her own legs and an inch or two of it over his.

'Can I offer you some lemon curd, Chief Inspector?' she said. 'I was making it when you were last here. I'm sure you remember. You said you liked it.'

As she spoke, Maeve Tredown came in with tea and a plate of biscuits and a jar of the lemon curd on a tray. There was a spoon on the tray too, rather as if she were a nurse bringing his medicine. The whole thing might not have been so odd if the lid hadn't been removed from the jam pot. Maeve, in her uniform-style clothes, her grey suit and white blouse, her blonde hair stiff and shiny as a yellow silk hat, stood over him, smiling, the nanny with her charge. Did they expect him to sit there and eat jam? He lifted Claudia's skirt off his legs and got up. He took the tray from Maeve and put it on the table. Then he turned round and spoke in the kind of voice no guest should ever use.

'Sit down, please,' he said to Maeve.

She did so. Claudia giggled.

'I don't know why you asked me to come here,' he said, 'but no doubt you'll tell me in due course. Meanwhile, I want you to tell me about the manuscript Sam or Samuel Miller gave or lent or sold to Mr Tredown in June 1995.'

'We never interfered in Owen's business dealings,' said Maeve.

Business dealings? As if Tredown had been an insurance broker instead of a world-famous author. Besides, it was a lie, Wexford thought. Any business there had been, he was pretty sure Maeve and Claudia had handled it. Claudia *or* Maeve or both had dealt with Tredown's agent, Tredown's publishers, accountants, financial advisers. In the matter of business, the author himself was a babe unborn, as the old phrase had it. 'So you never saw or heard of any such manuscript?'

Claudia was looking up at him earnestly. 'Dusty,' she said, lingering almost sensuously over the name, 'Dusty never saw much of Owen. Perhaps I should say Owen never saw much of him. You must remember Owen disliked being disturbed while he was writing – and he mostly was writing.'

'We saw to that,' was the unspoken sentence. Still standing over them, Wexford said, 'Miller came to see you again at the end of September, 1998.'

'Possibly,' said Maeve. 'About then. I can't be sure of the date.'

'I can. You gave him some money. Why?'

'Really! I told you why or my wife-in-law did.' Here a sly smile at Claudia. 'It was a wedding present. He had found some woman, one of the fruit-pickers, he was going to marry.'

'£1,000, I think you said?'

'Then you think wrong.' Claudia dissolved into silent laughter. 'We'd better things to do with that sort of money.'

He sat down again but this time on an upright chair well away from her. A wasp had got into the room, wheeled about slug-gishly before making for the open jam jar. He watched it crawl on to the jam's smooth golden crust. 'Miller had read the book Mr Tredown had concocted from his manuscript and was black-mailing you for plagiarism, for passing off his work as Mr Tredown's.'

'I know what plagiarism is, thank you very much.' Claudia shook even more with silent mirth. Then, suddenly she was serious. She frowned and swept the wings of charcoal-coloured hair away from her face. 'How did he die? Dusty, I mean.'

Didn't she know? Then Wexford recalled that, apart from him and his discreet team, Miller's death was known only to Irene McNeil and Bridget Cook. He was almost sure there had been some kind of sexual relationship between Miller and Claudia Ricardo, brief perhaps, a quick coupling in the bushes or in Grimble's house, but something. 'That I can't tell you,' he said.

'But he is dead?'

'I've told you so, Miss Ricardo.'

She said nothing.

'I'm sorry,' he said, 'if it upsets you.'

'Upsets me?' Her reply came as a strident shout. 'You must be mad. I'm delighted. I've a little holiday in my heart.' It was evidently a favourite phrase of hers. 'You've made my day.'

The wasp was satiated. It had crawled up to the rim of the jar. Maeve said, 'Claudia,' in a warning tone, got up and crossed to the table. The wasp was grooming itself, lifting its wings, wiping or washing traces of lemon curd from its legs. Maeve put out her hand, picked it up swiftly between finger and thumb and, before it could sting her, crushed the life out of it.

Claudia started laughing again. With an exasperated glance at her, Maeve dropped the wasp corpse on to the tray.

'He came away from here with the money you gave him,' Wexford said, 'and instead of going back to the site where the fruit-pickers were camped, went next door to wash himself and find other clothes to wear. Your delight, I suppose, is typically that of the blackmailer's victim when she or he knows the extortion can't be repeated.'

'For a policeman,' said Maeve, 'you have a most unusual command of the English language.'

This he ignored. Her almost clinical extermination of the wasp had disturbed him. Was he being too fanciful in thinking that if she could do that so ruthlessly she might be capable of other, more serious, executions? Probably he was. He got up. 'I shall visit Mr Tredown in the hospice tomorrow afternoon,' he said. 'Perhaps you'll tell him to expect me. I shall be on my own.'

H is evenings he treasured when he could spend them at home but when the case in hand was as important as this one, they were rare. To Selina and Vivien Hexham he thought he owed a visit rather than expecting them to come once more to him, and he arranged to call at Selina's house at seven. Hannah came with him. So difficult and prickly in some circumstances, she was an ideal companion for the coming encounter. Her sympathies were always with stalwart young women who postponed or refused marriage in favour of independence and a career.

During the day she had had another meeting with Bridget Cook, this time on a park bench about half a mile from where Bridget lived with Williams. The purpose had been to discover, if she could, where Miller had lived in the years between his first fruit-picking adventure in Flagford and his second and ultimate.

'Where was he living when you met him?'

Bridget had known that. 'In a trailer park outside Godalming.' Hannah noted with amusement how she used the American phrase, culled no doubt from television, rather than the British 'caravan site'. 'It was a van belonging to a pal who'd given him a lend of it.'

'Did you ever go there?'

'Once or twice. We was like in a relationship.' Seeing from her expression that Hannah wanted more, she said, 'My mum lives there. She went into the hospital to have her knee done. She'd fallen over and she had to have her knee replaced. I was stopping in her house and I met Sam. In a pub. Then he come back home with me.'

'Right. This – er, van he was living in, did he have a computer there or a typewriter, pens and paper, dictionaries and that sort of thing?'

Bridget stared. 'I never saw nothing like that. I mean, pens he had. Like a ballpoint and a pad for writing on. He wrote his poems there. That's when he wrote that poem for me.'

'And where had he been living before he came to Godalming?'

'He said he used to have a van.' Describing the difference between this shortened form of 'caravan' and the commercial vehicle eluded her. All she could do was point to the distant roadway where a red Royal Mail van was parked. 'Like that only bigger. He drove about, getting work where he could.'

'Did he sleep in it?'

'Sure. Why not? He had a mattress in the back.'

That some people, quite a lot of people, lived liked this was no news to Hannah but every fresh time she heard of it or witnessed it, her thoughts went to her conventional middle class mother and Bal's conventional middle class professional parents and she wondered if they had ever heard of these lifestyles. Her only astonishment came from her awareness that the man had never been in prison or even charged with any offence, as to her certain knowledge he had not.

It was in the report she had written, but she told Wexford about it later in the car after they had met on Barnes Common. 'I said you might want to see her and I've got a phone number and an address to contact her. Not her home address, of course. The dreaded Williams might be on the watch. She's got a cleaning job three days a week and I can get in touch with her any Tuesday or Thursday.'

'Where's the woman who employs her then?' Wexford asked, amused.

'It's a man, guv. You won't believe this but he's a cabinet minister and he's in his government department from 9 a.m.'

Selina Hexham must have been watching, for she opened the front door to them before they were halfway up the path. Vivien wasn't with her this time. Since coming home from work she had changed into a black tunic and tracksuit pants and her only jewellery, apart from the ring, were small gold studs in her ears. They sat down in that living room which had seen so much anxiety, hateful realisation and pain. It seemed not to touch Hannah who hadn't been made aware of it in the way he had and because she hadn't eaten since a kind of brunch at eleven in the morning, fell upon the milky coffee and biscuits they were offered, while Wexford took his coffee black and let his thoughts drift briefly to a glass of claret.

'I want you to tell me, Selina, why you think your father kept his – life up here in his study a secret from your mother. From you all really, but especially from your mother. If he was doing research for authors, as I think he was, what was the point of not being open about it?'

She seemed puzzled. 'You mean research in biology?'

'He was interested in various mythologies too, wasn't he?'

'Yes, but I don't think he had any particular knowledge. He just liked them. Do you mind if I ask you why?'

227

'You can ask me anything you like,' said Wexford. 'There may be some things I wouldn't think it right to tell you at this stage but if there are I'll let you know. I'm asking this because I have an idea – and it's only an idea at the moment – that your father may have gone to call on Owen Tredown after he'd left the Davidsons. And if he did, could it have been to advise him on the writing of *The First Heaven?*'

Selina frowned a little. She was very young but already two parallel lines were cut into the space between her black eyebrows. 'I've been thinking a lot about that. And I've come to rather a strange conclusion. I've been wondering if he did keep it a secret from her or if maybe she knew and they both kept it a secret from *us*. We were children. Maybe they thought it wouldn't have interested us and I suppose they were right.'

'But it was a perfectly respectable thing to be doing, a useful, valuable thing.'

She agreed rather reluctantly, 'Yes. Perhaps so. But Vivien and I, we'd have thought it a dull thing, we'd have thought it boring, and we wouldn't have understood how it could have been important enough to take him away for us almost every evening. I mean, I can understand now that Dad and Mum could have needed the extra money but I wouldn't have done then. They *never* talked to us about money. Mum said to me after he – well, after he'd gone, that children could have terrific anxieties if they thought their parents were short of cash. They imagined themselves without a home, sleeping in the street, that sort of thing. But then I thought, if he'd taken on this researching thing Mum would have mentioned it when Dad went missing – and she didn't.'

'We wondered,' said Wexford, recalling that this had been Burden's idea, 'we *also* wondered if your father had perhaps embarked on something which, if it was successful, would bring him a lot of kudos, but if it failed might make him seem ridiculous. Forgive me, but that's the way I have to put it.'

'That's all right. I'm past all that. But I don't know, I just don't know.'

He nodded. 'All right.'

Hannah, who had been silent up till then, spoke for him. 'Will you lend us your ring?'

There was no eager response. Selina touched the ring, covered it with the fingers of her left hand. Then, without answering, she pulled it off and handed it to him in one of those rapid gestures people make when they know they must relinquish something they desperately want to keep.

'Thank you. It will be quite safe.'

Hannah wrote her a receipt for it. Selina looked at it strangely, as if to receive this slip of paper was the last thing she expected to be given in exchange for a precious possession.

'What do you want it for, guv?' Hannah said when they were seated in the car and Donaldson was passing through Croydon.

'I'm not sure yet,' he said, not entirely truthfully. 'Is this your street or is it the next one?'

'This one.'

She got out of the car and ran up the stairs to the front door. Just as Donaldson pulled away, Wexford looked at the front window and saw her head and Bal's silhouetted behind the thin curtains. He rested his head back against the cushion and thought about the two women who called themselves wives-in-law. They had invited him to Athelstan House, he hadn't made the appointment himself. Why had they? There had been nothing they wanted to tell him he hadn't heard before and nothing they wanted him to tell them. He remembered the tray with the biscuits on it and the open jar of lemon curd and an unpleasant thought came to him. Would that wasp which had feasted on it have died if Maeve hadn't first crushed the life out of it? Was that why she had been so quick to seize upon it, even risking a sting?

Bizarre as it seemed as mid-morning refreshments, that lemon curd had been intended for him. Was it too far-fetched to think of poison? Of course it was. He must be overtired. Wearily now, he found himself fingering the ring in his pocket. It might have been one of those talismans which abound in fantasy literature, a magic ring which would make him invisible or give him his heart's desire. Perhaps he should make a wish.

'Keep Shamis Imran safe from harm,' he said under his breath, and added, 'What a fool I am.'

CHAPTER TWENTY-FOUR

Something dull and subdued about Matea made him ask. Very young people have a glow about them which starts to fade in the mid-twenties. Jane Austen calls it 'bloom'. In Matea's case, the bloom had clouded, dulling her eyes and turning her hair lifeless and lank. Though she was as polite as ever, there was a lassitude about the way she served them.

'How are you, Matea? Are you all right?'

The tone in which she said, 'Fine,' would have been funny if it hadn't sounded like misery. She came back with their naan and a jug of water in which she had forgotten to put any ice.

'I wonder what's going on in that family,' Wexford said. 'Akande's alerted the Social Services but there doesn't seem much to be done. According to Mrs Dirir, Shamis was running around as normal the day after they got back. She couldn't be doing that if she'd just undergone mutilation.'

Burden made a face. 'It's nasty, isn't it? It makes you wonder how feminists – all women in fact – can concentrate on any other aspect of persecution of women while female genital mutilation flourishes. Why isn't half the human race up in arms?'

'Is this my old friend Mike Burden talking?'

Burden didn't change colour. Blushing was a reaction he had left in the past. 'Well, those are Jenny's ideas. I can't say I don't agree, though.'

Matea brought their chicken tikka and Wexford poured them

glasses of water. He said nothing about the lack of ice. 'I'm going to see Tredown this afternoon.'

'Is that purely sick visiting or because you want a talk?'

'I hope he'll want to talk to me.'

'What, a deathbed confession?'

'It could be,' said Wexford. 'Last time I saw him I had a feeling he might say a lot if he could be apart from those two women. Realistically, though, I think only he can tell me how he found Hexham to do his research for him. Was it through some sort of advertisement or by word of mouth? How many times had Hexham been to Athelstan House and how and where did he go when he left on that particular day? In a taxi to Kingsmarkham station? On foot? Surely not. It was pouring with rain. Or did he never leave the place alive? Those are the things I want to know, or rather, the things I'm likely to find out.'

'Do we know how long Tredown has got?'

'You mean till the end? Till death parts him from those two wives of his?'

'I suppose I do, yes.'

'Weeks rather than months, I think. Do you want some halva? Or some yogurt? What I like about this place is that it takes its name literally, it's a passage to India and it picks up national dishes all along the way.'

Afterwards he wondered why he had chosen to go in his own car to Pomfret instead of letting Donaldson drive him. It had something to do with the awesome nature of this place, its function as death's waiting room, its humane and tender purpose. Officialdom should not come here and disrupt these last peaceful days where palliative care was all and hope was over.

When he came here before, just to have a look, he had noticed there was nowhere to park cars in the front of the building. He drove in through the gateway, past the pond with the ducks, the hostas and the bulrushes and followed the paved path which led round the side of the hospice to the back. Here was another arrow pointing to the rather distant car park, an area screened off by trees and shrubs. Five cars were already there and one of them was Maeve Tredown's, the dark red Volvo. He experienced a slight sinking of the heart, a feeling composed of exasperation and a sense of the futility of his coming here at all. He had told her he would be visiting that day. Couldn't she have taken the hint? Or was it rather that she (and possibly Claudia Ricardo too) had come *because* he was coming? He could see someone in the car but it was too far off for him to be sure it was Maeve.

Reflecting on this, he began walking slowly along the driveway towards an arrow marked 'Reception'. When he reached the side of the building and was between its brick wall and a tall chain link fence, wondering if there was any point in his staying, he heard a car behind him. It was going fast, too fast to negotiate this fairly narrow passage, and he leapt aside. As he did so, turning to face the oncoming vehicle, instead of stopping its driver accelerated. He shouted and threw up his arms but the car drove straight at him, scooping him up on to its bonnet and swerving to scrape its bodywork along the wall.

It was a bizarre, unreal happening, something he'd seen in films, only heard of in life. He teetered there, sliding, kicking on the slippery surface, trying and failing to get a grip on something, anything. Slithering off, making frenzied sounds, calling for help, he crashed on to the paving stones up against the fence, his right hand out to break his fall. Pain shot up his arm. Afterwards he said he knew he was alive because he heard a bone in his wrist crack. The dark red Volvo hesitated only for a moment before charging towards the gateway and out into Pomfret High Street with a roar and a gush of exhaust fumes.

H annah had slipped the ring on but it was too big for the third finger of her slender hand, fitting rather more tightly on the middle finger. It seemed an omen. She might wear the diamond Bal had given her for her engagement; no wedding band should ever replace it. If they wanted children she could have them without benefit of matrimony. She was too young to worry about inheritance tax and the law would be changed by then, anyway. No, she'd never marry, she thought, as Damon came down the police station steps and got into the driving seat.

'She's on a week's holiday and she's staying with her mother,' Hannah said. 'Godalming somewhere. Salterton Street. God knows where that is, you'll have to use the satnav.'

Fascinated by modern technology, Damon was delighted to get the chance. The satellite navigation voice, not unlike Hannah's own, directed him the opposite way to where he would have gone if left to himself. He sighed happily. 'This woman, isn't there some nutcase boyfriend who's paranoid about her knowing other guys?'

'You're quite safe,' said Hannah, laughing. 'It's only one particular guy. She's left him behind in my neck of the woods.'

The little house in a Godalming backstreet was found with ease but no more quickly, Damon insisted, than he could have done on his own. He was mildly disillusioned. A very old woman let them into the house, small, shrivelled, stick-thin, in a short-sleeved jumper and leggings which would have fitted an undersized twelve-year-old. It was hard to believe she and tall brawny Bridget Cook could be mother and daughter.

'You're not wanting to take my ring off me?' were almost the first words Bridget said.

'We'd just like to compare it with this one, Miss Cook,' Hannah said. She held out the ring Selina Hexham had lent Wexford on the palm of her hand.

'I don't know if it'll come off.'

Bridget struggled with the ring, twisting and pulling it, failing to move it over the swollen joint.

'Come on, love,' said Mrs Cook in her birdlike twitter, 'let me have a go. I've got just the thing. Wait a minute.'

A jar of Vaseline was produced, the finger anointed, and at last the ring began to slide. Mrs Cook gave it a final pull over her daughter's knuckle and the two rings lay side by side. Each had a chased design of leaves, as if a laurel wreath encircled them. Hannah looked closely, lifted each one in turn up to the light while the always-obliging Mrs Cook produced a magnifying glass. *For ever* was inside Bridget's and *For ever* inside Selina Hexham's, identical promises engraved at the same time, in the same italics.

'Let me see.' Lily Cook brandished her magnifying glass. 'I can't see that even with my glasses. Oh, look, fancy that. Who's that other one belong to, Bridge?'

'I don't know,' Bridget said sadly. It was as if some assumption she had made had been destroyed at a blow.

'May I borrow it, Miss Cook?'

'I knew you'd ask.' The sadness in Bridget's tone had deepened. 'I have to say yes, don't I? Tell me one thing. Did he nick it?'

In a manner of speaking, Hannah thought. 'I can't tell you that,' she said, but she was touched suddenly by unusual emotion, by fellow feeling for a sister-woman. 'The important thing is he gave it to *you*. He wanted you to wear it.'

I t is surprisingly difficult to crawl on two legs and an arm, easier (but more painful) when you bend the damaged limb at the elbow and swing it back and forth. He was afraid that if he stood he might find he'd broken more than his wrist but he tried and made it to the wall of the building where he hung on with his left hand to a drainpipe. Not an ache but an intense burning soreness shivered through his body. In the morning he'd be a mass of bruises but he was alive and not, he thought, much harmed. They would ask him, he knew very well, if he had lost consciousness. He wasn't sure. Had he? How was it that he didn't know? There seemed to be some missing minutes in his recall of the past ten, a black curtain coming down like a brief dropping off to sleep. Well, he'd tell them that. His phone was all right. As he began to key in the numbers a car turned in from the road and he recognised it as Raymond Akande's. It stopped before it reached him. Dr Akande jumped out.

'Someone tried to run me over in a car,' Wexford said.

'*Tried* to?'

'Failed, as you see. It was more a case of me running over them. I got tossed on to the top of the car and think I've broken my wrist. Look, I've got to make a phone call.'

'No, you haven't. I'll take you to the Infirmary myself.'

'Thanks but this is something else.' Akande helped him into his car and there, when the sharp pains associated with movement had subsided, he spoke to Burden. 'I want you to go to Athelstan House and arrest Maeve Tredown. What for? Attempted murder. That's right. Attempted murder of *me*.'

His notion that she had tried to poison him hadn't been so fantastic after all.

'Of course you have to stay in overnight if they say so,' Dora said in the mildly scolding voice she used when he was recalcitrant. She sat by the bed he had rejected in favour of the armchair next to hers. 'They've got to take X-rays and things. A scan, that doctor said. And they're going to put a plaster on your arm.'

'When Jenny Burden broke her wrist they put a pin in. She didn't have a plaster. Why can't I have a pin?'

'Don't be so childish, Reg. What were you doing at the hospice, anyway?'

'Visiting Tredown. Or trying to.'

'A corporal work of mercy, as the Catholics say?' She didn't wait for his answer. 'I'm reading *The First Heaven*. Sheila kept on saying I have to and I must say it's not a hardship. I'm loving it.' She hesitated, then said tentatively, 'Would you think I was mad if I said the only thing is he didn't write it?'

'My sentiments entirely,' said Wexford. 'Here, give me your hand. Two minds with but a single thought we are. I wish they'd let me go home.'

She shook her head. 'Don't get run over again, will you?' To his dismay he saw a tear in her eye but she said brightly, 'Here's Mike. You'll want to talk to him.'

'Don't go,' Wexford said but she was halfway across the ward. Burden kissed her cheek, came to the bedside and stood over him. 'What happened?'

'Court in the morning,' Burden said. 'Of course she denies it, says you walked – well, ran – out in front of her. Are there any witnesses?'

'Of course not. If there'd been anyone around she'd have postponed it till another day.'

'Sure.'

'Like I've had to postpone seeing Tredown. But she must be seriously afraid of me, don't you think? Did you have a look at the car?'

'Both of us did. I took Barry with me. There are scratches on the bonnet and a couple of scrapes made by the heel of your shoe where I guess you tried to get a purchase and both sides are scraped to hell. There's a long dent all along the nearside. But so what, Reg? She doesn't deny hitting you, she just says it wasn't her fault. And she's got the nerve to say she's not a very good driver. I don't think we've a chance of making it stick.'

'I don't think so either,' said Wexford, 'But that doesn't matter all that much, seeing that we'll very shortly have her back in court on an even more serious charge, she and her henchwoman, Ricardo.'

'And will we make that stick?'

'God knows, Mike. We can only try.'

CHAPTER TWENTY-FIVE

he two rings spilt out of the ziplock bag on to the lap of his blue check dressing gown. One was tagged with the name 'Cook', the other 'Hexham'. Hannah handed him a magnifying glass, apparently having no faith in his unaided eyesight.

'Did you notice the chasing on the Cook ring is very slightly more worn than on the Hexham?'

She hadn't. 'Why d'you think that is, guv?'

Dora had called him childish on the previous day and no doubt this was the word for his unreasonable hope that none of his fellow inmates of Frobisher Ward heard the title she gave him. Still, we all have our vanities and our touchiness, he told himself, we are only human. 'Because one was on someone's finger more than the other. Three years went by when Miller had the ring before he gave it to Bridget Cook and in those years no one wore it.'

The ward sister came up to them, told Hannah she would have to go as the doctors were doing their rounds. 'And I expect he'll let you go home, Mr Wexford.'

'I thought they always called people by their first names these days, guv,' whispered Hannah.

'I expect that like most of us,' said Wexford blandly, 'they call them by the name they prefer.'

At home he found a reception committee of daughters and grand-children. 'I haven't been at death's door,' he told his social-worker daughter.

'They all want to write their names on your plaster,' Sylvia said. 'What is it about the British that they always have to queue?'

'They learn it at their mothers' knees,' said Wexford, holding out his cast for the two boys. 'I don't believe you can write, you're too little,' he said to Amy.

Shouting, 'I can, I can,' she executed a bold squiggle in red felt-tip and he told her how clever she was.

Anoushka, in her mother's arms managed a scribble but Mary really was too little to do more than crow and laugh.

'I've been calling on the Imrans,' Sylvia said when he and she were briefly alone.

'*You* have?'

'I'm a Child Care Officer – remember?'

'And what have you found?'

'Not much,' she said. 'Shamis starts school next month. She's excited about it. I don't tell them why I'm visiting and they haven't asked. Maybe they think it's all part of the service, something that we do for every family with a pre-school child. If only we had the resources!'

'Do you tell them when you're coming?'

'Not to the time, Dad. I tell them I'll be along Monday or Tuesday, say. I can't tell them to stop at home for me. I've no grounds for that. There's just one thing to tell you and it's nothing really. They've got someone staying with them, a woman of about fifty. Mrs Imran calls her "auntie" so I assume she's a relative.'

'She came back with them from Somalia?'

'I think so.'

'Can't you ask her?'

'She doesn't speak a word of English,' said Sylvia.

'And you don't trust the Imrans to interpret?'

'What do you think?'

Karen Malahyde was also paying friendly visits to the Imrans and not always notifying them of the precise time she was coming. Possibly they thought this too was all part of the service.

*   *   *

239

T wo days later than he had intended, he walked into the reception area at Pomfret Hospice and asked for Owen Tredown. As he had predicted, he was a mass of bruises and his whole body ached. Though supported by a sling, the cast on his right arm felt heavy and cumbersome. He was all right sitting down, provided he was padded with a cushion but walking made him wince at almost every step. Returning to the hospice gave him a strange feeling and he told Donaldson to drop him outside the front doors. The sight of the fairly narrow defile – its walls scarred with dark red paint like a bloodstain – in which Maeve Tredown's car had trapped him and tossed him on to its bonnet showed him how easily, if she had been going a fraction more slowly, she might have run over instead of under him. Had her action been aimed at preventing him being alone with Tredown? Or was it designed to expel him from the inquiry altogether?

The advantage to the driver of a car as lethal weapon was that the intended victim doesn't believe until the very last minute that any fellow human being deliberately means to run him over. He, who ought to have known better, hadn't believed it. He'd simply set her down as the bad driver she boasted she was.

The receptionist directed him to the lift and told him he would find Tredown in Room Four on the second floor. It was only when he was past the first floor that it occurred to him Claudia Ricardo might be there. Tredown's request that he come, his urging a nurse to phone him ('He insists you come yourself,' the woman had said. 'He won't take no for an answer. And could you be alone please.') would have no effect on her. He hoped too that the other inmates of the ward might be far enough away for no conversation to be overheard or that curtains could be drawn round Tredown's bed. At least, this time, he wasn't an inmate himself but a visitor, free to come and go.

Tredown was in a private room off the corridor which led to the main ward. The door was shut. He knocked and, getting no answer, opened it. Inside it was light and airy, but excessively warm. A blue glass vase held white dahlias, another branches of red rowan berries.

Room Four had only one occupant and he, as Wexford himself had been when in the Infirmary, was sitting in a chair by the bedside with a blanket across his knees. There the resemblance ended. Tredown was asleep, his head turned to one side; and ill as the man had been last time he had seen him, now the advanced stage of his disease made him almost unrecognisable. All his flesh seemed to have been pared from him and the skin which was stretched over sharp but frail bones was a reptilian green. Tredown slept with his mouth closed, his face peaceful in repose and, in spite of wasting disease, protracted suffering and discoloured emaciation, remained handsome. So might be the sculpted face of some mediaeval ascetic carved from olivine stone.

Pulling himself out of these fanciful flights, Wexford sat down in the other chair. In the absence of a cushion, he took a spare pillow from a pile and stuffed it behind his back. That was better. He reminded himself that this time it was Tredown who had asked for him and not he for Tredown – though he would have asked next day – but still he hesitated to wake him. Perhaps a nurse would come and do it for him, but as yet there was no sign of one. The place was silent except for the occasional soft, steady footfall along the corridor outside.

Ten minutes went by. Outside, he heard a car arrive. In the corridor someone whispered to someone else. A petal dropped off one of the dahlias and fluttered to the ground. Tredown slept, his breathing light but uneven and once or twice he made a little sound which Wexford interpreted as distress without quite knowing why he did so. Next time he heard the footsteps he opened the door and asked a man in a white boiler suit if it would be all right to wake Mr Tredown. The man looked at his watch, said it was time he woke anyway, and entering the room, spoke gently and in a very low voice into Tredown's ear.

Stirring, Tredown muttered, 'It was so wonderful I was envious – no, I was consumed with envy . . .'

The nurse who had awakened him looked enquiringly at Wexford and Wexford stared at him too, slightly shaking his head.

'I'll leave you then,' he said. 'He gets very tired.'

'I'll try not to exhaust him.'

'Would you like a cup of tea? I'm bringing one for him.'

Wexford thanked him. He watched the man in the chair as he opened his eyes. Tredown had slipped down while asleep and now he struggled to pull himself up.

'I'm sorry I can't do anything to help you,' Wexford said, lifting up the arm with the cast and attempting a smile.

'I can manage.' Tredown heaved himself higher in the chair with difficulty. It was painful to watch but when he had raised his upper body an inch or two he seemed satisfied and he sighed. 'What did I say just now? I was half asleep.'

'You didn't say much,' Wexford said. 'Just that something was wonderful and you were envious.'

'Yes.'

The silence endured for a full minute, Wexford saw from the clock on the wall. All of our lives were ticking by, he thought, but for this man its passing must be more poignantly prescient than for most of us. Another precious minute would pass and another and another until one more of those last days was gone. Lord, let me know mine end and the number of my days . . .

Suddenly Tredown said, speaking in a strong voice, 'I'm going to die. I shan't last long now.' He looked hard at Wexford. 'Please don't say anything cheerful such as while there's life there's hope.'

'I wasn't going to.'

'I want to tell you about it before I die. It's weighed with me for eleven years, yet – I don't know if I did anything wrong. If I did it was a sin of omission. "I left undone those things which I ought to have done." I failed to ask questions when I should have asked them. I accepted.'

There was a knock at the door and the nurse came in with a teapot, milk and sugar and two cups on a tray. He poured the tea, suggested to Tredown that a biscuit would be a good idea but Tredown shook his head.

When the man had gone he said, '"Life is but a process for

242

turning frisky young puppies into mangy old dogs and man but an instrument for converting the red wine of Shiraz into urine."'

Wexford didn't recognise the quotation. 'Who said that?'

'Isak Dinesen. I may not have got it quite right but that's the gist. I suppose you think it very odd my wife and I and my ex-wife all living in the same house.'

'Unconventional,' Wexford said, 'but not all that odd. It's more common than you might think, though usually it's a husband and wife and her ex-husband. Men on their own find it hard to look after themselves.'

Tredown's laugh was a broken cackle. '"Like unto the crackling of thorns under a pot is the laughter of fools,"' he quoted. 'I'm good at quoting – maybe that's all I'm good at. I used that in one of my biblical books. I enjoyed writing them,' he said, 'but they were never very successful. They were a century too late. My publishers were always suggesting I try something else.'

'And you did,' said Wexford.

He drank his tea and took a fat-laden, sugary biscuit, reflecting in the ensuing silence that the food which is damaging to one may be, if not healthy to another, at least life-prolonging. Tredown ate nothing. He said, 'In a manner of speaking. When the manuscript came – it came in the post, you see – I did what I always did with these things, read the first page, meaning to read the first chapter. I did. I read the first and the second and the third . . .'

'You couldn't put it down.'

'You've read it?'

'Oh, yes. My daughter has a part in the film.'

'She's Sheila Wexford?'

He nodded, said, 'Go on.'

'Maeve read it and then Claudia did. Maeve acted as my secretary, you know. She wrote all my letters. We never – er, quite cottoned on to email. They read it and they said – well, things about its potential and how the author was a real find and that sort of thing. Claudia said, "What a pity you didn't write it, Owen."'

He took a sip of his tea, made a face and put the cup back on the tray. 'I don't want to blame them for this. It was my fault, entirely my fault – and yet . . . The upshot of it all, of our discussions, was that Maeve wrote to the author and asked him if he could come here and see me, have a talk with me about his manuscript. I don't exactly know what her precise words were, though I suppose I did at the time. They say we block off unacceptable memories – do you believe that?'

'I don't know,' Wexford said.

'I do. I know I do it all the time. And I've done it more since that manuscript – fell into my hands.' He gave a heavy sigh. 'That is an accurate description, carrying with it a certain menace. Fell into my hands – so much stronger, don't you think, than "came into my hands"? Well, he wrote back. He'd be in Sussex in a week's time and could he come then? He came. He brought another copy with him – the only other copy he had, he said.' Tredown's voice was losing strength, the tone cracking. 'I told him what we all thought of the manuscript and I said I thought parts of it needed rewriting and some careful editing. He said he'd do some work on it. No one knew he'd written a book. He seemed to think he'd be laughed at if anyone knew or else be told to do something that would make money. He'd sent it to me because he'd heard me speak on the radio and he thought – God help me – I was a good writer. He'd read two of my books too.'

'Mr Tredown, take it easy. You're tiring yourself.'

'What would it matter if I were?' Tredown pulled himself up with a gargantuan effort, leaned forward earnestly. 'Better if I tired myself to death. Sorry, I don't mean to be melodramatic but all this is painful to me, very painful. Anyway, he went. He took one of the manuscripts with him and I – I never saw him again. Maeve told me he'd gone and two days later she had a letter from him, saying he'd decided not to do any more about it. Writing it had been all he wanted. Having it published didn't interest him.'

Wexford shifted in his seat, trying to make himself more comfortable. 'You believed this?'

'I wanted to believe it, Mr Wexford. I desperately wanted to believe it. You see, I thought that if it was mine to do as I liked with I would rewrite it myself, keeping the story, the characters, the essence or spirit of it, but improving it, I thought I could improve it, make it perfect. I'd make it *mine.*'

'You saw the letter Mrs Tredown had from him?'

'I saw it. It was typed. It was signed.'

Wexford would hardly have believed that any more blood could drain from Tredown's face, but this is what seemed to have happened. He turned his head to one side, subsiding, slipping down the cushions of the chair.

'It was actually signed Samuel Miller?'

There was no answer. Wexford got up and rang the bell. The nurse came in, lifted Tredown's wrist and felt his pulse. 'Better go now,' he said. 'He's very tired.'

'Please come back tomorrow,' Tredown whispered.

T he call to the police station was put through to Karen Malahyde. But she had gone after paying a routine visit to the Imrans and it was Hannah who took the call. Two hours before she had come back from questioning two hospice visitors who might have, but evidently had not, witnessed Maeve Tredown's murder attempt. The day had been a long one and she had her usual drive ahead of her to home and Bal. It had been a dull, heavy day and at six in the evening was pitch-dark. A premonition that it would delay her made her very unwilling to take this call but Burden had already left, Wexford was not yet back from visiting Tredown and Barry Vine had begun his annual leave. A slightly tentative voice speaking fluent English but with a strong accent came on the line.

'My name is Iman Dirir. I have come from the home of the Imran family. I think – no, I know – something is going to happen in their flat – tonight. Yes, tonight. Please can you come?'

'Our Child Protection Officer isn't available,' Hannah began. She hesitated, said, 'Of course I'll come, I'll come now – but wait. Will I get in?'

'I'll be there,' Mrs Dirir said. 'They trust me.' Her tone was bitter. 'They never will again but – never mind.'

'Would you do something for me? Would you phone this number and tell the Child Care Officer. She's called Sylvia Fairfax.'

Karen and Sylvia had called at that flat two or three times a week and found nothing but an apparently happy family entertaining a middle-aged relative from Somalia. Shamis had been like any normal European child, free, playful, mischievous. If she had been circumcised she would have been confined to a chair with her legs bound together from ankles to hips. Driving out of the police station car park, her lights on, Hannah reminded herself of the commentary on female life Sylvia had repeated to her as coming from an elderly Somali woman she had met. 'The three sorrows of a woman come to her on the day she is cut, on her wedding night and the day she gives birth.' It made her shudder to think of it.

The block was brightly lit but as Hannah came to the top of the stairs and out on to the external walkway where the Imrans' flat was, she saw that it was in darkness. It was as if no one was at home. Sylvia Fairfax stepped out of the shadows to meet her.

'Dr Akande is on his way,' she said. 'I daren't ring the bell and there's no need. Iman Dirir will open the door at seven sharp.'

'And Shamis?'

'The woman they call auntie is a circumciser. Iman says she has seen the tools she uses, a razor, a knife and some special scissors.'

Hannah bit her lip. 'It doesn't bear thinking of but we have to think of it.'

'We have to stop it,' Sylvia said.

They stood outside the front door. There was no sound from inside. Next door they had a window open and music pounded out, the kind that has a steady regular beat, thump, thump, thump. Hannah's watch told her it was ten minutes to seven.

'It's horrible to think of,' she said, 'but will Iman let her begin? I mean, for God's sake, will this woman start on the child?'

'I don't know. I hope not but if she doesn't . . . Here's Dr Akande.'

He came running along the walkway. 'This can't be allowed to happen,' he said breathlessly. 'Even if it means failing to catch them, we can't let them cut this child when we're able to stop it.'

'She'll open the door,' Hannah said, 'the moment this woman picks up her razor.'

'That's too late. You don't know how fast a practised circumciser can do this – this atrocity. I do.'

'But surely they'll give Shamis some sort of anaesthetic?'

'I doubt it, I very much doubt it,' Akande said and with that he put his finger to the bellpush, holding it there so that the chimes it made rang loudly above the thumps of the music.

The door flew open. Iman Dirir shouted in a loud clear voice, 'Come in, all of you, come in. In here!'

Akande went first, Sylvia behind him. The hallway was dark, the only light was in the kitchen at the end of the passage, showing round the edges of the door. They ran towards the closed door and, thinking it locked, the doctor kicked at it. But it flew open and he almost fell into the little room. The woman in a long black robe who had been bending over the child, a cut-throat razor in her ungloved hand, took a step backwards, exposing to their view a small girl, entirely naked, lying on a spread towel on the kitchen table. Reeta Imran, the child's mother, made a shocked sound and flung a sheet over her. As Hannah said afterwards to Wexford, she was more affronted by a male, even though a doctor, seeing her little daughter without clothes than she was by the rite which the circumciser had been on the point of performing.

Totally covered, face and all, by the sheet, Shamis began to scream and struggle. She fought her way out and threw herself into her mother's arms. Mrs Imran once more grabbed the sheet and swathed her in it. Hannah walked up to the table and eyed the circumciser's other tools which lay there, a knife and a pair of scissors. There was no sterilisation equipment to be seen, no medication of any kind. A length from the reel of sewing thread would be used, she supposed, to stitch the raw edges of the wound together, a length from the ball of garden twine to bind Shamis's legs together once the deed had been done. The circumciser, a woman of perhaps no more than fifty, though she looked seventy, her face brown and wrinkled, most of her front teeth missing, fixed on Hannah a stare of absolute impassivity. She laid the razor on the table and said something to Mrs Imran in Somali.

I ought to arrest her, Hannah thought. Or Reeta, or both of them. But charge them with what? They've done nothing and I can't wish they'd begun what they were going to do for the sake of charging them. But I can't leave them here with the child either. All she could think of was that this woman had been in possession of a an offensive weapon – could she arrest them on suspicion of intending to perform an illegal act? Hardly knowing what she was doing or the consequences, she snatched Shamis out of her mother's arms and pulled off the sheet. There was blood on it. And a long streak of blood across Shamis's left thigh where the razor had just touched her. They had got there just in time.

'You do not have to say anything in answer to the charge,' she began, and glancing at Sylvia, saw tears running down her face.

CHAPTER TWENTY-SIX

Wexford went back to the hospice in the morning, feeling he had had a lucky escape. If he had gone ahead and Amara Ali and Reeta Imran had appeared in court, the case would have been dismissed and contumely heaped upon him for racism, sexism and jumping to unjustifiable conclusions. Anger against Hannah had been strong at first. Karen wouldn't have done it but Karen hadn't been there. Hadn't it occurred to Hannah that the women would say Shamis was sitting on the table after a shampoo and prior to having the hair on the nape of her neck shaved? The trace of blood? The shock of three people bursting into the flat had made Amara Ali's hand slip. Halfway home on the previous evening, he had answered his phone to be told that the two women were in custody and he had turned round and gone back, letting them both go with scarcely a word.

Now as he waited to be admitted to Tredown's room, he thought of things which had hardly occurred to him before. Naively, he had supposed he could prevent the mutilation of girls and so perhaps he could, but only after a number of them had already been mutilated, for in order for a prosecution to succeed a circumciser would have to be caught either in the act or when it was in the recent past and the poor little child crippled, her legs bound together. Later he would read through the Act of Parliament and see if there was provision for a charge of intention to commit mutilation, though, without going any further, he could see all the problems and pitfalls this would entail.

Tredown had had his shower, been shaved and was propped up in his bed this time. A drip had been inserted in the back of his hand. Surely pointless at this stage? But no, perhaps it was painkillers which travelled down that tube to make his last days more bearable. Tredown's greenish pallor was even more marked today and his sad smile more revealing of the skull beneath the skin. This time he noticed the cast on Wexford's arm and remarked on it.

So no one had told him. The last thing Wexford wanted was to tell him that his wife had been charged with attempted murder. 'A fall,' he said. 'It's just a simple fracture.'

This satisfied him. 'I was telling you about the letter,' he began. 'I told you it said I could have the manuscript to do what I liked with. I took that to mean I could – well, make it mine.'

'But he'd taken the copy away with him, hadn't he? If he meant to give it to you why would he do that?'

'He took it out of my – the room where I work. That was where we'd talked. That evening my wife brought it to me. He'd given it to her before he left.'

'Mr Tredown, do you mean he'd given it to her or she said he'd given it to her?'

Tredown frowned. 'It's the same thing.'

'Not always,' Wexford said.

'I hear what you're saying. And, yes, I'll tell you now that I did have doubts. Oh, more than that, more than that.' The agonised note in his voice came from mental, not physical, pain. 'I did write to him – that is, I got Maeve to write to him, saying it was too enormous a gift and telling him again how good it was and how very likely it was to be published and perhaps make a lot of money.'

'You never saw him again?'

'Not in the flesh.' The words and the way in which they were spoken brought Wexford an unpleasant feeling that someone or something was watching them. Tredown shivered. 'It was just my fancy,' he said. 'In the evenings – when I was alone upstairs – if there was a heavy rainfall – but this is pointless, I mustn't go on like this.'

Indeed you must not, Wexford thought, or I shall begin to think you not quite sane. 'So you went to work on the manuscript?'

Tredown nodded 'Yes, I did. I cut it. I gave some scenes more weight and others less. I took out a lot of technical stuff about the prehistoric creatures and early men. There were episodes in it I thought weren't consistent with Homer and Ovid, I . . . But why go on? I made it mine, as you say. Maeve was enthusiastic and so was Claudia. Maeve spent hours typing for me – I'm not much of a typist. She transcribed my handwriting and the changes I made to the original manuscript.'

Wexford was anxious not to sound judgmental. The man was at death's door. He was a wreck of what he had been and, in spite of the palliative drip, he was no doubt in pain. But, if he wasn't precisely shocked by what he had heard, he was astonished at what he saw as villainy. Tredown had been so set on money, urged on by wife and ex-wife, so desperate for fame that it meant nothing to him that the celebrity he achieved would not be his own but stolen from another. 'Fame is the spur that the clear spirit doth raise . . .' but it wasn't only the clear spirit that was raised by that prospect but sometimes greed and theft. For, of course, Tredown had known there had been theft and perhaps worse than theft but it hadn't stopped him making *The First Heaven* his own work. Wexford heard his own voice cold and condemning.

'Didn't you wonder when you never heard from him again?'

'Maeve told me he'd said he wanted to put the whole thing behind him. Maybe he'd read the book when it came out but he had no wish for it to be acclaimed as his own.'

'Perhaps we can leave Samuel Miller for the time being and talk about the man you found to be your researcher. I take his job was to deal with the passages which weren't consistent with Homer and Ovid and with the prehistoric detail.'

Tredown's frown was back. 'What do you mean? I did my own

251

research and I don't know any Samuel Miller. I think we're at cross purposes here.'

'I think so too.' Wexford got up, stiff and aching. He stumbled, clutched the back of the chair with his left hand. 'Thank you for your help,' he said. 'I won't take up any more of your time.'

The death's head smile came again. 'No, it isn't as if I've much of it left.'

'That was when things fell into place,' Wexford said. He had already passed his discoveries on to the assistant chief constable and was talking to Burden in his office; Hannah and Barry had been sent for. 'As in most cases when the truth becomes clear you wonder how you could ever have seen things differently.'

'But for matching the rings,' said Burden, 'would we ever have known it?'

'Maybe not.'

Wexford moved behind his desk as Hannah came into the room. It was the first time she had seen the plaster and the sling. 'Please may I write something on your cast, guv?'

'I'm afraid not. It's strictly for persons under twelve.'

The chances were that she'd have written something along the lines of 'Best wishes to the guv'. He watched her settle herself into the chair next to Burden's, leaving the remaining one to Barry. He'd have had to carry that 'guv' about with him for the next five weeks. 'I'll start at the beginning,' he said, and as Barry hurried in. 'I'd say good of you to join us except that I know where you've been.'

'Claudia Ricardo is in Interview Room One with Lyn, sir. I asked her about Alan Hexham and she said, "Don't be ridiculous. I never laid a finger on him."'

'If laying a finger on someone was a prerequisite for a murder conviction,' Wexford said, 'we'd have a lot more room in our prisons. We wouldn't have 80,000 banged up.' His sigh was inaudible. 'Now for the beginning. It begins, of course, with Alan Hexham living in that house in Barnes with his wife and his two small daughters.

For they were still small when he started writing the novel we now know as *The First Heaven*. He wrote it secretly up in that tiny room of his where everyone else in the household had learnt to respect his absolute privacy.'

'Why did he do it in secret, guv?'

'Some people have secretive natures. We have plenty of evidence for that. Acting in secret satisfies something in their temperament and adds a spice to what they do. On a more practical level, if no one knows they won't ask the sort of questions that may be very damaging to the project. And I imagine there's always the fear of being scoffed at – even laughed at. They may ask what's going on behind the closed door. But they can be fobbed off with tales of marking homework, filling in forms, preparing lessons. I don't think Hexham did much of that. He wanted it to be thought that he was doing research for authors, advising them, but again his wife must have wondered when he earned nothing by it. Maybe he told her he'd tried and failed.'

'What did you mean about "damaging to the project"?' Burden asked.

'Some writers thrive on making the people close to them aware of exactly what they're doing, reading their latest chapter to them, discussing it in detail, but there are others for whom the whole creative process is ruined if it's – well, brought out into the light of day. I had a writer say to me once that she'd written ten chapters of a novel when her boyfriend found it and read it. He was delighted, loved every word, could quote from it at length but it ruined it for her. She had to abandon it and start afresh.'

'Abandoned the boyfriend too, I should think,' said Hannah.

'I believe she did. Anyway, this seems to have been Hexham's attitude too. It's part shyness, part dread of ridicule and part a fear that the person who reads it will begin with high hopes and be disappointed. Hexham seems to have had a happy marriage but we don't know – his daughters certainly don't know – what the precise relations between the two of them were when they were alone. Isn't it possible that Diana Hexham wouldn't have understood what he was getting at? They were never very well off and she didn't work until after he disappeared. We know he took on the occasional tutoring job. Perhaps if she'd known about *The First Heaven* she'd have wondered why he was wasting his evenings playing at writing a novel which might never be published rather than taking on more coaching for exams. Whatever the answer to that is, he did keep it secret, kept it entirely to himself until it was finished and beyond.'

Burden said, 'A pity he chose Owen Tredown to send that manuscript to. Why did he? Why choose Tredown?'

'We're never going to know that. Tredown says Hexham had heard him speak on the radio. That may or may not be true. Possibly he just liked Tredown's books – he had two of them in his house – or he may have read an article in a newspaper about Tredown saying that unlike many authors, he read the manuscripts which were sent to him. Anyway, he did send it. He'd have been wiser and safer if he'd thrown it on a bonfire.'

'Put it in the recycling, guv,' said Hannah in a reproving tone.

'Or put it in the recycling as you say, Hannah.' In a few words, he thought, she wiped away centuries in which the only way to get rid of paper was to burn it. Was she aware there was life before modern planet-saving measures? He almost laughed. 'Tredown read it and thought it wonderful. He told me he was envious. He was jealous of someone who could write that but I don't believe he had any idea of plagiarism, of stealing someone else's work, at that stage. He wrote to Hexham, praising the book and asking him to come and see him. Or, rather, he got his wife to write. Apparently, she did all his secretarial work. What exactly she said in that letter – or, come to that, subsequent letters – we don't yet know. We may never know.

'The date Hexham got this letter was in late May. He might then have told his wife, but he didn't. I imagine he was waiting to surprise her with a fait accompli. His old friend Maurice Davidson died and his funeral was fixed for 15 June. This, incidentally, was three days after John Grimble was refused permission to build more than one house on his deceased father's land. The trench for the main drainage had been dug and now there was no option but to fill it in again.

'Hexham wrote to say he would be in Sussex on the fifteenth and could he come to see Tredown at about three in the afternoon.'

Here Barry Vine broke in with, 'Why wasn't any of this done by phone, sir?'

'Presumably, because of maintaining the secrecy. Diana Hexham might have taken the call. Besides, then Tredown would have spoken to Hexham and Maeve would have had no control over what he said. You have to remember too that a lot more letters were written eleven years ago than are today in the email age. Be that as it may, Hexham was told that would be fine and in that letter, written of course by Maeve, he was asked to bring the other copy of the manuscript he had with him. She must have asked and been told he had just the two copies. Remember too it had been typed on an old-fashioned electric typewriter, so unless Hexham possessed a photocopier, which we know he didn't, the number of copies would have been limited.'

'Wouldn't Hexham have asked why they wanted a second copy, guv?'

'Probably, but there are answers to that. Such as, so that Tredown could send manuscripts to two publishers or to an agent and a publisher. Anyway, Hexham was satisfied and he brought the second manuscript with him in his briefcase, taking it with him first of all to the funeral and then to the Davidsons' house. He left that house later and caught the 2.20 train to Kingsmarkham. It was pouring with rain. There was no bus for an hour so he took a taxi which brought him to Athelstan House at a few minutes to three.'

Burden, who had been fidgeting, took this opportunity to break in. 'While all this letter-writing was going on there must have been a good deal of discussion between Tredown and his wife – Claudia too, I expect – as to what line they were to take with Hexham. I mean, I suppose there was a point where Tredown acknowledged to himself and maybe to the two of them that he wanted to pass it off as his own work.'

'This is one of the things we have to find out,' said Wexford. 'If we can. The trouble is that two vital witnesses are dead and another one soon will be. However, decide they did. Not, I think, to murder Hexham, not then. At that point they seem to have had some plan to try and buy the manuscript from him and have him relinquish all rights to it.'

'They'd never have been safe then, sir. When the book came out what would there have been to stop him telling some newspaper Tredown had stolen it from him?'

'Nothing, probably, Barry. Nothing to stop him saying that, but with both copies gone and no member of his family knowing he'd written anything, what evidence would he have had? Anyway, even if they did plan that it came to nothing. Hexham came and apparently saw Tredown alone. At first. Again we don't know and probably won't know what they said to each other but it appears that Hexham took the second manuscript away with him, having learnt all he wanted to learn, that his novel was good and very likely worth publishing. The rest, he probably thought, he could handle himself.

'It seems he was given tea by Maeve and Claudia and as it was still raining, promised a lift to Kingsmarkham station. Not in a taxi this time but in the Tredowns' own car, that same vehicle Maeve used as a lethal weapon on me. Only it wasn't as lethal as she hoped.'

'Was it lethal to Hexham?' Barry asked.

'You'll have to wait a while for that. To be continued in our next, as magazines that ran serials used to say. Inspector Burden and I have an engagement with Miss Ricardo in Interview Room One.'

'I never laid a finger on him,' Claudia Ricardo said again. 'Funny, that phrase, isn't it? As if touching someone would kill him. The touch of death.' She laughed musical peals. 'Be useful, wouldn't it? Like a ray shooting out of one's forehead you get in those films about aliens. *Noli me tangere* would have some real meaning.'

Priscilla Daventry, her solicitor, was looking grim. One's clients were not supposed to behave like this. One's clients should be rude or truculent or abusive or frightened, in need of reassurance or comfort, preferably silent, though that was rare, but not light-hearted and speculative as this woman was.

'Who drove Mr Hexham to Kingsmarkham station?' Wexford asked her.

'Maeve couldn't drive then. She's a terrible driver now,' Claudia giggled. 'I mean, I can't drive at all but I'd still be better at it than she is, if you get my meaning. And of course you get my meaning! I was forgetting. She did that to your arm, didn't she? Poor Maeve, she shouldn't be allowed out at the wheel of a car.'

'Just answer the question, will you, Miss Ricardo?'

'I wasn't there. I went up to Owen.'

'Answer the question, please.'

'My client has answered the question,' said Priscilla Daventry. 'She said she wasn't there.'

'Tell me about your relationship with Samuel Miller.'

'I suppose you mean love affair. That's such a terrible expression, "relationship". I mean I have a relationship of sorts with you, though I'd rather not. I have a relationship with Miss Daventry and I certainly have one with Maeve. But I don't fuck them which is what you mean by the word, isn't it?'

Wexford just stopped himself shaking his head. He glanced at Burden and Burden said, 'Did you have sexual relations with Samuel Miller?'

'Well, I did in 1995. When he was doing our garden. Sometimes *in* the garden. That shocks you, I can see. Policemen are such prudes.'

One of the most irritating things someone can say to you is to tell you you're shocked when you're not. Burden reflected on this without rising to the bait. 'And when he came back three years later?'

'Not then,' she said. 'He'd taken up with that Bridget woman and I'd – well, I'd moved on. That's the contemporary expression, isn't it? Moved on?' She looked at Wexford and smiled, turned the smile on to Burden and then, broadening it, on Priscilla Daventry. 'I'm not going to say any more. Silence is about to reign. It's no good asking me because I'm going to keep silent.'

And she did. He tried to move her to answer but she remained speechless. She sat smiling, and contemplated her long, claw-like, unpainted fingernails. She crossed her legs, right over left, then left over right. She said nothing. Burden took over the questioning. She smiled at him. When he asked her if she had killed Alan Hexham she smiled more broadly and when he asked her if Maeve Tredown had, she closed her eyes. Staying there was useless and after half an hour the interview was terminated, Claudia Ricardo returning to one of Kingsmarkham police station's two cells and the two policemen going back to Wexford's office. Hannah and Barry had left, but returned when sent for, and Karen Malahyde came with them. Claudia Ricardo had been given refreshments but there had been none for Wexford and Burden and Hannah sent down for tea.

'As I said, Hexham came to Athelstan House and saw Tredown alone,' Wexford resumed. 'I don't really know how Tredown could have been so confident this story of his could become a best-seller. Of course this may be because I couldn't see much in it myself, but the fact remains that Tredown fell in love with it. He more or less told me so. And, as we know, he was right. He had to get his hands on it and make it his own. Maeve and Claudia appear to have been as enthusiastic as he was. But whereas Tredown, left to himself, wouldn't, I'm sure, have contemplated anything criminal to get hold of it, they would and did. Tredown may have thought of buying it from Hexham or simply persuading Hexham that whereas he could easily get it published because of the name he already had, Hexham himself would have had great difficulties.

'Did Hexham waver? Up in that room at Athelstan House did he listen to some proposition Tredown made to him but decided against it and to have a go at getting it published on his own? If he did so he condemned himself to death.'

'Signed his own death warrant, guv,' said Barry brightly, using the cliché Wexford had avoided.

'Yes, thank you, Barry. Hexham took his second manuscript away with him, no doubt very much encouraged by what Tredown had said to him and confident he could handle the rest himself,' Wexford resumed. 'There was a 5.30 train to London and probably he aimed to catch it. It seems possible that Maeve told him someone would drive him as she couldn't drive at that time. Did those two try dissuading Hexham from trying to publish his own work? I don't think so. After he was dead Maeve must have told Tredown not to worry about him again because he had said before he left that he was making them a present of his book. And here was the second manuscript to prove it.'

'Would he have believed that?'

'We tend to believe what we want to believe, Barry, and Tredown passionately wanted to believe it.'

'So who did drive Hexham, guv?'

'No one,' Wexford said. 'He was taken to their car all right. Or taken in the direction of the car which was in the garage. Claudia is maintaining a useless silence down there. She might as well not bother. Maeve admitted everything when Inspector Burden spoke to her before she was charged with attempted murder of me. Isn't that so, Mike?'

'Not everything,' said Burden, 'but a lot.'

'Hexham was taken to the garage and his briefcase containing the second manuscript was taken from him and put into the boot of the car. There, as he bent down to get into the passenger seat, he was stabbed in the back with a knife, probably repeatedly stabbed.'

'You mean by Maeve or Claudia?' Barry asked.

'I mean by Samuel Miller. I mean by the lover of Claudia Ricardo and later on of Bridget Cook, Sam Miller, the so-called poet.'

'M iller may have stabbed him in a frenzy – God knows why – because one blow of the knife seemed to have cracked a rib. That broken rib is the only sign Carina could find that Hexham met his death by violence.'

'But we knew he must have,' Karen said, 'because someone buried him.' Picking up Hannah's usage, she added, 'Who was that, guv?'

Wexford sighed a little. 'That was Miller. Grimble's trench had been dug and partially filled in by Bill Runge. Miller didn't really have to bury him. The grave had already been prepared. All he had to do was wrap the body in a sheet – Claudia's purple sheet, there was of course no bedlinen burglary – carry the body to the trench after dark, take out a few spadefuls of earth, lay poor Hexham in there and cover him up again with, say, six inches of soil. Next day, 17 June, Runge finished filling in the trench. Someone must have helped Miller carry the body and I daresay that was Claudia. She'd be stronger than Maeve.'

'They must have paid Miller,' said Burden.

'Indeed they must. I doubt if sex with Claudia would have been sufficient inducement. But how much? Unless they tell us we'll never know and we'll never know even then because lying seems to come naturally to them. We do know that Miller took the ring off Hexham's finger and kept it. Maybe Claudia told him to. She wouldn't have dared keep it herself.

'He took it and three years later he gave it to Bridget Cook, having first gone back to Athelstan House to blackmail those two women. For all I know at present, he may have been back several times in those three years to blackmail them. Over the plagiarism, of course, not the murder. He was too deeply involved in that himself. I don't suppose he threatened them with the police – it's more likely that he'd tell his story to a tabloid. They paid up and this time we do know the sum Miller extracted from them – £1,000.'

'What happened to Miller after he'd buried Hexham?' Hannah asked.

'We must assume he went back to his fruit-picking poetry-writing career with possibly occasional forays into Sussex to demand money with menaces from the Tredown women. By this time of course *The First Heaven* was starting to be the success Tredown had predicted for it and, when Miller came back three years after Hexham's murder, they could pay up without too much pain. By this time too Miller had engaged himself to Bridget Cook. He may have genuinely meant to marry her. She had a caravan and a car. She wasn't a bad option for someone like him.

'With the £1,000 in his jeans pocket he went into Grimble's bungalow. Who knows how often he'd been in there before when he was camped in Grimble's Field? Bridget's shower was broken and he stripped off his clothes in the kitchen, left them on the counter and went into the bathroom to wash himself in the trickle of water that came out of the tap. He had no intention of putting those clothes on again – with the exception of the t-shirt, he'd have worn that again to please Bridget – though he didn't intend to leave them behind either. The £1,000 was in the pocket of his jeans and that too he intended to take with him.

After he had washed, he meant to help himself to whatever he fancied from Arthur Grimble's wardrobe. In fact, he had already been into the bedroom and put the contents of his anorak pockets, keys and a watch and his wallet, into the pocket of a sports jacket. It was in the bathroom that Ronald McNeil encountered him.

'Now Irene McNeil says he menaced her husband with a knife and the knife we took off Darrel Fincher may certainly have been his. But would a man who believed himself alone in a house, a man who was in his underwear, in a *bathroom*, carry a knife with him? I don't think so. I think what happened was that after he'd shot Miller, McNeil found a knife among the clothes in the kitchen and put it in the bathroom to give credence to his story. The £1,000 remained where it was, in Miller's jeans pocket. Pity it never found its way to Bridget Cook.'

'She had a lucky escape,' Hannah said.

'And maybe even she will think so,' said Wexford, 'when all this gets to be public knowledge.'

I n A Passage to India Wexford said to Burden, 'We come in here because it's more or less next door – well, you come to feast your eyes on beauty and I must come because you do. I can't think of any other reason. I'm getting sick of Indian food.'

'There's a new restaurant opened on the corner of Queen Street. It's Uzbek. We could give it a go.'

The bead curtain was pushed aside and Matea came out, followed by Rao in a tight suit and a bow tie. Matea stopped when she saw them and whispered something to her employer. He seemed to be arguing with her but, after a moment or two, he spread his hands out, shrugged and let her go back the way she had come. Two menus in his hand, he came over to Wexford and Burden, all smiles, bowing to them.

'What was that about?' Burden said when Rao had taken their order.

'God knows. Before we say any more, I have to tell you that Tredown is dead. Barry told me as we were coming out.'

Burden was silent. 'I think this is a case where you could truly talk about a merciful release.'

'Yes. Poor wretch. Stealing Hexham's work didn't bring him much pleasure, did it? It brought him money. Money for those two hell-cats. But when you come to think of it, they didn't know what to do with it when they had it, did they? Flagford is a pretty village but they lived in the ugliest house in it. As far as I could gather, they never had a holiday. They hadn't got a decent piece of furniture. Their car was fifteen years old. When Tredown wanted to change his consciousness he didn't use an expensive opiate but a herb you could grow in your garden.'

Always interested in sartorial matters, Burden said, 'And one of his wives dressed like a bag lady and the other one from Asda.'

Two more couples had come into the restaurant, followed by a man on his own. Matea emerged from the kitchen area, setting the bead curtain ringing, she moved so fast, her normal grace lost. Her face seemed deliberately turned away from their table as she went to hand menus to the newcomers.

Without commenting on her behaviour, Wexford said, 'It's an image I shan't soon get out of my head, that poor devil sitting up there in a room – which, by the way, we never got to see – with someone else's manuscript in front of him, re-typing the whole thing, making a little change here, a different word there, altering Hexham's no doubt superior style to something more like his own writing in those Bible epics. Maybe making those changes made him feel what he was doing wasn't all that wrong. He must have told himself that the finished work – think of it, Mike, over 500 pages when it was a hardcover book, how many manuscript sheets must it have been? – but think of it, think of him labouring away, turning someone else's work into his own, so that he could tell himself in the long watches of the night that what he was doing wasn't so bad, wasn't real plagiarism, because its author had said he could have it – hadn't he?'

No wonder he saw ghosts, he thought, but didn't say aloud. Their chicken tikka and lamb korma arrived, brought by the proprietor. He seemed nervous. It was as if, Wexford said when the man had gone, he feared being questioned about Matea's conduct. An explanation for it awaited them next door in the police station but first they had their lunch.

'Poor Charlie Cummings was never found,' said Wexford.

'A great many missing people never are found. Darracott was never found.'

'I know. But all through this case I've had a sort of absurd hope that one of us would come across Cummings somewhere, alive and well. I suppose I should be glad we didn't find him dead. Yet somewhere he's dead. In some pond or lake or cave or deep ditch his bones are lying and it seems wrong, though I'm not sure I could say why, for anyone's body to lie unburied.'

Burden always felt uncomfortable when Wexford talked in this vein.

'What do they eat in Uzbekistan?'

'Camel,' said Wexford who didn't know. 'Yak. Abominable Snowmen. Noodles. I wish I knew what was wrong with that girl. It worries me.'

They walked across the police station forecourt. 'D'you think they'll still make the film?'

'It'll be a blow to Sheila if they don't. But they will, Mike. When did you ever see a film where the name of the author mattered or anyone even knew it?'

Wexford was talking to the duty sergeant when Karen Malahyde came up to them. For the first time in months she called Wexford 'sir'.

'Kingsmarkham Social Services have taken Shamis Imran into care, sir.'

Wexford was very still. He seemed turned to stone, the heavy cast on his arm held across his body as if defensively. 'Was that necessary?' he said at last.

'I thought you'd be pleased,' Karen said.

'Did you?'

'At least she'll be safe, guv.'

'I suppose so. In one way.'

He walked towards the lift where Burden caught up with him. 'So that was what was wrong with Matea. It can't be helped, Reg. While she was at home there was nothing to prevent her parents trying again. Another "auntie" would have been fetched from Somalia.' Wexford looked at him, surprised. 'Yes, I know. I've been reading up on genital mutilation. I think I've got some idea now how strongly these people feel about it. Not having it done would be like us not having our daughters immunised. Worse than that – not sending our daughters to school.'

Once again Wexford said he supposed so. As the lift climbed slowly to the second floor he seemed to see the Imrans in their 'penthouse' flat, hard rock beating out from the place next door, the two parents silent, not understanding why this had been done to them, bewildered by inexplicable laws. They had been doing the very best for their daughter, ensuring her acceptance in the community and her eligibility for a good marriage, but she had been taken from them. They were unfit to have the care of her. Where had they gone wrong? *Le métier d'homme est difficile.* The job of being a human being was indeed difficult. It sounded a lot better in French.

O n a gloomy day in late November, the day John Grimble heard from the Kingsmarkham planners that his application to build more than one house had again been refused, Jim Belbury and Honey came cautiously back to their truffle-hunting ground. The trench had been filled in, the crime tape had gone, but the season wasn't quite over. Jim had a nice cut off the Sunday joint, hygienically wrapped in a recyclable plastic bag, to reward Honey if she struck lucky.

Their hunting ground it was but not the same location. Jim would have felt a bit squeamish about that. They went prospecting round the field and among the trees until Jim saw a swarm of flies buzzing about under an oak tree. The oak was right up against Pickfords' fence but no one was about in the Pickford garden. It was too cold and too damp. Jim could see the television screen glowing behind the French windows and Mr Pickford and his son watching the cricket from Australia.

Jim said what he always said, 'Get digging, girl.'

Honey waited for those words. Perhaps no others would have served as a trigger. But those three words were enough. She snapped at the flies and began a busy rooting in the fallen leaves, the leaf mould beneath and the soft loam under that. Jim thought they weren't going to be lucky. Not this time. It was too late in the year. But Honey was enjoying herself. He tugged at her collar, pulling her away to where the banished flies had regathered and once more begun their frenzied dance.

He slightly varied his command. 'Give it a go, girl.'

She took longer than usual about it. She dug deeper. He could hardly believe his eyes when he saw the enormous truffle she came up with. It was almost too big for her to hold in her mouth, it was as big as the largest corm of celeriac Morella's had in their farm shop, as big as a Hallowe'en pumpkin.

Without protest she let it drop into Jim's cupped hands. He sniffed its aroma, the scent that one of those posh London chefs that went on the TV would pay more for than the whole of his winter fuel supplement. 'Good girl,' he said and popped into Honey's mouth a thick slice of prime Scottish beef.